I

I hope you will like this Italia story

Franco

The
Wise Men
of Pizzo

The Wise Men of Pizzo

Francesco M Marincola

Edited by Paula Marincola

Library of Congress Control Number: 2014909706
ISBN: Hardcover   978-1-4990-8627-0
                  Softcover   978-1-4990-8626-3
                  eBook   978-1-4990-8628-7

Printed in the United States of America by BookMasters, Inc
Ashland OH
July 2014

Rev. date: 06/02/2014

To order additional copies of this book, contact:
Xlibris LLC
800-056-3182
www.Xlibrispublishing.co.uk
Orders@Xlibrispublishing.co.uk
614403

Contents

Letter to the Publisher

I am a firm advocate of equal opportunities for little towns, particularly those along the southern coast of Italy. Take for instance Pizzo, the place where I spent a significant part of my youth. Beyond a fifty-kilometre diameter, almost nobody has ever heard of it, and one has to patiently explain to strangers that it is Pisa where the Leaning Tower is situated and that Pizza, not Pizzo, is a kind of food. Historians would argue that Pizzo has no place in their books for the simple reason that nothing of relevance has ever happened during its 3,000-year history, save for the execution of Joachim Murat—too indirect of an achievement to contribute sufficient status. Although it is difficult to disprove with inexistent facts this premise, I would argue that something does happen indeed in this little town where the best ice creams in the world are served and where people carry existences that, compared with the rest of the world, are almost as dignified.

By having this novel published by a respected publisher, I could prove that even in neglected little towns something happens that may be of sufficient significance to grant them a corner, albeit minuscule, within the big scheme of things. I would also have the opportunity to repay Pizzo for restoring identity to me, an anonymous city dweller, during my occasional homecomings. Finally, this success may inspire others who at the verge of retirement, having little else to do, may want to apply the same principle to revive the glory of their respective little town.

FOREWORD

It is a special honour to write this brief foreword for the first novel of a very dear and wonderful friend.

Sandra Demaria

For readers like myself, who left the country we grew up in and have been living in the States for long enough to count the time not in years but in decades, the novel *The Wise Men of Pizzo* resonates deeply with our experience. We can relate to the feeling of belonging to a place we still consider our only true home and at the same time feel surprisingly at odds with it. The masterful description of the first day of Giuseppe in Pizzo and his difficulty in accepting the stillness of the *cuntrura*, being used to the frenetic pace of an intensely busy life, connects readers conducting a similar existence, often governed by a number of electronic devices, with the main character of this story. Empathising with Giuseppe, we see through his eyes the small town and become distracted by the oddities and contradictions of a very different existence, soothed by the natural beauty, tempted by the good food, and amused by the colourful characters who meet at the bar Gatto. As the story unravels, the perception of what is meaningful and important in life begins to change, and the busy frenetic existence feels distant and insignificant, while the human wisdom of the old men becomes larger than us, forcing a reflection on our own lives.

The story of Alessandro, which becomes the centre of the wise men and of Giuseppe's attention, consists of three levels. One is the historical context of a post-war generation of young Italians embodying the great expectations of their parents and grandparents for a future of change, but becoming disillusioned by the realisation that true change seems to never be possible. A second level is more universal. Alessandro's story is paradigmatic of the hopes that the great potential of children generates and the sorrow we feel seeing them going nowhere. The third level is deeply personal. It is a story of friendship and love and of the pain of realising that we cannot change other people, only accept them and embrace who they are. In a way, Alessandro tickles our consciousness and makes us reflect on the question what it means to be 'honest to oneself'.

Despite the tragic conclusion of Alessandro's life, the novel is full of characteristically southern Italian irony, which makes the reading extremely pleasant and entertaining. The main characters understand, albeit in different ways, what is wrong with the world. With a mixture of fatalism and wisdom, they accept that if there is not much they can do to fix it they might at least enjoy the very human pleasure of having a good drink together.

Although the novel portrays an old-fashioned 'men's world', the only unquestionable hero is a woman. Nonna is the only one to show true determination and to fight, with nobility and intelligence, in order to change whatever she can of her world. Respected, admired, feared but ultimately loved by everybody, she is the most significant positive point of reference, not only for Alessandro but also for the entire town.

Similarly to other existential struggles narrated as novels (and I am thinking about some of Gide's works like Paludes and L'immoraliste), The Wise Men of Pizzo does not really have a beginning or an end; it simply 'is', which brings me to its end which, quite appropriately, is a conclusion but not an end.

There is something timeless and comforting about cemeteries, at least the old ones in small towns where few people live and, therefore, die, so there is no need to rush out the poor bones after a fixed number of years, as in big cities. Families can be together and nothing else matters any more, but the name that links them. The cemetery of Pizzo is a clever place for the last meeting of the three characters connected in very different ways to Alessandro. By virtue of its sombreness, it takes the story out of the triviality of everyday life and restores the nobility to the tormented yet dissolute Alessandro. In the simplicity of the grave, all three characters, Ophelia, il Marchese, and Giuseppe, are enhanced and become more meaningful than ever.

It follows naturally for Giuseppe to feel a need to seek the forgotten yet familiar ritual of the confession before he leaves town. Despite the deep philosophical discussion between him and Don Pino, the real benefit is for him in the rituality, like remembering a prayer one recites in childhood, the same feeling of redemption that symbolism can inspire.

The inevitable metamorphosis of Giuseppe that starts as the plane takes off is again something that emigrants like myself, who have lived between two worlds, can recognise, as is the desire that the 'old world' we left behind temporarily (we like to believe) will exist unchanged forever or at least until we want to go *home* again.

Beyond the appeal of the nostalgic memories of youth and beyond the affection, or contempt, the reader may feel for Alessandro and for Giuseppe himself, there are many layers within this novel. The final conversation between Giuseppe and Don Pino highlights one of the main themes of the novel, i.e. how choices we make or do not make will shape our life and the lives of people close to us. The admonition of Don Pino—'*You cannot assume that by not making decisions you are not to be blamed. I see that your indolence is self-centred; it may even be an excuse to protect yourself from engaging with the challenges of life*'—could apply to all of us procrastinators and deniers who get immersed in countless daily tasks, feeling justified for avoiding the discomfort of addressing the real problems in our lives. On the other hand, to make choices we need to first answer Don Pino's question: '*But what is your goal? [. . .] If you are unhappy about things that are under your control, exert your power and make yourself content [. . .] or if you decide not to do it and to sacrifice yourself for the happiness of others, then all the same do it with all your heart and be consistent with this choice.*' Despite the wisdom of Don Pino's exhortation, in the background is the tender story of Anita and Il Marchese, who decide to sacrifice themselves for the happiness of their child and are consistent with this choice to the end. By a twist of fate, however, their child will never be happy.

So neither Don Pino nor the other wise men of Pizzo provide easy solutions to the complexity of life; they know better. It is Giuseppe who, while escaping towards his troubles, comforts us with the thought that eventually any problem will be solved by waiting until it will become *irrelevant.*

It is the human paradox that since birth, as children, we struggle to be noticed, to be important—first, just for our parents, then, as we grow up, for a larger and larger audience. We want to cure people or amuse them or make them think or educate them or dress them smart, feed them, make them beautiful . . . driven by the need for accomplishments that make us feel important, if not for parents we have lost or children we may not have but for the entire humanity. And as we are approaching the end of life, we finally realise that all the effort was just a way to postpone the inevitable time when we have to confront our irrelevance.

As I am considering this true but difficult to accept thought, I think about the one person I still trust the most, despite the fact that he is only a memory now for many years. For all of his life, my father maintained an enthusiasm for a few things he always liked and enjoyed—things that make you feel alive, feel like a wild kitten let loose in a garden after it has been constrained in a small room for a while. And I am cheered by imagining that I am going with my father for an aperitif in the small cafe near his place of work in Turin. We chat with a few old men, as we used to do, before going home for dinner.

PREFACE

When I originally conceived this story, I named it 'The Wise Guys of Pizzo'. I then changed the title to the current one in deference to its characters who, once upon a time, not having much else to do, embarked on the honourable task of academically discussing and systematically solving some—if not all—of the most outstanding of life's problems. Nonetheless, the readers should feel in absolute liberty, upon completion of their task, to choose for themselves which designation they consider most appropriate.

Indeed, this manuscript is based on a true story but not one of a particular man or woman, hero or heroine, prince or princess, marionette or Cesar. It is instead a cumulative story narrated by voices who fancied leaving a legacy for generations to come. This is also not the story of my life, although it may appear to be so at some juncture. With few exceptions, every word—noun, adjective, or verb—is pure fiction. Yet this story is denser in truth than the pedantic life we are accustomed to, which predominantly follows a flat course with rare picks from where one could oversee its essence. Here, I have endeavoured to deplete the story of the distracting annoyances that spring from the shallow waters of daily existence to focus on episodes that occasionally elevate our thoughts and resonate in the mysterious abyss of our consciousness. To ask whether the characters truly existed or whether they are just the fruit of imagination is as vital as asking two centuries from now whether any of us truly existed, like asking whether the notes of a musical composition are real; such information has no bearing over the appeal of a symphony.

THE WISE MEN OF PIZZO

I

The Chiazza

Pizzo is a little town sitting on a rock by the Tyrrhenian Sea. Its ancient name is Napitia, which derives from the name of the leader of the Focesi,[1] Napeto, who founded it in the twelfth century B.C. Accordingly, its citizens are either called Pizzitani or Napitini, depending upon the educational level, the mood, the inclination, and mannerism of the interlocutor. In Italian, some would even call Pizzo 'ridente' which literally means 'smiling'. In fact, seen from a distance on a sunny day and with a good deal of imagination, one could catch a smile drawn by the irregular architecture of houses piled on top of each other like a Nativity scene. But this should not leave the observer with a false impression about its inhabitants, as Pizzo shares the same ratio of smiles and tears, happiness and sorrow, with every other town in Italy and in the world.

To the visitor, upon arrival, Pizzo offers a gratifying impression of yet undiscovered splendour. In the terrace, one smells a mixed fragrance of basil and jasmine blended with the saline marine breeze. The lemon tree carries a few humongous lemons in the pensile garden, and together with its shadow, the dark green of the leaves and the yellow of the fruits draw an Italian kirigami over the spotless white wall where a solitary gecko basks under the sun undisturbed by the new arrival. The eyes search for exotic charm, scanning over a myriad of pixels of light scattered by the choppy blue sea. The evolving clouds enliven the deep blue sky,

---

[1]   Phoenicians.

hinting that a considerable affair is about to begin. Robins storm above, exhibiting their aeronautical skills, and a pigeon, alerted by the voices, lands on the terrace testing the newcomer for his generosity. Admiration erupts from the visitor's paunch as hope swells that something special and genuine, something never previously experienced, is about to happen.

But soon the eye is satiated by the beauty and the snout by the fragrances; the spirit is quenched by the returns of contemplation, and a second phase begins that follows a crescendo and diminuendo like the surges of waves slapping the sand as the storm builds under the power of the unbridled winds. Subtly first and overwhelming at last, a flagrant feeling of boredom supervenes at the realisation that not much can be accomplished in Pizzo save for eating, drinking, admiring the landscape, and periodically listening to the church bells that pace the time of the little town. Of the latter, it is possible that somebody had engineered a link between the clock and those church bells to disrupt the absoluteness of the silence and thereby discourage the preposterous deduction that absolutely nothing happens in Pizzo.

The ennui grows in the still hours that follow lunch. This little town has been sitting astride the rock rising from the sea for centuries and perhaps more. Whether the rain washes its red roofs or the sun roasts its white walls, not much has changed in Pizzo, and only habits, like the ivy engulfing the walls of the castle, prosper to embody the frame of the town's life. Among the rituals, the 'cuntrura', which literally means 'the time against time', is the magic moment in the early afternoon when all sojourns and the men, taking a well-deserved break from the morning duties, go to their women and to a Lucullan lunch waiting at home. I realise as I write that in modern times, even for the forgotten town of Pizzo, the concept of women servants waiting at home for their man is unrealistic, archaic, and inappropriate. However, I would like to take the literary liberty here and henceforward, for the sake of this timeless story, to persevere in the well-established prejudices that embroider the perception of Southern Italy.

After lunch, the habit demands an equally deserved nap embellished by the peaceful rhythm of snoring in various tones and intensities that echo the sounds of the waves beating the shore. An occasional stray dog or a cat roams the streets knowing that there is nothing to do, so it sniffs around, sighs, and lies in the shade, and being the most ambitious of the animals, it meticulously licks its fur until the contrura is over.

Returning to our visitor, who is still not adjusted to the new life, time seems to never pass. Checking with his own clock, he realises that the bell tolls every fifteen minutes to signal the time, and he appreciates how long such periods can be. He calculates that this periodic event will have to recur ninety-six times per day for a fortnight before it is time for him to leave. Something to fill the space should be creatively sought soon, before an irreversible damage is done to his mind. Therefore, the visitor looks around his room first and then the whole house. There is plenty of reading material that he had diligently carried through customs and security checks from country to country. There are more treasures in the old and dusty shelves of the den. But then our visitor thinks, 'What was the point of coming all the way to Pizzo to do exactly what I could have been doing at home?' He vaguely recollects that there was a purpose to the visit, but it seems so far away now. He needed a break, some time to gather his thoughts. Things were not well at home. He had even suggested a separation from his wife due to perpetual unsolved problems. It was a very painful status of affairs—a status against which he coped with a strange kind of compensatory narcissism, self-indulgence created and maintained to protect a fragile ego. But now, in the stillness of the cuntrura, in the holiness of the silence broken by the church bells, it all seems so far removed, distant, and trivial. The noble resolution gradually evaporates into a lethargic cloud that hovers in the back of his mind.

At last, our friend tentatively approaches the window to observe the little square that Italians call 'piazzetta' or, as called in the dialect of the town, 'chiazzetta'. And there, with his elbows on the banister, his hands supporting his chin, he waits, like the cats and the dogs, for the end of the time against the time. There the eye, similarly to the adjustment to the darkness, becomes conscious of things that would have never passed the threshold of awareness in the light of regular life: A few pigeons are pecking at invisible crumbs, while robins circle above to catch those unfortunate bugs that could not rest even during the cuntrura. Encouraged by these promising signs of life, our visitor softly drags a chair to the window to avoid waking the other inhabitants and like a patient fisherman casts his attention down on the chiazzetta, waiting for something to happen.

He does not have to wait too long. In the blazing sun, a stray cat is stalking a mouse, the only moving object, while a dog is dozing at the other corner of the chiazzetta. The cat's tail is still except for its tip that nervously ticks. Then . . . a sudden pounce! But the mouse slips into a hole just in time. The seemingly disinterested cat licks its fur at the torso and, wetting its paws, refreshes the ears. The cat goes to rest on a step in the shade. The dog that had raised its head—tricked by the commotion—sighs and goes back to sleep, cynically reminding itself that nothing happens at this hour in Pizzo. The cat, feeling unobserved, wanders back to the mouse's hole. It inspects it with its nares for some time, and then sits in front of it. The dog exhales a larger breath as if to express sorrow for the triviality of worldly things and once more goes back to sleep. Nothing happens for some time until the cat yawns and so does our visitor while the shadow of a robin sweeps over the floor of the little chiazzetta: It is indeed the cuntrura.

Suddenly, a woman carrying a gozza[2] to fetch water at the fountain appears in the middle of the chiazzetta followed by the village idiot, who cannot talk or hear. He touches her inappropriately while she is bending to fetch the water; she turns and slaps him in the face. He holds his hand up in between his mouth and the sky as if to grasp a word that does not want to come out while the other hand covers his burning cheek. Once again, peace is restored. These and similar affairs of comparable consequence occupy our visitor for a while until boredom once again knocks and he resolves to do what he should have done from the beginning: get into bed and wait for merciful sleep.

* * *

I will now switch the narrative to the first person under the guise of the visitor and to a mixture of present and past tense to further entangle the reader's experience, magnify the realities of this Lilliputian world, and indulge my ambivalence in parting the present from the past, the antique from the contemporary.

---

[2]   Gozza is a clay jar.

                                *   *   *

. . . The doorbell woke me up suddenly; it was still daylight, though with
a fainter tone, and a pleasant cool breeze parted the curtains to softly
caress my skin. I waited for somebody to open the door, but nothing
happened. They must have all gone out. A second prolonged, violent,
insolent, and insulting ring obliged me to get up. I distractedly organised
my steps towards the gate controls and without enquiring who was
waiting outside I pushed the button that opened the door downstairs.
A shuffling sound announced a person coming up the stairs and Ciccio
Percuoco—an old family acquaintance—appeared. Because of his looks
being peculiarly similar to those of some members of my family, it has
been insinuated that there was an illegitimate relation between his
existence and our family due to some understandable escapades of my
grandfather, which were not entirely unheard of at those times. He had
been a loyal servant who cared for us while we were in town.

'We kiss your hand, Signorino.[3] Giuseppe, your father is waiting for you
at the Chiazza.'

The Chiazza[4] is the parlour of Pizzo. It is ancient and its origins are
obscure. On one side, it draws the roads from all verges of the town and
on the opposite side it ends with a staged opening towards the sea in the
western direction where the sun, day after day, salutes the Napitini with
the most creative of kaleidoscopic sunsets. The Chiazza disproves the
visitors' opinion, including mine, that nothing happens in Pizzo and that
the law of its land is boredom. Now its citizens, past the curfew of the
cuntrura, materialise and busy and bustling about give the impression
that, no matter how irrelevant their business may appear to the foreigner,
it is all a matter of great importance to them.

Just as in a major city, there is a policeman. He tries to control the
traffic, which comprises an assortment of vendors, people, motorcycles,
little carriages, vans, cars, tricycles, children, cats, dogs, and pigeons, all

---

[3]   Signorino is a conventional Italian title of respect for a young man.

[4]   Chiazza is dialect for piazza, meaning square and referring to the main
       square of Pizzo.

zipping through made-up stands coloured like butterflies to attract the tourists. Everybody enthusiastically bends the rules with the primary purpose of keeping busy the otherwise bored policeman who floats like a buoy above the waves of the sea he cannot control. There are 'one way traffic' signs, but which way remains to be clarified and they should more properly read 'one way or another'. One such sign points directly upwards towards the sky. It is not clear if this was a mistake or if it was done purposefully to comfort the agnostics that there may be a God up there supervising this chaos. The little shops reopen after the cuntrura and will stay open until very late when at an undefined time the owner will become tired and find something better to do than linger like a proud spider on its own web.

Business flourishes at those hours. The green grocery lady piles grub on the scale and without looking at the results transfers everything into a paper bag, asking for round figures. Nobody questions her because nobody wants to embarrass the poor lady by testing whether she can read the results. Besides, everybody knows that the scale is there only as a decoration, an embellishment to give credibility to the store. The shop has been there for generations, passed from parent to progeny that overlapped for decades to assure that all nuances of the business were conclusively learnt before the elder departed. Often, the elder did not depart at all but stayed as a supervisor settled in the shade on a woven wicker chair at the entry of the store, where he would greet by name each of the patrons and offer a cherry or, according to the season, a comparable treat to the younger apprentice customers. Eventually, a picture on the wall replaced the chair that supported the elder till he had not departed for better pastures.

And then there is Uncle Sarino's shop that sells unknown entities buried under layers of dust of archaeological appeal. Uncle Sarino is another elder sitting on a wobbling and condemned straw chair at the doorway. There is no progeny inside: first, because he has none, and second, because none is needed since nobody ever enters to buy. When no one talks to him, he observes the Chiazza from his dejected cathedra—the post from which he has observed a few changes over the past sixty years. His transparent blue eyes are resigned like those of an animal caged for life. There is no use in grasping further than his reach from this virtual enclosure made of obsolete memories and missed opportunities. I ask him, 'Come va[5]?'

Stroking the dark mane of a little boy who is playing at his feet and who probably reminds him of the son he lost half a century ago, with a gentle smile he mechanically replies, 'Accussi', meaning 'so-so' according to a metric without gauge. But one can barely distinguish his voice in the loud music erupting from the balcony up above, the honking of car horns, the yelling of salesmen, and the swelling sound of townspeople's chatter. From the left comes a lady balancing a canister of eggs on her head, from the right a buffalo mozzarella boy. They say it is a business owned by the Mafia, but then what is not in this town?

Many other things on which I will not further dwell happen at once in the Chiazza while the sun relinquishes its undisputed diurnal control and the cool marine breeze takes over to transform a dormant little town into a bustling hive of metropolitan ambitions, where only the cats keep composure, continuing to yawn and rest wherever they had dwelled during the cuntrura. Within this combustion, I found myself submersed as I responded to the call of the paterfamilias.[6] These flashes of real lives can only be sketchily reported as they remain spattered in my memory as graffiti on a dirty wall as I walked with haste towards my destination: the bar 'Gatto'.[7]

I should at this juncture prepare the unaware reader to the fact that going to il Gatto is no ordinary business. It is an experience worthy of ablution as il Gatto is not just a bar but a shrine that should be elevated among those places of holiness that others, according to their own beliefs, reserve for the Parthenon, the Temple of Minerva, St Peter, Mecca, or the Taj Mahal. For the unaware tourist, il Gatto is just a gelateria where epic ice creams such as the black or white Tartufo[8], the

---

[5]   'Come va?' means 'How are things going?'
[6]   Paterfamilias is Latin for 'father of the family'.
[7]   Gatto means cat.
[8]   Tartufo is truffle, name given to this ice cream because it looks like a truffle.

Cassata Siciliana,[9] or the Torta Belvedere[10] are served with wafers and ice-cold San Pellegrino. But not so for the locals and those like myself connected to them. Il Gatto is the place where common life is discussed and elevated to concepts that are then assembled into grand philosophy and regurgitated into recommendations for hypothetical beneficiaries who might be roaming on the outskirts of existence. As I approached the tavolino[11] around which my dad was sitting with his friends, I knew that I was about, willing or not, to learn lessons that not even Mr Pratt could have imagined extracting from the Herkimer's handbook of indispensable information.[12]

Towering over the tavolini was il Gatto himself or, for historical accuracy, Sig.[13] Belvedere belonging to an estimated reiteration of fathers' and sons' gelatai,[14] whose family tree had its roots in the abyss of the Mediterranean Sea and whom everybody had been calling 'Gatto' for decades for forgotten reasons. His ears were droopy like those of a hound dog rather than pointy like those of a cat, and although the Italian ingenuity that created the Renaissance could have assimilated his squinting eyes to those of a cat caught by the sunshine, Sig. Belvedere wore no whiskers. Perhaps the most compelling prerogative to such appellation was his posture, as like a cat, he tirelessly scrutinised the Chiazza, seemingly prepared to pounce on potential clients and carry them by the nape of their neck to the first free tavolino.

'Signorino Giuseppe, it is a pleasure to see you back!' said il Gatto as he exhaled a large cloud of smoke generated and digested from a cigarette that was just one among an incalculable number that, judging from his nicotine-stained fingers, he had undoubtedly held that day. As far as I could remember, I had always been called 'Signorino'. When I was a little boy, it seemed precocious. Then for a short while, the appellation was

---

[9]   Cassata Siciliana is Sicilian ice cream.
[10] Torta Belvedere is Cake Belvedere for the name of the owner of il Gatto.
[11] Tavolino is a little aluminium table.
[12] O' Henry short stories.
[13] Sig. is the abbreviation for Signore, which is Italian for 'sir' or 'mister'.
[14] Gelatai are ice cream makers.

appropriate for my age. But as the years passed, it stuck, and even now in my fifties, I was still Signorino Giuseppe.

'Come va, Angelo?' I said, as this was Sig. Belvedere's proper name and nobody could dare call him Gatto in his presence.

'Volaru acei!' was his answer, as il Gatto was never satisfied with the number of tables filled with customers, even when they were about to stack them on top of each other because no space would remain in the crowded Chiazza. 'The birds flew away!' is the translation, suggesting that like birds following the ancestral migratory patterns towards the end of August, as the day of my arrival just happened to be, summer dwellers were starting to return to their metropolis or, according to his hyperbole, had already completely vanished.

Trying to demonstrate the deepest sympathy for the upcoming famine that was about to follow this cyclical course of catastrophic events, I said, 'Well, I hope the next season will come again soon', or something of comparable gravity.

Don Paolo was sitting, leaning back in a plastic armchair, his legs crossed, one hand holding his chin and the second lazily tapping the tavolino: That was my dad. Close to him was his brother, Don Giusto, whose posture was perfectly symmetrical to my dad's. He was also leaning back, with the opposite legs and hands inadvertently doing the same as if there was a mirror creating the vision. A man clad in white was sitting in front of them. He was il Marchese, called 'marquise' not just because of his birth, which had been rather forgotten in time, but because elegantly dressed in white linen suits in summer and dark grey wool suits in winter, with a bow tie and a cane, he graciously appeared in the Chiazza with the regularity of the church bells after the cuntrura day after day for God knows how many decades. He royally distributed his presence in different bars, graced their patrons with his company, dignified audiences, and enlivened conversations, thus elevating the appellation given to him by birthright into a legitimate and honourable profession. At his side was Don Ciccio, 'il Professore', who was the retired school principal and a self-proclaimed scholar of classic literature. Allegedly, he had written and published a dissertation on Greek dwellings in Calabria,[15] which nobody to my knowledge had ever read or even seen. A little apart from the four but still belonging to the same congregation was Mastro[16] Antonio, who owned a carpentry business. Being the only one representing just a trade rather than a profession or a rank by birth, he upheld the least entitlement to the honour of sitting at the tavolino. But just like many inconsistencies adorning the life of Pizzo, this also had no obvious explanation or at least one that would be worth exploring.

'What a pleasure!' said il Professore, seeing me weaving my way among other tavolini.

As I reached my destination, il Marchese was the first to rise. Holding my right shoulder with his left hand and tapping the right one with the ivory handle of his cane, he kissed me on both cheeks and said, 'Onorato, onoratissimo.'[17] Angelo's son came to readjust the tavolini and to accommodate the additional party. The usual rituals began to ensure that everybody would be given the most equitable seat around the tavolini, including Mastro Antonio, who instinctively kept an appropriate distance.

Just about then, Dr Riga appeared. He was a plump old man who stood as a testimonial to metabolic syndrome. Being a smoker and drinker as well as the town's primary care doctor, he thought it useful to educate his patients on harmful behaviours by example. He grunted and snorted continuously, only occasionally interrupting his performance with words or—even more rarely—complete sentences. He was best known for his left wing political views: He was a communist. Like all communists, fascists, other '. . . ists', and croakers who participated in creating the political landscape of Italy at those times, their *raison d'être* was more for the purpose of conversation or, more precisely, to annoy those with milder views. Indeed, none of them withstood any illusion that whatever view they might nominally share with those who represented them in the

---

[15]　Calabria is the south-western region of Italy in which Pizzo resides.

[16]　Mastro is the appellation denoting a person with a specific technical skill.

[17]　I am honoured, I am truly honoured.

government would ever correspond to any substantive action or factual change.

With an ironic smile, Dr Riga asked me, 'Che si dice in America?'[18]

As I attempted to mumble something that would fairly characterise the voices of over 300 million people distributed over fifty states, my uncle, who—contrary to my father—leant politically to the left and always enjoyed provoking me helped by saying, 'America is doing always well. They are pragmatic. They do not waste time chatting like we do. They just mind their business!' Being thankful to my uncle for saying something on my behalf, although with sarcasm, I sat in between my relatives as I did as a child, expecting protection from further inquisition.

'Yes, we need some pragmatism here!' said Mastro Antonio. 'I am not saying somebody who could run the trains like Mussolini, but I think we have gone too far the opposite way . . . Where is the common sense?'

'My dear Mastro Antonio, let's not dust the past. Let it rest in peace, and, in any case, I ask permission to say,' il Professore piped in, turning next to me. 'America has done a lot of great things for the world, but don't you think that it has lost the value of culture along its way?' And so it was that I suddenly found myself engulfed, once again, in some unsolicited conversation about an exoteric subject whose 'pragmatic' value was beyond my willingness and desire to discuss.

As I was once again caught in a corner, trying to come up with a coherent answer, Angelo, who without asking had brought me my usual negroni[19] with olives and chips, saved me. 'Double gin for il Signorino! We hope he will come more often!'

'There are no intellectuals in America,' added il Professore. 'This is the problem! Doing, doing, doing . . . but to what avail? All engineers there,

---

[18]   Literally: 'What do people say in America?' but more generally: 'What is worthy of news in America?'

[19]   Northern Italian drink from Milan made with one-third Campari, one-third gin, and one-third Vermouth and served with a slice of orange and ice.

there is no classic education. This is why they end up not even believing in evolution! Their education system has problems. It restricts their thinking. It educates about how to solve problems, but not about how to find the problems.'

'And to think they have the best heath care system in the world! Meanwhile, they go bankrupt every time they get sick . . . ,' added Dr Riga, in between coughing spells.

I tried to nimbly survey all of my acquaintances in America, wondering which one of them did not believe in evolution, thought we had the best health care system, and was not an intellectual. As I could not think of one, to buy time, I asked, 'How do you define an intellectual?'

Il Marchese, who since I had been a little boy had a particular preference for me, smiled and patted me one more time with his cane across the tavolino. 'Somebody just like you! How can these gentlemen say that there are no intellectuals in America when we know at least one?'

Il Professore interrupted il Marchese but answered my question more directly. 'An intellectual is somebody who is interested in learning beyond the scope of its own sustenance.'

'But then I could name plenty of idiots that could be called intellectuals. May be being interested in learning is necessary but not sufficient,' I replied, instantly regretting the words that had come out too freely, a hint at my mounting irritation. 'What I meant', I tried to correct myself, 'is that there should be some system to the desire to learn, but I do see your point . . .' I did not continue because I was distracted by a sudden thought. I saw myself as another person, immersed in a strange conversation with a number of people from another generation whom I had not seen for many years. I felt thankful to be included so naturally among them in spite of being a fish out of water in this little town by the sea. Still, I felt sorry for not taking a stance to more strongly defend my fellow Americans. In the beginning, I felt an impulse to point out that Italy itself a much smaller country was populated by a colourful assortment of people. Italians, like candy, come in innumerable colours and tastes, of which good examples were sitting at this very tavolino. It would have been all the same unwise to populate a country as big as the

United States with 300 million clones of Uncle Sam wearing a beard, a stars-and-stripes hat, all singing together, 'Oh, say! Can you see? By the dawn's early light . . .' I stuck to my negroni not for lack of patriotism, but rather because I lacked confidence my words could convince these stubborn men that Americans do not come out of an assembly line at the General Motors plant; instead I felt contempt for their provincial minds. The combination of those two sentiments simply interfered with my debating skills. Becoming disinterested, I let the conversation fade into the background, dialling down my auditory channel and up the visual one as I do too often in similar situations.

As I let the conversation float ashore carried by those Aeolian[20] minds, I noticed that il Professore was holding a notebook in his hands. The book was bound in black leather with a golden inscription that stated, in English: 'To my beloved self'. I automatically enquired as to what it was. 'It is a story I am working on. I do not know if I will ever finish it. The truth is that I did not even start it myself, but it was an autobiographical attempt by a student of mine,' said il Professore after looking at il Marchese who replied with a consenting smile.

'He never finished the story, but left these notes, sort of a diary. I have been contemplating the idea of completing the story to honour his memory. Maybe you do remember him? He was about your age. His name was Alessandro.'

'Of course, I know him!' I cried. 'May I see the book?'

'Sure, take it with you. I would love to know what you think.'

As I took the book from his hands, I asked, 'What happened to him? What is special about his story?'

Il Professore began to tell me, but just as he parted his lips to begin his story, other people came to join the tavolino, friends and families, who joyful and clueless interrupted our conversation. Shortly thereafter, my

---

[20]   Aeolus is the Greek God of Wind.

father stated that it was time to retire home for dinner. My uncle stood up; the negroni glass was emptied, and hands were shaken.

As I said goodbye to il Professore, I asked, 'Am I going to see you tomorrow?' So it happened that the magic of Pizzo pounced upon me once more. While the disproportion between the trifling affairs of this little town and the weighty concerns of the rest of world was gradually adjusting, I forgot the boredom, the cynicism, and complacency for the provincial life, and walking home with my relatives, I thought of an old friend whom I had, until now, completely forgotten.

That night, as I called home, I tried to seem cogent, but I instead sounded distracted and I managed, in a new and creative way, to still annoy my wife. I felt sorry for her and for me, not for the essence of our problems but because of my inability to focus on them from this distance. I felt remorseful for being detached and for my personality tainted by an autistic inability to empathise verbally on the phone. As I looked at the silent phone, the church bells paced the time. I left my books piled in an orderly manner on the bedside table while I turned my Kindle, iPad, and other electronics off. Holding the old notebook, I then lay down in bed.

It consisted of notes typed with an old typewriter on collated sheets that were almost transparent, made for carbon copying. There were scattered overlaid corrections. The story had a title: '*The Room*' and went like this:

*　　*　　*

It had four walls, cold even in summer, and two windows. Those were the limits, but the horizons were within because children's imagination does not require expanses. As life takes its course, knowledge chains the imagination, and as our experience expands, larger distances are needed to approach the novel. As the mysteries of youth dissipate, the limits converge into an event horizon where nothing new can be imagined. As a black hole, our essence folds and disappears.

In the centre of the room was a long wooden table. All of the children sat on either side. At one head sat the Future, at the other the Past. At first, the children only talked to the Future and the Past had to shout to be heard. As time went by, they listened more often to the Past. Then some of them did not come to the table, and one day, the Future did not bother to appear. Memories sat on both sides and the Past had nobody to talk to.

This is the story of one of those children and what happened to him that made him leave the table to follow a faraway path. His name was Alessandro. He had an elder brother named Achille. His sister was never born. They had told the two brothers that she had died a short time before birth. He used to fantasise that she would have been the best among them. That was the way he envisioned her during his childhood. She was his best friend, a trustworthy companion, and the only being in whom he would confide.

Compared with Alessandro, his elder brother Achille knew more and knew better. When Alessandro was four, Achille told him that Gesù Bambino[21] did not exist and proved it by showing what their parents hid in the closet before Christmas. Since then, betrayed by his parents and by Santa, he never believed in anything that could not be proven, and for a long time, he blamed Achille for his lack of faith. He never sat close to his brother at the table. The two brothers had cousins, several of them, who shared the wealth of the family. An older one had a particular reputation among the youngest. It was said that she was predisposed to teach and her teachings were quite appreciated by the budding male cousins. She taught sex to the stallions, allegedly providing practical demonstrations during individual lessons. Most went through such teachings without complaints, and as an adolescent, Alessandro looked up at her with the respect reserved for a college professor. She had always been nice to him but somewhat distant, encouraging with her body, unreachable in her soul. When his turn came to be trained, he didn't say no. In the beginning, there was inexperience. He drank with devotion every drop from her spring of knowledge, but since he was a diligent student, it did not take too long to incorporate the teachings and move to uncharted domains. Still, even years later, he viewed her with a mixture of embarrassment and respect, like his first grade teacher who had witnessed his spelling hesitations. When they would run into each other in the Chiazza, she was nice and natural about the past, like nothing had ever happened. Eventually, she made a mistake: She impulsively got married. But as one would expect, she soon betrayed her husband. The simple fellow killed himself when he discovered the truth. She

---

[21] Baby Jesus—believed to carry presents during Christmas Eve, being the Italian counterpart of Santa Klaus in other countries.

then took the children and the furniture and moved away from the angry town. Somebody may know where she went and what happened to her, but her story left a deep mark in Alessandro's life.

The cousins sat at the table following an order that could be best explained by the principle of entropy. However, some gravitational power kept the older boys together at one side of the table while the youngest children spun around the older girls with the excitement of comets belonging to a tiny solar system. Adjacent to it was another dining room reserved for the adults. This was where relatives and guests ate. It was not clear at what point in time each of the children would become adult and move to the other room. It was Nonna's[22] decision to invite. It seemed that boys moved there earlier than girls, perhaps because they were more interested in talking politics or perhaps because they were not needed to take care of the little ones. Most likely it was because that was the way it was supposed to be at those times in that little town. Nobody really knew why or how those decisions were made, probably not even Nonna, but nobody ever argued. Alessandro vividly remembered the day Achille was swallowed by the other room. He did not miss him and he was comforted to have an idea of when, more or less, he would become an adult himself.

The children were not allowed in the adult dining room during meals. The adults did not like to have their discussions interrupted. 'Children should be seen but not heard,' Nonna would say. Occasionally, however, by some principle of reverse osmosis, the adults, as conversations languished, trickled from their dinner room and sat at the children's table, particularly in the evenings, and talked about business, politics, or other stories that would never end. Alessandro's parents rarely came to the table. They did love him immensely, but their father believed that children should look up to their parents and try to become like them, not the other way around, and their mother would not dare to disagree. All of that made sense to him then.

There was wine at the table, regular wine for the older ones and a special wine for the younger ones that Nonna carefully selected with the farmers. It was real wine, but sweet and sparkling and was mixed with water. Perhaps it was because of the wine that meals at that table were always animated.

---

[22]   Italian for grandmother.

Discussions were endless, arguments were without purpose, and agreement was never achieved. It was a noisy pinball game whose apparent randomness is partially controlled by the law of gravity. What came out of the mouth of one child sparked nimble and seemingly purposeless reactions like a ping-pong game. Yet much of what was said carved indelible holes in everybody's soul, with the gentle, effective strokes of dripping water. Things never heard before were brought up by the older cousins, and for the younger children, those 'things' were true life. Around that table, discussions, laughs, arguments, fights, and screams were like breezes and storms, suns and clouds, rains of fall and aromas of spring in an atmosphere without forecast. When the noise reached a certain, yet undetermined, threshold, Nonna would knock on the other side of the wall with her special stick. This was the simplest way to end arguments, the storm of words, and the war of principles.

Among the cousins was Anna Maria, a delicate soul in a delicate body. Her brown eyes were large enough to contain all of Alessandro's childhood dreams. Her smile was the centrepiece of the table. Her delicate voice was the solo violin in that commensal orchestra. According to family legend, she had been struck by lightning that almost killed her when she was a young girl. Fortunately, she survived. But the power of nature was still in her and made her different from the others. She could not be frightened because that could stop her heart. She could not be touched roughly because that could make her body shake. She could not be chased because she was not supposed to run. There was only one thing left to do: love her. And Alessandro loved her fervently for years, silently, peacefully, until one day he got bored. And so it was that the biggest love of his life never knew how he felt.

That day, as Alessandro turned his eyes towards the sea through the window between geraniums and basil leaves, he squinted to reach the horizon through the shiny waves. He wondered what was in the future. That was the end of the room, of the cousins, and of Anna Maria. When he looked back, with the glare of the sun still in his eyes, he could not recognise those familiar shadows. As his pupils widened, embracing the darkness of the room, those faces, voices, and stories became stiller and smaller and quieter and remoter. They disappeared in the distance, as if an imaginary boat was taking him away forever. And this is where our story begins . . .

*   *   *

The typewritten pages ended and scribbled notes followed. But of those we will refer in the following chapter, as we do not want to disturb Signorino Giuseppe, who is by now dozing unaware of the church bells striking half past eleven.

II

The Story of Alessandro

A drizzling rain was rinsing the streets, and being the first of the new season, it was washing away whatever memories were left of the summer, preparing locals and visitors for the advent of autumn with its cool breezes and clear skies. Down the street, the sea, grey like the sky, was receiving its portion of fresh water with complacency and returning foam to the air in gratitude, while the robins, fulfilling Mr Belvedere's prophecy, were setting off for their migration to distant territories. Drops of rain were patiently following in line their course along the gutters, resisting gravity for a few extra moments of altitude before their dive, while a soothing aroma of brioche and croissant saturated the street. The smells rose towards Signorino Giuseppe's open balcony. The fragrances travelled towards his nares, gently rousing him from his slumber. It is to Signorino Giuseppe that we humbly return the narrative.

*   *   *

. . . Thanks to my dependable antidepressant, I slept profoundly all night while Alessandro's memory patiently awaited my awakening. I had known him quite well in my youth before leaving for the Americas. He was an extraordinarily handsome man: tall, with delicate feminine features tempered by a naturally masculine conduct, and inconsistent shaving habits. He had black, curly hair and light blue eyes enveloped within long dark eyelashes that when he stared at you penetrated the soul and distracted the perception of beauty in favour of depth and intelligence. His hands were poised, gracefully accompanying his words without exaggerated Southern affectation. His athletic figure was slim and inconspicuous while his magnetic personality and charisma could be better described as distracting. No matter the topic of discussion, his presence was sensed as the dominant element, and the listener was automatically soothed by a sense of belonging to an elite aristocracy of divine elegance. But perhaps the most remarkable was his smile that, when it suddenly appeared flanked by playful dimples like sun rays breaking through the clouds, bestowed a feeling of confidence and hope, of reassurance that all worries could be forgotten in favour of enjoyment of life, which in turn was beautiful under his kingdom. His elegant demeanour, his comfortable affability, his self-confidence were strikingly in contrast to the nervous coyness that would define most of us during our teen years.

Though his peers universally admired him, he inexplicably stood in a class of his own. He was reserved, did not associate with any exclusive social circles or 'clicks', and was all in all not a particularly popular student. Most regarded him as a snob at best or socially retarded at worst. Despite his interpersonal shortcomings, he had the eye of all the women, and our girlfriends coveted him from our embrace. As a prince, he stood above all not because of the size of his harem but for the number of women who desired to belong to it. In reality, little was known about his relations with the other gender, and although he had been spotted occasionally in the company of older and beautiful women, he never offered a single word or confession to enlighten the gossip. Thus, Alessandro lived a parallel life to his peers for years. He was respected by men and admired by women while simultaneously being neither a man's nor lady's man.

Our relationship deepened serendipitously during our time as teammates on the high school soccer team. We played a similar position as mid forwards, he on the left while I covered the right. He was a fantastically talented player whose technique, athletic skill, and endurance outshone that of everybody else, and I, being a strong player as well, accepted a secondary role to support his play. This mutual understanding of our roles on the field developed into a parallel friendship of sorts off the field. We respected each other and exchanged occasional words before, during, and after games.

I was baffled by his flat disposition during games. As we worked together to get through exciting wins and devastating defeats, I never once witnessed a flinch in his emotions. No matter how stellar his performance, he reliably disappeared at the end of each game with apparent disinterest in any celebration. Although others may have interpreted his behaviour as arrogant or condescending, I believed that it was instead the result of his incoercible propensity for privacy, loneliness, and seclusion. Not being particularly communicative myself, I easily adjusted to this relationship by avoiding judgment and unrealistic expectations—that is, until the last game of the season changed everything.

I remember that night well, as we were ahead in the standings and needed a tie to win the championship: A loss would not suffice. With about fifteen minutes left in the game, we were losing by one goal. I was angry with the passion of young age and equally annoyed with Alessandro's apathetic play. He had been approaching each tackle tentatively, passing carelessly, and taking distracted shots all through the game. On the other hand, I was putting my heart and soul and felt as though I was about to tie up the game with a goal when I found myself on the ground with a most painful sensation coming from my ankle. The next thing I knew I was sitting on the bench, with tears stinging my eyes. I watched the inexorable ticking of the clock and with it the demise of what had been a glorious season. As my hope dwindled to nothing, Alessandro suddenly began to rouse. For the first time all game, he played with the energy and skill we knew he had. With just a few minutes left in the game, he invented a goal from where it was not meant to be. With the utmost grace, he turned to take a thirty-metre shot, and there was nothing for the goalie to do. The ball sailed into the upper corner of the goal and into the net to tie up the game.

The joy and excitement of the team was immediate and immense. There were yells and screams, congratulatory punches and slaps, and tears of joy. But consistent with his character, Alessandro shied away from the celebratory hugs and handshakes. Instead, he coolly walked towards me, and with the widest smile, he pointed his index finger at me, pressing the thumb against it to mimic a shooting gun as if to say, 'Bingo! This goal was for you.'

The game finished in a tie just a few moments later: We had won the championship.

After the game, I ended up in the Emergency Department for X-rays of my ankle. In the waiting room, as I was distracting myself from the throbbing pain with a trivial magazine, I suddenly perceived a shadow. It was Alessandro standing in front of me, wearing his signature warm smile flanked by dimples. He asked, 'So what should we do after you get this leg of yours wrapped up?' And this is how we became friends.

Gradually, we became lovers rather than friends—not in a physical sense, as neither of us bore such tendencies, but in a spiritual way, and at the same time we became accomplices. As easily deduced by the introductory typewritten notes, Alessandro belonged to a well-to-do aristocratic family that for generations had towered in the region. Like many aristocracies of the day, it remained enveloped in an island of paranoid contempt for the rest of the world, and as such, Alessandro had access to the most exclusive circles and elite villas where scores of high-class and fashionable women were waiting to be seduced by his gaze. In his wake, I had my share of harvests from sequential orchards, seducing or being seduced in turn. Despite the self-absorption of youth, I had retained some vague memories of those adventures: a smile, a whispered word, a tear, a squeeze of the hand around my arm, a letter, a shy attempt at poetry. Such flirts did not seem to falter Alessandro, who, on the other hand, with the proprietary boldness of an orang-utan, going from tree to tree, would pick a woman after another like a banana, peeling it on sight, eating it, and discarding the waste before moving with arrant ease to the next without a need to keep record of previous meals.

He once told me, 'In regard to women, there are two kinds of men: the hunters and the lovers. The hunters see women as trophies and move from one to the other just to brag like cowboys putting tags on their revolvers for every Indian they kill or the Indians collecting, vice versa, the cowboys' scalps. The lovers, on the other hand, want to please the woman as if she is their mother, still remembering the comfort of her bosom. They want caressing and approval. I am neither. I am not sure even why I do all of this. Maybe curiosity? What can I learn that I do not already know from smelling this fresh new flower? One has to practice to maintain his skills! But in reality, I get no satisfaction or pleasure but just an ephemeral sensation of being alive and absolving a duty beckoned upon me by destiny. I do it because I feel it is expected of me and it is one of the few things that I can do well . . . I had good training.' He then told me the story of his 'professorial' cousin, with whom the reader is already acquainted through the typed notes. He did not, however, mention her tragic end at that time and simply stated, 'I wonder what happened to her.' Yet in his tone I sensed anguish and a fragile emotion that I had never observed in him when he spoke of other women.

He continued, 'I muse listening to women's flatters. The man that women see when they look at me is a totally different person than who I really am. He looks like me on the surface, but inside him they see whatever suits their fantasy of a prince charming that, in reality, does not exist. These women like me until they know me. But even then, when they finally realise that there is nothing here . . .', he gestured to his heart, '. . . they continue to work on my redemption as if they are a Katarina Ivanovna who could not renounce rescuing Mitya Karamazov.[23] But contrary to Dostoyevsky's character, I have no heart.'

I regarded Alessandro's nihilism as an affectation; then, and in my devotion for him, I was as amused as I was sceptical. In my curiosity, I asked him once, 'Have you ever loved anybody?'

It was then that he mentioned Anna Maria. 'There was a cousin when I was a little boy. I still think of her once in a while, but I am not sure why. She was pretty and shy then, and I was happy just looking at her or sitting close to her. But this changed. Maybe she changed or I changed. I never told her anything, and when I look at her now, she does not stir any emotions in me, as if she is another person entirely.'

'So I love an image buried in the past, and I recollect that sweet feeling of anticipation waiting to see her, of closeness when I was with her, of peacefully sharing time, telling stories to each other. Where has all of this gone? I do not know. I look at those times with the impotence of a boy who looks at a balloon lost from his grip while it climbs the unending sky.'

---

[23]   The unfortunate and unappreciated fan of the eldest of the Karamazov brothers Mitya in Dostoyevsky's novel: *The Brothers Karamazov.*

'It is painful to feel incapable of reciprocating love. I do understand the logical importance of giving, but at the moment there is nothing in me—no happiness, no sadness, no fears, no hopes: just comforting emptiness. I see my life with the detached interest of a person watching a documentary or a boring TV show. Each morning I turn the TV to the channel of life and I passively watch as if I do not exist except as a third person until night when I can turn off the soap opera and reunite myself in the darkness.'

When we were not harvesting, we spent evenings dining at our favourite trattoria that hovered as a palafitte[24] above the sleepy sea. Gradually, we developed a proclivity to betray Venus[25] for Bacchus[26]. We had simple but unending meals with cold bottles of house wine as we talked for hours about every possible subject connected to existence. There were periodic interruptions by friends who dropped by the table to report on mythical conquests in the feminine challenge. We listened to one such braggart with complacency until he departed, after which Alessandro said, 'See? Another hunter! Too bad he did not bring pictures of his prey hanging by her feet.' Then he added, 'But lovers are not any better. An illusion is often created in the mind of worldly men who, upon recognising how much emotional and physical pleasure they can offer to a woman in a relationship, conceive the charitable thought of spreading such joy to other women by evenly distributing their time to effectively satisfy to the broadest reach the other gender. Unfortunately, such generosity is not appreciated by members of the latter gender who seem to put more weight on the exclusivity of a relationship than the practical pleasures that can be derived in the passing moments.' Then noticing that my gaze was lost as I was trying to follow his Messianic teachings through the vapours of alcohol, he turned to the rest of the imaginary group of eager pupils to complete his thoughts. 'This discrepancy of views between genders may be worth debating in another occasion, but for the moment let us simply admit that this comprehensible misunderstanding has brought several misfortunes in the documented history of mankind (and likely even

---

24   Stilt House.
25   Roman Goddess of Love and Beauty.
26   The Greek God of the grape harvest, winemaking, and wine.

earlier), among which several I have had the opportunity of experiencing first-hand.'

Admittedly, his words were not as polished as I represent them here. Nonetheless, they portray the demeanour of those light-hearted ironic moments when Alessandro, taken by that uncontrollable surge of creativity that occasionally grips the human soul, let himself go along the paths suggested by the splashing waves that, just a few feet from where we were, continued their motion unaware of human anguish. In retrospect, I strongly suspect that those carefree conversations, tainted by full bellies and empty bottles of wine, were likely the only speckles of unbridled happiness that Alessandro experienced in all of his life.

Eventually, there was a common finale to all of our discussions that converged into an agnostic view of one's existence. Seen from the point of view of youth and provincial innocence, Pizzo seemed large compared with the rest of the world that being never before seen appeared trite and irrelevant. It seemed to us that past Pizzo's narrow alleys and little alcoves, behind the fragrant bushes, taverns, and beaches, a whole universe breathed an autocratic life in dramatic contrast to the reality of our planet that like an insignificant marble wandered the verges of a galaxy lost in the expanses of the infinite. And when we forgot about the grandeur of Pizzo as we looked up into the night, we felt no relief: The skies symbolised walls of infinite thickness that hovered as a quadri-dimensional prison from which we would never escape, compressed forever by space and time. For others there was God; for us there was only doubt. Faith was nothing more than the ultimate lie that opened the door to a wishful truth. We wondered where we should draw the limits of our imagination. On those moonlit nights, as the emotions grew, we imagined something bigger and unreachable, for life itself was too small and did not fit the horizons of our imagination.

But Alessandro could not endure his own lies for too long. He would test me: 'Imagine that you are in a Jeopardy game . . . And now, the hundred million Lira[27] question! Sir, does God exist or not? With that money at

---

[27]   Lira is a now obsolete form of Italian currency, since it has been replaced with the euro.

stake, what would you guess?' And he would answer himself, 'I would definitely guess that there is no such thing as God. I would not want to lose the money! . . . But we will never know for sure. We could go at the speed of light, shooting up into the sky from now until we die and never get farther than our celestial neighbourhoods. As soon as we are born, we are condemned to a life in prison for the simple sin of existing.' He would conclude thus. As we will see from his notes, there were deeper roots to his pessimism that he never shared with me.

Therefore, at the ripe age of seventeen, Alessandro was a mythical figure to the locals, an idol to the girls, and a leader to the boys, but in himself, he reserved an uneasy feeling of failure and low self-esteem. He floated on the surface of the little town by the sea, searching the horizon for opportunities that he doubted would ever materialise. To be a hero in a town forgotten by God and by the world, to be a leader of a non-existent army was like being a teacher in an empty classroom. He once told me, 'As Machiavelli said of Hiero of Syracuse—he lacked nothing to be able to reign, save for a kingdom.'

He was the first to leave our town. He moved to Milano,[28] nominally to study, but in reality to explore the world 'out there'. I was the one who drove him to the train station. As I arrived at his family home, I found Alessandro waiting outside with his parents. As I pulled up in the car, Alessandro's dad cleared his throat and said, 'Take care of yourself and work hard. You do not want to be like a plant that bears beautiful flowers but never yields fruit.' Taking that as a contorted encouragement, Alessandro hugged his dad, then his mom, placed his bags in the trunk, and turned away.

In the car, he admitted, 'I do not know what I want to do. They want me to be a lawyer or a doctor. Perhaps doing what they want is the best solution. But in some ways, I feel that this is what I have been doing all of my life. It feels like a vortex that is pulling me down deeper and deeper with each turn. When I start accepting one thing, this leads to another and then another against which I have no recourse because the same false logic that made me accept the first will apply to the following.

---

[28]   Milan, a large city in Northern Italy.

And little by little my feet get heavier and heavier, the sky looks farther and farther, and I realise that I am becoming accustomed to breathing the polluted air of my own decisions or lack thereof. Yet as time passes and I am deeply sunk into my life of default, it becomes more difficult to soar and easier to keep falling towards the end of the vortex. I am tired of looking towards a prettier future. Somebody said that "most of the future lies ahead", but for me during these past years, the future has simply evoked the past: the good but mostly the bad times, the achievements and the failures, trying to find answers to questions that I cannot clearly formulate but which continue to erode my soul. These reflections are selfish ghosts who suck any possible happiness from my veins. But now it is time for me to forget the past and move on.'

We shook hands but did not hug. He punched me below the left collarbone, and I can still feel the pressure of that mark of friendship. He climbed up the train and immediately pulled down the window to salute me. As the train started its slow and clanking path towards the unfamiliar territories of the future, he stretched his hand out with his index finger pointing at me, pressing his thumb as if he was, one last time, shooting at me: 'Bingo!'

* * *

As I was sipping on my espresso under a large umbrella on the terrazza of my childhood home, the rain continued to lazily tap, and I opened the notes, curious to find out what more there was to know about my lost friend. To my disappointment, the notes were almost undecipherable, written in a hurried and unstable style, and I decided to defer to my encounter with il Professore, who, like all of the men of his generation in Pizzo, was retired with nothing else to do and was therefore likely to appear in the Chiazza for a light colazione[29] in spite of the discouraging rain. So I walked the fifty meters to join my dad who had already been tapping his right hand on the tavolino for a while now, my uncle's left reliably performing in synchrony. All of the patrons were bunched under an awning that pitched from the old walls of the bar Gatto and came out for approximately eight meters. Water droplets falling off its edges on to

---

[29] A light meal, in Italian.

the wet ground heightened the feeling of cosiness for the fortunate who had found reprieve from the admonishing drumming raindrops.

Il Professore was not there. Instead, under a disproportionate umbrella appeared l'Avvocato,[30] who, like Dr Riga, juggled an unremitting competition between alcohol and cigarettes. Unlike Dr Riga, l'Avvocato embodied a later stage of erosion ascribable to these gusts of pleasure, with a consumptive body, a notable tremor, and the barrel chest of a man with obstructed airways. With Dr Riga, he shared a propensity to snort, grunt, and cough in creative cadence. Interspersed with these noises, he had a proclivity to expectorate at regular intervals into a large unfolded handkerchief that he subsequently refolded elegantly—to protect its contents—enabling his utterly cacophonic symphony to begin again.

As I approached the tavolino, my father, who had clearly been waiting too long for this moment, eagerly jostled the *Corriere della Sera*,[31] turning it open to the third page where there was a long article explaining that an Italo-American had discovered a cure for cancer. I knew instantly that this was a false alarm, and I clarified that this tremendous breakthrough was once again for the benefit of another—much luckier—mammalian species and that, for those of us who are not mice, patience remained of the utmost importance. Having committed years of my life to cancer research, I felt quite confident in my conviction and explanation on the matter, but my comment nonetheless stirred a corollary dissertation from l'Avvocato. Being the retired town lawyer, he felt compelled to exercise his dialectic skills now that in retirement he had few opportunities with more relevant audiences. Holding his first Sambuca above his head with one hand and a cigarette between the middle and index finger of the other, he began his proclamation by stating that, in America, there were many successful scientists who received prestigious prizes and led the world in research but that he failed to see the results. 'This reminds me of the story of the two wine sellers who were taking ten bottles of precious wine to the market . . .'

---

[30]   Italian for lawyer.
[31]   Quotidian newspaper from Milan but popular all around Italy.

Meanwhile, il Marchese appeared, holding an umbrella instead of his cane, but all the same using his new weapon for greetings and for scratching his sideburns in moments of contemplation.

'It was a hot day,' continued l'Avvocato, 'and as they were walking to the market, one of the men said, "Say, what do you think if we drink a bottle of wine?" His friend reminded him that they made the wine in order to make a profit and he did not want to just give it away for nothing. To this, the first wine merchant replied, "How much are we going to sell it for?" "One euro," said the other. "I just happen to have one euro. Give me the bottle and take the money." Satisfied with such impeccable logic, the second businessman accepted the transaction and so they continued. But as they walked along under the sun that beat down, he eventually recognised a similar longing for something cold, liquid, and flavourful to be administered as soon as possible to dissipate the effects of the hot day and the idleness of the path ahead. Considering that good business requires fair transactions, he returned the euro to his friend for a bottle of wine. It is said that wine is not a good thirst quencher and that when a bottle is emptied another is needed to retain the effects. By the time the friends reached the market, there was no wine left and just one euro in their pockets.'

As we sat trying to distil the wisdom into a concise and meaningful argument, l'Avvocato helped us. 'Just the same, it seems to me that all of these "scholars" live a self-congratulatory existence, exchanging prizes, patting each other on the shoulders for their self-proclaimed achievements, all the while neglecting to substantiate whether they are actually doing any good by returning a tangible gain to those who are supporting their self-indulgent pastimes.'

Il Marchese, who had been patiently awaiting the end of the narrative, waved his umbrella at Sig. Belvedere and said, 'Will you bring us two latte di mandorla?[32] One for me and one for Signorino Giuseppe—many thanks.' Turning to me, he added, 'I bet you even forgot what it tastes like.'

---

[32] Southern specialty that consists of squeezed almond juice and sugar that looks like milk but tastes more like the nut from which it originates.

I had intended to drink a cappuccino, as was consistent with my deeply entrenched morning routine, but I had no courage to displease il Marchese. I sipped my latte di mandorla patiently. As I remembered, it offered a sensation of freshness as it smoothly followed its path towards my stomach.

By this time, l'Avvocato's personal competition was tied at three Sambucas and three cigarettes; the rain had reverted into a light drizzle that made my uncle proclaim, 'Zaccalia[33]!' And the lady carrying eggs in a basket on her head reappeared as the undisputed queen of the Chiazza. When a tourist appeared and asked permission to take the queen's picture, she lifted her hand up and rubbed her thumb with her index and middle fingers in a gesture that meant 'money'. The tourist gave her some change from his pocket as she smiled and posed for the picture. And now we know why, even in these modern times, such an obsolete practice of freight remains alive and well.

The combination of the absence of il Professore and the overwhelming inertia of a sleepy town so different from the world to which I am now accustomed together caused me to be overtaken by my typical edginess that so much annoys my family members of all generations. As I began to recognise this within myself, I excused myself from the tavolino with the pretence of finding something interesting to cook for dinner.

Despite the fact that shopping does not come naturally for me, it is strange that when I go to the shopping mall in America around Christmas time, I find myself feeling temporarily and mysteriously happy. Perhaps it is due to the confusion and bright lights that momentarily distract me from the chronic depression and boredom that often overtake me before the holidays. In any case, I do a very poor job at shopping. The sensory overload—caused not just by the 'things' but also by my fellow mall shoppers—overwhelms me. I find it fascinating to observe the variety of species and subspecies of consumers, and I find myself wondering whether spending behaviour is mostly the result of nature or nurture.

---

[33] Dialect expression to describe a drizzling rain.

There are the experts who seem to know everything about everything in the mall. They can do comparative shopping with other malls in the area and even those in California where they might have been last summer or because they have checked the Internet. They can precisely point out the pros and cons of every item and accurately differentiate between true and pseudo bargains. Although objectivity is the most apparent feature of this phenotype, the vibration in their voices when they describe the most recent gadget for sale on the top floor betrays deeper emotions.

Then there are the sceptics. No matter how good something may seem, they do not fall for it. They know that the pink plastic mask for their cell phone, although very handsome looking, should cost at least fifty cents less than the posted price. Not to mention that it could break easily if you are not careful because the parts assembled in China are probably not well glued together: Their sister-in-law bought a similar one several months ago and had to take it right back with a crack down the middle. Fortunately, she got her money back. In general, it is always prudent to watch out for the big conspiracy that is trying to sell you mediocrity at an inflated price like those Redskins socks that would not last one washing without shrinking and are in any case overpriced, particularly considering how poorly the team is doing this year.

Then there are the compulsive buyers. They buy things because they are 'so cute', like the bobble-head doll with the president's head. One definitely could not do without it, not to mention that it is twenty per cent off! It is easy to justify such compulsions when you feel that the more you spend the more you save.

This brings me to the bargain hunters. I believe this is a subspecies of the compulsive buyers who collect only things for sale whether they need them or not, whether they can fit in their house or not, and whether they like them or not. The logic behind this behaviour is that a bargain is a bargain and the chance of getting a twelve pack of pink plastic sunglasses with snowflakes painted on top for fifty per cent off may never materialise again.

Obviously, the best kind of mall shopper is the practical buyer. At an efficient pace, she follows a pre-planned path across the mall, emerging from each store with additional bags and packages that she efficiently fits inside her other bags like a Russian babushka doll until the external bag breaks. She can fill up the trunk of her car in only a few hours, having spent an appropriate amount of time and money to achieve the ultimate holiday shopper's goal: burying the dullness of Christmas with colourful junk.

Then there are the desperate ones. I believe I belong to this group. They appear lost in the crowd. They look at 'things' that they do not see. They do not really know what their spouse or kids would want, not only for Christmas but also for life, which makes them wonder whether they really know them at all. Everything looks the same to them. They look for new ideas, but nothing matches their hopes, perhaps because they have none. They think of past Christmases and they see the repetitiveness of the game: the desperate struggle towards a concept of happiness that inevitably will not materialise. They think with nostalgia of those times when Santa took care of everything and Christmas Eve brought trepidation and surprise. They do not understand what happened to Santa, who now sits at the corner of the mall posing with children for minimal wage. They question what they are doing there, forgetting that they have nowhere else to go. In the end, they identify a kind soul in a candle shop and ask her to sell them something—anything—so they can finally go home without feeling that their day was once again a failure. And when they emerge from the mall with the bells jingling and the lights shining, they feel once again happy because, after all, it is Christmas time.

. . . But shopping in Pizzo is none of that. First of all, as I walk along the shops in Pizzo, I am not one in a crowd but rather I am promoted from Signorino Giuseppe to Signor Dottore[34] or Signor Professore, according to the social status of those who address me. I wonder what title I could be promoted to if an even lower caste existed. To validate conclusively the irrefutable reason for such deference, to the wondering and unsophisticated customer the shop owner would avow, 'He is Don Paolo's son', thus settling any residual dispute about the need for special attention. Despite what it would appear, it is not fawning but rather

---

[34]   Italian for doctor.

sincere appreciation for something far and exotic that can only be shared indirectly by demonstrating the deepest reverence.

Second, there is far less to choose from, completely mitigating the sensory overload of the American mall. Then almost nothing is on sale, although everything is open for bargaining. But this is a skill beyond my greatest ambition. What suits me best, however, is the freedom from decision making. Any indecisive character is in paradise here. 'This fish just arrived. It is still flapping its tail,' the storekeeper said, and before you know it, the fish is in a paper bag and in my hands. 'And what about these eggplants? Have you ever seen anything that big? They will do just fine for a parmigiana. Let me add this mozzarella cheese right away and some tomatoes, and let's not forget a few leaves of basil. By the way, let me go in the back. I have some good house wine. Now do not tell anybody because we have no license to sell it! You have to try it, Signor Professore. It is a good new wine. It is called Critone. Take a bottle, compliments of the house.' In the end, with bags full of goods for which I paid a total of exactly ten euros, I found myself walking home, trying to remember what I had intended to buy for dinner in the first place and wondering what I would do with the flapping creature from the sea that was too big and unlikely to adapt to the limited ecosystem provided by our little fresh water tank in the study.

At this point, I can hear in the background the reader asking where this story is going and whether such diversions are warranted. But I would ask in return: Isn't this the way that our life is? Don't we so often have to put on hold what we most care about to deal with trivialities that keep us busy, whether we want them or not? And besides, this is the way things go in Pizzo. Here, only the church bells are predictable and everything else has to wait for God's time.

Fortunately, as I returned to the Chiazza, I found il Professore at the tavolino ready for the continuation of the story of Alessandro who, I hope, has not been already forgotten. This will be the subject of the next chapter. But before turning the page, I am compelled to conclude the saga of my shopping spree.

Patiently waiting for me at the corner of il bar Gatto was Ciccio Percuoco. He was sitting on a chair with his legs crossed just like my dad and uncle, looking towards the barber's shop and compellingly arguing with himself, with the most polite demeanour and possibly, if he could be heard, the most reasonable eloquence. Walking towards the monologist with my provisions, I could not avoid noticing the similarity between his piercing blue eyes and those of my dad and uncle, particularly under the frame of the characteristic receding baldness of my ancestors, and once more I wondered. But there was no tavolino at his side and, therefore, the penetrance of the 'tapping' phenotype previously discussed could not be tested and confirmed on this occasion. Therefore, I just delivered the comestibles to his dependable care, including the fish that said 'goodbye' to me from the bag with one last flap.

III

Alessandro's Coming of Age

The story now stumbles into a delicate matter about which the readers are asked to keep confidentiality and to refrain from divulging it beyond the threshold of these pages. At the tavolino, together with the by now well-known crowd, sat Don Pino, il Sacerdote[35] of the Church of San Giorgio[36], this being the Cathedral of Pizzo from which the famous bells marked the time. The reason for such sensitivity was Don Pino's reticence in being recorded as participating in the profane setting of pleasurable human consumption, since he represented Pizzo's top ecclesiastics. In fact, he never gave in to such temptations, save for those not so exceptional occasions in which he was forced by his own kind nature to reach out to his flock, particularly when forcefully and insistently invited by the *noblesse oblige*[37] of il Marchese. Therefore, in accordance with Dr Riga's efforts to educate by example what to avoid in the corporeal matters, Don Pino made an effort to illustrate on the spiritual ones, also on account of that merciful facet of Catholicism that incorporates remorse, penitence, and redemption for any sin without specific limitations on nature or number.

---

[35] Head clergyman, minister.

[36] The Cathedral of Pizzo which sits just in front of my house and is known for hosting the grave of Joaquin Murat (about whom we will hear more later).

[37] French phrase literally meaning 'nobility obliges'.

This is not to say that Don Pino was a bad shepherd. In fact, he was just what Pizzo—a town that could not tolerate a chauvinist—needed: somebody with credentials for empathy for all imaginable sins, as Don Pino allegedly possessed hands-on experience with most of them (not that anybody would dare question him on the matter). What the town needed was a clergyman who baptised at the early stages, conducted marriages when they were utterly unavoidable, and offered comfort and hope to those preparing to leave Pizzo and never return. Death, according to him, was not the end but the beginning of a better life, provided, of course, that potential disputes with the Omnipotent had been settled before departure. 'Dio perdona tante cose per un atto di misericordia'—*God forgives many things for an act of charity*—he would remind the penitent, paraphrasing Lucia Mondella's words from *The Betrothed*, hinting that even a modest donation to the Church of San Giorgio would suffice to compensate for a lifetime of accumulated endeavours that may not meet exactly the requirements for trespassing the gates of heaven.

Don Pino was popular in the entire town, even with those old ladies who dressed in black like cockroaches chanted melancholic litanies in Church with high-pitched bleats, perhaps out of respect for God but unquestionably in contempt of any musical deity. Standing in front of them, he would bend his neck forward, followed by his head and chin, displacing his cervical fat and touching his chin to his breastbone while crossing his hands in front of his heart. With his eyes thoughtful, sad and even moist at times, he looked at them and temporarily, as abruptly as a cloud covering the sun, substituted his jovial demeanour for that of sorrow in a gesture of sympathy for those bigots. And one could clearly see that he was genuinely sorry for these poor ladies who had nothing better to do than wasting their time in such a predicament.

But such contrition was too much in dissonance with Don Pino's jolly temperament to last for long. As such, whatever service he was conducting, he performed it efficiently so that the congregation—himself included—could be relieved of their spiritual duties and return to the fresh air once again, leaving those who retained further matters to discuss with the Father, the Son, and the Holy Ghost to do so in the privacy of the elated enclosure of incense and without further and unnecessary terrestrial interference.

Don Pino judged that l'Avvocato embodied the neediest of the current flock of congregants. As an archetype of his charitable nature, he decided to demonstrate empathy and allegiance by ordering himself a Sambuca to match his neighbour's. Meanwhile, Don Pino's presence aroused in Angelo Belvedere an unsettling presentiment in that his own life may one day end, particularly on account of his own habit of indulging in smoking and drinking that may expedite the process. In an attempt to ingratiate himself to the master negotiator, Sig. Belvedere took it upon himself to bring an ice cream sandwich—consisting of a brioche cut into half and filled with homemade vanilla ice cream—together with biscotti and pasta di mandorla[38] cakes. These, in turn, forced Don Pino to release his white plastic collar by shoving two fingers behind it, to unleash it and, thus, facilitate the progress of food down his oesophagus, following the path originally suggested by gravity but impeded by the clergyman's traditional garment in resemblance of the snare of the cormorants.[39] To further facilitate the progress of the grub towards its destination, Don Pino ordered a second Sambuca followed by a grappa-spiked espresso since, according to his modest opinion, the liquorish taste of Sambuca would not go well with the bitterness of coffee. 'Grappa in coffee is like Mary's tears diluting the bitterness of the Passion of Christ,' he would say, leaving his audience in awe of the poetic portrayal of this otherwise profane vision, while he continued his mastication with gravitas.

As I approached the tavolino, I was welcomed by a row of warm smiles. As I observed them on this particular day, I felt a sense of love for the old wise men that had gathered, waiting for me, on a rainy day. I realised what I must mean to them: I was a representative of their own progeny who were scattered around the Italian boot and beyond, most of them successful on account of the immigrant's pride or, in any case, better off than if they had stayed in Pizzo, where opportunities are scant and of comparatively diminutive proportions. This time, with this in mind,

---

[38] Almond paste.

[39] Birds that have been used for centuries by fishermen in China, Japan, and Greece. A snare is placed at the base of the neck, allowing only small fish to be swallowed. When a large fish is swallowed, it becomes caught in the neck, prompting the bird to return to the fisherman's boat, where the fisherman relieves the obstruction and brings the fish to market.

I did not seek shelter between my relatives, but rather sat in between il Marchese and il Professore.

'Dear Don Pino,' Dr Riga, who had also joined the group, was saying, 'you should not feel bad about this. Things have changed because of the Internet.'

Don Pino had observed that the size of his flock had been shrinking over the years, as the diminishing elder contingent was not replenished by the seeds of youth, and expressed concern that this vanishing of the mystical verve was, at least in part, his own fault.

'Let us be honest!' continued Dr Riga. 'Why do people become Christians in Italy and not Muslims, Jews, or whatever else? Because they are baptised just out of the womb, before even getting a chance to pass the meconium!'

'And then they remain Christian by default,' added l'Avvocato, 'because while they are preoccupied with more important things most of the time, Christianity—with its gamut of sacraments—works as a panacea by keeping their mothers and wives busy. Our generation passively followed what was served to it on a plate, and I conclude that "religious choice" is a circumstantial affair. Do not try to convince me that it is more than coincidence that religious preferences follow geography and ethnicity. It is absurd to assert that each individual member of each ethnic group around the world converges on to a common conclusion after considering all of the options.'

The glass of Sambuca was by then hovering over us while l'Avvocato stood in a statuary pose resembling the Statue of Liberty, save that I had yet to see the latter cough and expectorate with the same majestic might.

'But these modern kids are different! They are showered with information as soon as they learn to use a computer in kindergarten, things we could not have even imagined when we were young! Being different is the fashion these days, and while this may be good for the new generation, it is harmful, with all due respect, to the business of Christianity and other institutions that depend upon habit. Therefore, my dear Don Pino, I do not think you should blame yourself. It is the times that have changed.'

'I totally agree with l'Avvocato,' intervened il Professore. 'We should teach our children all religions and philosophies and let them choose which they prefer in the end. Let them compare the allegorical and patronising jargon of the parables that all religions share. Let them examine the pseudo-logic that all religions share with the common goal of enforcing something that could not otherwise be proven by logical thinking. Dear Don Pino, with your common sense,' continued il Professore, 'you made more proselytes and saved more souls than all the prophets put together because, at least, you keep your teachings relevant to what your flock needs, and you bring positive affirmation when and where it is most called for.'

'And you keep it short!' interjected Mastro Antonio, nodding his head thoughtfully.

'I know what you mean,' replied Don Pino. 'Sometimes I see myself more as a Buddhist than a Christian. A few years ago, I went with a Christian delegation to China and visited the oldest Buddhist temple in Beijing. I loved being there for those few hours of meditation. I loved the silence and simplicity of the monastery. There were just a handful of monks around. The Buddha—with an encouraging smile on their faces—were sitting or reclining in peace. The smell of incense and monotonous chanting put me at ease, in synchrony with the Eternal Spirit. I felt an overwhelming desire to change, although I was not sure from what to what I would be changing. I promised myself, right then and there, that the goal of my life and serenity would be to never hurt others and to alleviate spiritual and emotional suffering on Earth, as the returns of such practice are easier to measure for us mortals.'

'It seems to me that Buddhism could just be summarised as "take it easy"—an ascetic version of Prozac!' added Dr Riga.

'Sometimes I feel that I am a Buddhist myself, but for other reasons. I feel that the Chinese are right that we exist in different lives, but I would amend the concept ever so slightly: We do not live our different lives sequentially but rather in parallel. Sometimes we are mice, sometimes tigers, dogs, or cats and most often pigs,' added l'Avvocato, confusing Buddhism with the Chinese Zodiac and adding cats to the mix, possibly in honour of Sig. Belvedere, who standing on his mound, with the thousandth cigarette in his hand, was scrutinising the Chiazza for potential clients now that the rain had subsided and the sun was poking through the clouds.

And so it was that non-sequiturs around a common theme filled those lazy mornings in Pizzo. Problems that could not be wholly embraced by philosophers and scholars were dissected with simplicity by the good-hearted wise men, who having lived their entire lives in that little town were sheltered from having to confront their logical solutions against the rigor of science.

'Yes, Don Pino, take it easy. You are exactly what we need,' said il Marchese.

Mastro Antonio added, 'You see, Don Pino, you may not be perfect, but as il Marchese said, you are just what we need. In fact, you remind me of Berlusconi.[40] They can say whatever they want about him, but nobody could ever accuse him of giving Italians the reputation of being boring.'

Despite the undisputed affection we all shared for Mastro Antonio and his unwavering honesty in spite of all diplomatic considerations, we all felt that his well-intentioned testimonial directed at our town's most prominent ecclesiastic figure had gone too far. I silently pledged— and I am fairly confident that most of the others did, too—that next time Mastro Antonio opened his mouth, I would shove an ice cream sandwich—vanilla or chocolate, whichever was most handy—in it before it was too late. I say most, but not all, of the others because, as the rest of us shifted uncomfortably in our chairs, il Marchese, staring at his shoes and scratching his right sideburn with the handle of his umbrella, produced a subtle smile at the corner of his mouth that I caught only because I was sitting at his side.

---

[40]   Silvio Berlusconi, Italian Prime Minister for a total of nine years, making him the longest standing Italian Prime Minister (1994-1995, 2001-2006, and 2008-2011) and whose life has been characterized by colorful rumors regarding his relationships with the other gender.

It was il Professore who first brought up Alessandro's story. 'Did you read the notes?' he asked, smiling.

'Certainly. Only the typewritten part, though. It was too difficult to decipher the rest. I was hoping that you could summarise it for me.'

'Ah yes. Frankly, it took a lot of studying and, more importantly, talking to Alessandro during the late stages of his illness to turn those scrawls into a coherent story.'

And so it was that il Professore, after looking one more time at il Marchese for encouragement, started, 'I am sure you all remember Donna Giovanna . . .'

'Of course we do!' exclaimed Don Pino. 'We were all so scared of her!'

The readers are already familiar with Donna Giovanna, being the character described in Alessandro's notes as 'Nonna'. As il Professore told his story, my relatives restrained their tapping, Dr Riga and l'Avvocato toned down their coughing and snorting to their minimal necessity, Mastro Antonio inched closer to the table, and il Marchese rested his chin on his hands that were crossed over the handle of his umbrella that stood in front of him. I will paraphrase his narrative from here on, interjecting only relevant salient contributions from the audience.

*   *   *

Donna Giovanna had lived through World War II, floating above the tempestuous sea in a coastal town that served as a stronghold for the Germans while the Allies bombarded them regularly. However, it was not the bombs that shook the town to its core. Rather, it was the derivative unsettlements associated with the devastation, chaos, and poverty that accompany war that had the greatest effect on the town's citizens.

Following the death of her husband because of tuberculosis a decade before, her firstborn son died when he was taken down by enemy fire while flying in a raid over the Tyrrhenian Sea. They felt lucky when his body was found badly burnt on the shore a few days later, his identification tag still hanging from his neck, as he could be properly buried in the family chapel. Together with these losses, a large portion of the family's old estate dissipated as a result of the evolving rulings by the ever-changing factions, which altered the previously untouchable political landscape of Southern Italy. Unfortunately, these rulings could not be contested in the absence of the patriarch or the eldest son who would have carried both the political connections and the savoir-faire to stabilise the sinking boat and preserve their property during the chaotic and unstable environment created by the civil war within the regular war. Despite all that was stacked against her, Donna Giovanna managed. She made ends meet by turning the palace where her family had prospered just a few years before into a boarding house for Germans and later Americans. It has been rumoured even that for a brief period of time after the Americans landed in Pizzo, she boarded both nationalities simultaneously for those few days when a handful of Germans had to stick around for mainly administrative reasons and were caught by surprise by the swift invasion. Allegedly, she negotiated between the two factions that her home would be a sanctuary of tolerance during the overlap, serving the respective factions their meals at two different times in their respective wings of the palace and leaving the German clerks the time to organise for their departure—with the understanding that they would leave as soon as possible—in peace.

Following the devastation of the war, her surviving children migrated to the north while she stayed in Pizzo to restore the family's empire by herself. The old mansion slowly regained the majesty and respect that had belonged to the family for centuries before. In the process, Donna Giovanna became a tough woman. She learnt to lead and control those around her, and people simultaneously feared and respected her. In the Church of San Giorgio, she had a private balcony that sat empty most of the time, waiting for those special occasions when she honoured the cathedral with her presence. On those rare occasions, people made way for her as the sacristan opened the gate to her balcony and the altar boys came to kiss her hands, among them being the young Don Pino. She often asked Sara, her faithful servant, to light candles and give donations while she scanned the cathedral from her bench with an inquisitive eye, as if to ask the *nouvelle* post-bellum leaders of the town sitting in the front row, who had also come to pay they respect to the Omnipotent, 'Where were you when I needed you?'

Thus, Donna Giovanna lived as a fearless governing queen, dictating the undisputed rules of her queendom. But Alessandro was not fearful of her. To him, she was simply his Nonna. She was a Nonna with whom he lived, as his family had reunited in Pizzo after their wealth and status had been restored. Truth be told, the invincible Donna Giovanna nurtured a weakness in the vest of Nonna. That weakness was for Alessandro. Though he did not closely resemble any of his ancestors, his beautiful eyes and gentle demeanour were disarming, even for the tough and stoic Donna Giovanna. Alessandro's special place in her heart was well hidden from the world by her stern countenance, save for Alessandro's elder brother Achille, who secretly resented the discrimination.

In his defence, it should be admitted that Alessandro was an exceptionally agreeable boy. At any age, no one could recollect his involvement in a temper tantrum of any kind. Even the rebellious behaviours in which any child may be involved were often defended by a disarming logic that, though not necessarily correct, demanded respect and required thoughtful negotiation.

*   *   *

As an example of Alessandro's compulsive logic, il Professore offered an anecdote that he had heard from the boy's father and that he thought contributed 'compliments of the house'. At the age of four, in the parlour where most of the family activities took place, Alessandro's mother had said, 'Your father and I are so lucky to have the best children in the world!'

To this, Achille replied with courteous enthusiasm, 'And we, too, are lucky, since we have the best Nonna and the best parents in the world!'

Happiness was preparing to settle around this impeccable discovery if little Alessandro had not interjected with a thoughtful utterance. 'Wait a minute. That would be an *impossible* coincidence.'

*   *   *

In regard to Alessandro's agreeable personality, there stands another revealing anecdote, this one directly contributed by his own diary. Among

Nonna's many rules, one in particular was unassailable: the need for complete stillness during the contrura. Whether summer or winter, hot or cold, children were expected to eat at the table dressed, after taking a shower if they had just returned from the beach, according to her code: freshly ironed and starched shirts. They were expected to behave appropriately, with their legs under the table, hands but not elbows over it, and chewing with their mouths closed. Following the family meal, they were expected to retire to their rooms, undress, and lie down until the time against the time had ended.

Rest and sleep during the contrura was an ancestral custom, alleged to have an effect on a child's health and growth. No scientific argument could have supported this theory, as Achille's mind soon realised. Thus, cursing Nonna and the accomplice ancestors, Alessandro's discontented brother would doze off in the deepest gloom, day after day, and year after year. This was not the case for Alessandro, however, who learnt to enjoy this tranquil time. Every day, during those quiet hours, he placidly brought a chair to his bedroom window where he could observe the outside world peacefully. He stared for hours at life in the third person, a manner that suited him well and that he brought forward into his adult life, as we have already discovered in the previous chapter.

As a result of the agreeable personality that defined his childhood, Alessandro never took advantage of his charismatic power over his Nonna, accepting amicably her rules. But this agreeableness was shaken by the dawn of puberty. In those years, as might be expected during this complicated age, he developed a vague compulsion to explore uncharted aspects of the complementary gender. This drove him to favour spending evenings in the Chiazza or—even better—in the secluded alcoves of the Marina[41] instead of sitting in the family parlour to listen, again, to rehashed family tales. As a result, he became progressively less keen on observing the 8 p.m. curfew imposed by Donna Giovanna and policed by Sara.

---

[41]   Original fishermen's dwellings right below the town and along the seashore, an area with several bars, restaurants, and nightlife.

Sara had been with the family since they had adopted her at age six. She had served originally as nanny for Alessandro's father and subsequently for his two children. With time, she had risen in the family ranks to acquire the stature of what in modern times might be referred to as 'Nonna's executive assistant'. As part of this important role, she took command of all chores with firmness and loyalty. She was perfectly suited to work for Nonna's dominant personality. Over the years, she had adjusted by accepting any order or guideline from Donna Giovanna without question, digesting it, and then sweating it out as if it was of her own genesis. The execution occurred as a unidirectional flow, like a fish gulping water from their mouth and pushing it out through their gills in one smooth movement. Sara, dressed in a characteristic red and black servant's gown, wobbled rather than walked and wore a braided bun that crowned her head. She was dependably followed, from a distance, by two disproportionate rumps that she exploited when she rested her retroverted hands behind her back. One hand carried a wooden spoon that, like a monarch's sceptre, demanded obedience. She called the tool 'la ragione',[42] and it served as a deterrent against mischievousness.

On one particular evening as the church bells signalled eight o'clock, she wobbled into the Chiazza to collect the two boys and marshal them to their stable only to find that the thirteen-year-old Alessandro was nowhere to be found. In no time, the Chiazza dwellers were encircling Sara to offer their comfort and to support her for several reasons. First, the missing child was an unprecedented indication of a loss of respect for the wooden spoon and for the woman who carried it. Second, the prospect of having to confront Donna Giovanna with the news of a lost child, the townspeople knew, was unbearable. And third, and perhaps most important for the simple and kind-hearted woman, was that Sara had genuine and deep concern for the whereabouts of her prince.

While Achille sincerely contested any insider knowledge of the current predicament, Alessandro appeared at the doorstep of Carmelo Natti. Sig. Natti was Pizzo's electrician, who maintained a relationship with Alessandro's family comparable to Ciccio Percuoco's with my own, probably on account of similar escapades by Alessandro's grandfather.

---

[42]   La ragione: colloquially meaning 'being right'.

With regal deportment, Alessandro informed Sig. Natti that he had initiated a revolt against Donna Giovanna and that he planned to move into Sig. Natti's house because he trusted that he was a man of honour that could provide him asylum from his despotic grandmother. Carmelo Natti, realising that it was prudent to host the rebel to prevent him from concocting an even dumber plan should he be left to his own devices, allowed Alessandro to establish the headquarters of his insurrection in his home where he lived with his devoted wife, two daughters—of which the elder, Mariuccia, was one year older than Alessandro and quite pretty—and their little mutt dog.

The dice already being cast, and with not much else left to do at that early hour, Sig. Natti proposed a game of bingo. While the entire family, now one person larger, was settled around the table with their cards and little pieces of tangerine peel and seeds to cover their Bingo card numbers, the poor electrician, who had been living a most peaceful life up to that moment, positioned his wool hat on top of his head and announced that it would be pleasurable to celebrate this historic occasion. With that, he left the small apartment under the pretence of fetching some gelato.

Alessandro's family palace sat just a few turns away from his own home. Sig. Natti walked along narrow alleys which, at that hour, were populated only by stray cats and dogs that, strangely, seemed to continue living their lives untouched by the historic event. Similarly, the whole town appeared unchanged from a few hours before, save for the fact that when Carmelo Natti reached with trembling knees the mansion where Donna Giovanna reigned, he noticed that more than the usual number of windows were illuminated. This was most likely on account of the fact that Donna Giovanna, like Napoleon in circumstances of similar gravity, was meditating while shuffling her feet back and forth along the top floor where the headquarters of the counter-revolution stood.

As he climbed the stairs, after being announced, wondering how Donna Giovanna would take his resolution to offer asylum to her insubordinate grandson, he overheard her state in front of the portrait of her defunct husband something that made his knees shake even more forcefully. 'Maria Santissima, that boy would never have thought of doing something so foolish and irresponsible if you were still alive. You would know how to take care of him and whoever is helping him in this despicable rebellion.' It was clear to Sig. Natti that the rumour that Alessandro was alive and well somewhere had already spread. As such, Donna Giovanna could focus the entirety of her energy on re-asserting her authority.

Having received no help from the admonishing but detached portrait of her deceased half, Donna Giovanna realised that, as it had been the case for many decades before, she would be forced to deal with the current problem on her own. Returning to her pacing, she stumbled into the presence of Sara and Sig. Natti, who was nervously holding his hat in one hand and turning it around with the other. As he was preparing to say, 'Baciamo le mani, Donna Giovanna',[43] she cut him off by saying, 'Un uomo coi baffi[44] told me that he came to bother you!'

While Sig. Natti racked his brain to unearth the best way to admit his fault, Donna Giovanna continued, 'Great! Keep him in your home like house arrest until I decide what I will do with him.'

Like all great commanders in the past, Donna Giovanna knew she had to develop a swift and unforeseen manoeuvre to reassert her supremacy over her audience and, subsequently, over Alessandro. Taking another walk along the corridor, where the council of ancestors looked inquisitively at her from their portraits, and not being able to come up with any punitive action against her adored grandson that she would have the muscle to carry on, she returned, and holding her right hand open towards the door as an indication that Sig. Natti was free to leave, she proclaimed, 'Let the boy worry all night. Tomorrow I will send Sara to communicate that if he returns without further nonsense, I will forgive him.'

Like Napoleon before her, satisfied with the established plan of attack for the following day, Donna Giovanna went to bed and rapidly fell asleep,

---

[43] An expression of respect meaning literally 'kissing the hands'.

[44] 'A man with moustache'—mythological figure out of Napitinian folklore feared by all youngsters because without being seen, he dwells everywhere and hears everything to report naughty pursuits to respective Nonnas.

feeling proud of her diplomatic ability to turn her first defeat in a long time into an honourable compromise.

Just a few rooms apart, Sara also had fallen asleep. Her sleep, however, was not peaceful. Instead, it was interrupted by sudden falls from a tree, by gestures of anger from strangers, and most importantly, by the reproaching stares of the ancestors who, having come out of their portraits, were pacing up and down the hall sharing with one another their discontent with Sara who had let them down.

In yet another room, not so far apart, Achille was instead completely awake. He lay in bed, relishing the thought of Alessandro's impending punishment with the subconscious hope that following his brother's mischievous escapades he could gain a better ranking within the family hierarchy.

Alessandro completed the bingo game, and holding the bowl up against his face, he licked every last drop of ice cream clean down to the very bottom in quiet recognition that neither Nonna nor Sara was there to monitor his behaviour. He then went to bed and slept deeply, not as a reward for a well-designed plan to confront the upcoming events, but rather on account of the naivety of his privileged youth that caused him to presume that something supernatural would fix everything in the morrow. In a bed close to him, Mariuccia lay awake, observing Alessandro's curly hair.

The following day, Alessandro woke up to learn that life's problems do not just evaporate on their own. As the light came through the curtains, it occurred to him that not only did he miss the comfort of his room, decorated with frescos of beautiful and friendly cupids and plump goddesses, but also he was floating adrift the waters of a complicated affair of his own creation from which he had no idea how to concoct an escape. To validate for himself the previous evening's status of affairs, he went in his head over the series of events that had precipitated the revolt. In doing so, he reassured himself that it was truly not his choice to pursue this fight for freedom. Instead, he felt that it was his moral duty, much like during the American Civil War the Union took on the responsibility to fight against the Confederates who like Nonna upheld the practice of slavery.

Comforted by the thought that this quandary was in fact not his fault at all, he turned around to find Mariuccia's big brown eyes staring at him, distracting him completely from his current predicament. As was his usual manner, he countered with his charming smile.

You can imagine his surprise when the doorbell rang, disrupting the tender moment. Sara appeared at the door, informing him that Donna Giovanna had granted Alessandro amnesty, provided that he would retreat without further discussion. All of her strengths aside, it was clear that Nonna lacked the strategic shrewdness of the great conquistadores who would not dare to concede even the smallest sign of weakness to their adversary. In fact, the unexpected concession brought forth by Nonna's messenger restored Alessandro's confidence. The boy, who was already taller than the stubby Sara, held her right shoulder with the disproportionate paw of a teenager and staring in her eyes said, 'Please tell Nonna that I will come home only when she agrees to let me stay out at night until 11 p.m. and until midnight on weekends. Until then, I will stay here . . . even if that means staying here for the rest of my life.'

It is difficult to accurately portray the devastating effects of such a cyclone on all those who were present. Sara simply dropped her jaw and patted her clammy forehead with a calico handkerchief while she wobbled to the first available chair. Sig.ra Natti crossed herself while Sig. Natti thought best to pretend he had not heard. All the while, their little dog, sensing that something ominous was hovering above the Natti household, circled from person to person while whining, tapping its tail, and licking whatever hands or body parts he could reach from his squatting position. The youngest daughter appeared unaffected by the conversation and stuck a finger in her nose while Mariuccia blushed and turning her big eyes downward silently imagined a life with her prince and had no quandaries.

After partially recovering, Sara was the first to break the silence. 'Do not upset Donna Giovanna any further. Nobody has ever defied her. She knows what she is doing. Mayors, professors, Onorevoli,[45] and all men

---

[45] Appellation used to address members of the Italian Parliament,

with moustaches do not dare to confront her. Do not challenge the woman who took care of this entire family during the war!'

As she went on, regurgitating testimonials that she had heard before in similar circumstances, Alessandro's resolve remained unshakable. One more time, he touched Sara's shoulder, and gently squeezing it with a reassuring smile, he told her, 'Do not worry. *Il Diavolo non é brutto come lo si dipinge.*[46] Donna Giovanna is not as bad as they say. Everything will be fine. Just refer to her my message.' With that, Sara, wobbling at a record pace with both hands resting on her rumps, went back to relay the message of defeat to her previously invincible commander-in-chief.

But courage waxes and wanes, and after Sara left him in his asylum, Alessandro wondered, 'What will be next? Will I really spend the rest of my life here, playing bingo and eating ice cream?'

Meanwhile, in the confederate headquarters, Donna Giovanna was preparing to magnanimously receive with open arms her prodigal grandson. She rehearsed the scene over and over, walking up and down the ancestors' hall, taking a sniff of pepper powder,[47] sitting with composure on the leather arm chair that contained the family emblem, but in the end ruining everything by rushing to the door when Sara's return was announced. The internal turmoil that followed Donna Giovanna's discovery that Alessandro did not return with Sara could not be portrayed in words, even if those words were written by a committee of experts including Omer, Virgilius, and Dante, nor even by asking for prominent international contributions from Shakespeare, Dostojewski, Chekov, Hemingway, or Steinbeck. Therefore, I will circumvent this part by humbly describing the factual portrait of Donna Giovanna resting in bed, with the shades completely shut and a cloth soaked with vinegar on her forehead, moaning like a pregnant cow and complaining of a most horrific headache. The only comfort for the defeated queen came from Sara, who testified on the souls of all the family's ancestors that in the

---

[46]   '*The devil is not a bad as they paint it*' (from the third chapter of *The Betrothed* by Alessandro Manzoni).

[47]   Used as snuff in the olden times to stimulate the senses and avoid fainting spells.

Nattis' hands, Alessandro was well fed and nurtured. To this, Donna Giovanna would whimper, 'Bonu, Bonu',[48] before returning to her moaning.

A fact that can only be appreciated by those who did participate in historical occasions such as this one is that although the prominent moments may be elating, the course of events interposed between the beginning of the journey and its end is often not as exciting. In fact, the facts of the voyage may, at several junctures, turn unbearably boring. As heroism may sometimes germinate from desperation, defeat may all the same spring from boredom.

As the day wore on, Alessandro began reckoning this sobering lesson. After a few more games of bingo, even glances at Mariuccia's beautiful brown eyes and the charged smiles that accompanied them failed to restore his mood. As he wondered what the rest of his life in the Natti household would be like, he also began to believe that historians had failed to communicate to the masses the real reason for capitulation during a siege. Unlike what our history textbooks have led us to believe, the reason is not necessarily famine, plague, or discomforts purposely inflicted by the assailant. It is merely the desperation to move on with life beyond the barriers that faithfully shelter us.

His was not a real siege, of course, because unlike the heroes of our favourite tales, Alessandro was free to leave the apartment at any time. Still, there were a few things that kept him inside. First, there was the fear of having to confront his ridiculous situation when he inevitably stumbled into friends or foes, both of whom he knew were out there, talking about his little adventure with smug smiles. Second, he knew that 'uomini coi baffi' would be dispersed about the town, waiting to spy on him and report his latest movements to Donna Giovanna. Although these reports may not necessarily be compromising, the simple idea of it gave Alessandro an uncomfortable feeling of being watched.

In addition to the boredom, a slight sense of guilt and anxiety that could not be easily explained began supervening. He remained as determined

---

[48] Well, well.

as ever to be right, but each time the church bells paced the rhythm of life, he was nonetheless reminded that his Nonna was waiting at home, that his parents were likely questioning his logic, and that the entire town was also undoubtedly expecting some catharsis to this unprecedented conundrum. As a result of the unease building, Alessandro decided that he needed to seek validation from someone older, wiser, and at a more mature stage of life. He believed his own father was the person for such counsel, and so he informed Sig.ra Natti that he would step out of the fortress to make a call from the bar Gatto. You see, the Nattis did not own a landline, and this was all far before the time of cell phones.

As he patiently waited his turn at the phone booth, he observed with envy the lucky people who were living ordinary lives without the burden of an increasingly uncomfortable conscience. When he finally had his turn on the phone, Alessandro dialled the number of his father's office in Milan, where the family business was settled and where his parents spent a considerable amount of their time.

Alessandro's father was an easy-going person. As was in alignment with the image expected from a person of his rank, he appeared severe and detached from his children, as was the convention of the time that saw parenthood more as a task than a relationship. Despite his icy exterior, he was in reality quite benevolent when difficulties arose in the household and he often preferred to work towards a solution rather than aggravating the problem. With this in mind, Alessandro anticipated that when he called to provide convincing clarifications of the situation at hand, his father, whom he believed to be both a clever and fair person, would (after objectively reviewing the facts that led to the current impasse in their entirety) decidedly stand by him. In fact, his father might even offer to intercede with Donna Giovanna to reach a historical compromise that could save both factions' repute.

Caught in the middle of a meeting, Alessandro's father quickly returned to his office, where he was summoned by his secretary to talk to his son. 'Ciao, Alex. How are things?' said his father, pretending not to know anything about the ongoing revolt.

This open-ended greeting unlocked the gates for a flood of information from the other side of the phone on the tremendous *Battle of Pizzo* that according to Alessandro was bound to be more infamous than the Bastille, the American War of Independence and the Civil War, the Italian Risorgimento, and the strenuous Resistance of Partisans against Fascism combined. As Alessandro was dutifully attempting to provide all the necessary details around his own predicament, equating it with valid arguments to previous occasions that unquestionably merited a legitimate place in history and that were undoubtedly needed to develop a fair and unbiased ruling on the matter (even if their relevance to the current predicament might have appeared somewhat arcane and difficult to grasp for most listeners), his father had an understandable reaction. A few minutes into Alessandro's monologue, the father politely interrupted, asking him, respectfully, to get to the point. Such a request seemed reasonable to Alessandro, as he had been trying to do just that but was somehow inexplicably impeded from allowing the aforementioned concerns to reach the open air from the high spheres of his intellect.

Finally, Alessandro presented the events that had led to his current predicament with the utmost impartiality. After all, in his opinion, facts could speak for themselves in the assertion of the rightfulness of his cause. When Alessandro finally paused and waited in trepidation for his father's reaction, he heard an unconcerned voice on the other end of the line. 'Alex, I am really sorry but I am not going to get in the middle of an argument between you and my mother. If I did, she would probably kill both of us rather than just you. Since you started this, you should work out a resolution. Your Nonna is a reasonable person and you are trying to become one, too. Nevertheless, I wish you a lot of good luck.' And with that, Alessandro's father sent him an exaggerated kiss through the phone and hung up.

Left alone in his quest for freedom, without help from the Allied Forces, Alessandro felt butterflies in his belly. With his hands in his pockets, his head bent forward and his forehead corrugated, he slowly walked back towards another bingo game and Mariuccia's comforting smile at his headquarters. As he made his way along the narrow alleyways, he recapped the dialogue with his dad and he reckoned a suggestion of irony in his father's voice that forced him to finally question his own position. When he arrived back at the safe house, he found the little dog welcoming him back with a stretch towards him while he barked, leapt, and yelped for returns of affection. This restored in part his confidence that at least his own little army remained loyal.

It should be noted that it did not cross Alessandro's mind to call his mother. Alessandro loved his mother dearly, but he saw her, even at that age, as a meek woman who would have never confronted Nonna on his behalf and would have likely cried at the other end of the phone as she would have begged him to go back and make peace with his grandmother before it was too late. When Alessandro was a young boy and his father was out of town on business, she used to cuddle in bed with him and hold him in her arms until she fell asleep. Her sleep was never peaceful. With his eyes wide open, Alessandro would listen to her talk in her sleep and whimper. Sometimes when screams would burst from her mouth, he would caress her head until she could calm down once again. She treated him more as a doll than a son. In jest, she would sometimes put make-up on him before guiding him in front of a mirror to tell him that he looked like a handsome prince. This lasted only until her husband was out of town, at which time she would regress into the little girl that she had little chance to be, as she had been married young through a well-concocted arrangement among families of stature. As Alessandro grew older, he reversed the roles and treated his mother as a daughter. He cared for and protected her from the vicissitudes of life that she was not prepared to confront. In the end, he looked upon her as just another woman who needed love and attention, who could not lead but would follow him wherever he went, and in spite of his love for her, he did not respect her.

By the time Sara reappeared later that evening with a new message from Donna Giovanna, Alessandro had, so to speak, prepared his suitcase. Sara related that to preserve the family honour and avoid further embarrassment created by Alessandro's perseverance Nonna begged that he return home where negotiations could be continued behind closed doors, thereby hanging the family's dirty laundry out of sight of the whole town. Alessandro, who had lost his original vigour as a result of boredom, guilt, and lack of support, welcomed the compromise.

As he walked in front of Sara towards the patriarchal mansion, his spirit kept swinging from disappointment with himself for so easily capitulating to uneasiness in anticipation of having to confront Nonna's magnificent power. As he climbed the long staircase to the big hall where he knew she was waiting, his courage faded, and for the first time, he realised what he had done. He had gone against the most powerful entity he had ever known, against a woman that was afraid of nothing and was respected and admired by the entire town. He walked as slowly as he could in an attempt to delay the worst, counting the well-known white marble steps in reverse order, calculating how many remained before he reached the top where capital punishment awaited him. As he climbed the last steps—three, two . . . , he thought of the last steps of Robespierre[49] and all the characters that history condemned for their impulsive actions.

Eventually, the stairs ended and Donna Giovanna stood in front of him, Achille peeking from behind her, wearing a grin in expectation of the impending punishment of the impudent rebel. Alessandro could not tell which hurt him more—the humiliation he anticipated from Nonna's words of admonishment or the condescending smile that Achille wore. But to his surprise, Nonna pronounced, 'At least there is somebody in this family who will stand up for his principles. Your grandfather was just like you, you know. Let's have lunch now. You will eat with the grown-ups from today forward.'

Nonna had made her homemade pasta dipped in chicken broth. This was Alessandro's favourite meal, and that day he knew it would taste even better than he remembered. As he made his way to the dining room, he caught a glance of Achille, who was left with a frozen smile that questioned whether any justice was left in this world.

* * *

'Well, this ending does not surprise me a bit! She was an astounding lady,' said Don Pino. 'You could never tell which side of an argument she was going to take, except that in the end it was always the one that made the most common sense, independent of any conventional wisdom. She was the one who pushed for my promotion. She told the bishop on my behalf, "That young deacon may not spend much time on books, but he understands the human soul better than any of those cockroaches that, with all respect, are coming out of your seminaries nowadays. When I

---

[49] Hero of the French Revolution who succumbed to the guillotine.

die, I want him at my bedside for the last sacrament and a cup of champagne!"'

*   *   *

From that day forward, the curfew was lifted for the two brothers. Alessandro never returned to the children's table, but instead sat quietly with the grown-ups; he avidly listened and rarely spoke. With his gentle resolve and scrutinising blue eyes, with time, he progressively became the second in command of the household.

But the irreversible process known as 'puberty' that triggers so much unrest in most adolescents had just begun. Several tribulations lay ahead about which we will learn in the following chapters, as by now the congregation of wise men had adjourned in deference of the advent of the time against the time.

*   *   *

Back in my room during the contrura, I paced back and forth, waiting for Hypnos to sway my edginess. As I had the day before, I took a glance down at the Chiazzetta from my balcony. Perhaps because the weather had changed from sultry heat to a light breeze from the mountains, or because my mood had followed the same course, today life in the Chiazzetta appeared lively and purposeful. Frequently a passerby crossed the Chiazzetta to disturb the pigeons. The dog who had been lazily sleeping the day before now eagerly followed an indiscernible path back and forth, seemingly determined to pursue its lifelong detective mission, all the while wagging its tail and when appropriate lifting its hind limb to return in approbation scent to scent in response to cryptic clues.

Even the cat was less self-absorbed. The dog approached him to offer a salute and the feline responded by arching its back, straightening its tail and rubbing its side against the canine's chest. When the canine respectfully, but perhaps a little too intrusively, took it upon himself to sniff the feline's rear end, the cat (in an even greater affirmation of affection) stood on his hind limbs and slanting his ears backwards like wings of a fighter jet delivered three swift boxer's jabs to the dog's snout with the fore ones, which made its friend sneeze. The canine responded affectionately with one lap of its big and foul tongue that covered half of the feline's fur, thus giving the latter an opportunity to spend the remainder of the contrura restoring order with its own.

At the opposite corner of the Chiazzetta, sitting on an old chair tilted against a wall, the village idiot saluted a passerby at the time. His growl had lost the harshness of the previous day and was somehow transformed by the breeze from a monotonous litany into a harmonious serenade, following its own string of melodies and rhymes that caused even the pretty lady—who had slapped him the day before—to smile.

It seemed, however, that the differences from the previous day were trivial in contrast to the ageless Chiazzetta that had endured for decades, unaware of time. And gradually I began to recognise at the different corners of the Chiazzetta my old friends and acquaintances whose existence had evaporated with time. They continued to dwell here as ghosts, invisible to the eye but vivid in my own memory. I reckoned that the dog, following their trail, wagged its tail to indicate the site where a furtive kiss, a gentle act, or a friendly handshake had occurred God only knows how many years ago.

I did not sleep that afternoon. Instead, I lay in bed, comparing the present with the past and the evolving with the durable. I wondered how much future was left here for my relatives, my friends, my acquaintances, and for the old wise men who had embraced me with their affection for the short period that I would spend in this corner of oblivion.

IV

A Life Behind the Scenes

The *Spuntone*, or *La Pizza Punta*[50], is the bow from which Pizzo's dreams originate. From that point high above the rocks, the dreams are set free to navigate over the shiny carpet laid over the sea by the sun towards the horizon. It is the promontory from which squinting eyes observe every evening the setting sun. From there, one can oversee the coastline as it twists amongst the waves and in the distance Stromboli[51] with its periodic plumes of smoke. It is where the clouds display creative impressions and reverberations, empathising with the dying source of light. It is at this spot that one wonders what the next day will bring and the following day to the following one.

Most of these dreams, of course, will remain such and will never materialise, and this is in fact a godsend because fulfilled dreams inevitably lose the effervescence of imagination as they become flat along the progression of customary life. Those who have left Pizzo to create their future elsewhere, following the blueprints of youth, and periodically return discover in the twilight that ensues from the sunset that the flavour of their childhood dreams did not accompany them to their new homes in faraway lands. Instead, their dreams remained where they originated, patiently waiting for their creators to rejoin them at the *Spuntone*.

---

[50] Literally meaning the tip of Pizzo.
[51] A small island in the Tyrrhenian Sea, off the North Coast of Sicily, containing one of three active volcanoes in Italy.

The *Spuntone* sits at the staged end of La Chiazza in the direction of the sea. Sitting along the perimeter, overlooking the waves, there are concrete benches that become scorched under the sun in daylight but become hospitable at sunset. Most are occupied at that time, but somehow, mysteriously, there always seems to be one last bench left free, apparently waiting for the lonesome, who will sit there to attentively scrutinise the horizon, mistakenly equating distance with time, and search the horizons for clues about the future that will inevitably remain elusive, no matter how far his squinting eyes may reach.

It was in that exact spot that I found il Marchese as I returned to the Chiazza that afternoon. He sat in his characteristic posture, his chin resting atop his hands that were crossed over the handle of his cane. His handkerchief was displaced from its decorative position in the front pocket of the linen jacket and instead was held in his left hand. His eyes appeared moist, and as I approached him, I asked, 'Tutto bene?'[52]

Swabbing his right eye with the handkerchief, he smiled, and scanning the horizon one more time, he simply said, 'Daftness of old age! Let's go! Your father and the others have been here for a while and are waiting for you. Let's go to the Gatto.' And with that, forgetting to tap me on the shoulder with his cane, he grabbed my left arm to lift himself from the bench. Arm in arm, we walked towards our friends at the tavolino under the watchful eye of the austere bust of Re Umberto Primo,[53] the inspiration for the legend of the 'men with moustache'. On our way to the middle of the Chiazza, il Marchese, who had recovered from his flash of melancholy, repaid the respectful salutations of passers-by with his usual enigmatic smile.

The old men were all there, including Don Pino, who had swiftly concluded his vesper functions and, bypassing the need for persuasion by his friends, was already sitting at the tavolino with his dependable and reassuring smile. It was obvious to me that these men had eagerly

---

[52] 'Is everything okay?'

[53] King Umberto I reigned Italy from 1878 to 1900, when he was assassinated by an Italo-American anarchist in Monza, near Milan. He characteristically wore a conspicuous set of moustache.

gathered to hear more about Alessandro's story. An odd mixture of warmth and jealousy for my old friend came over me with the realisation that Alessandro, even after his death, would take centre stage, displacing once again, at least for the time being, il Signorino Giuseppe.

Il Professore was evidently impatient to continue his story. 'Buona sera, buona sera cari signori miei,'[54] he said, greeting il Marchese and me. 'Sit down and enjoy the cool evening! The negroni is coming for il Signorino and the Kahlua for our Marchese.' Having therefore concluded the preambles, we sat to listen.

'So much has been said about sexual abuse of women, but do people realise that men can also be the victim of rape by a woman?' started il Professore.

'Of course I do! If I do not, who would?' interrupted Don Pino enthusiastically. As he immediately observed fourteen baffled and wide open eyes staring inquisitively at him, he elaborated, 'I mean . . . because of the confessional, of course! It is incredible the kind of fish that can come out of the net!' And having restored the focus of the audience on the original story, he sheepishly added, 'Sorry for the interruption, Don Ciccio. Please go ahead.'

'This was the first encounter that Alessandro had with sex . . .'

* * *

Alessandro's family owned property along the coast just a few miles south of Pizzo. It covered over a kilometre of private beach and extended up into the hills for quite a distance. It was lush with banana and fig trees, centuries-old olive trees, prickly pear cactuses, and agave that bloomed once in a lifetime. The tomatoes and grapes were irrigated by gently mumbling trenches—built anew each day by the farmers who carefully tracked the changing needs of the crops in the torrid days of summer—that channelled fresh spring water. There were shady areas that—together

---

54 Good evening, good evening, my dear sirs.

with the breezes that swept in from the sea—made long walks through the property pleasant even on the hottest days.

The two young brothers found countless mysteries to uncover in the privacy and solitude of the vast property. There they spent the long days of summer with little to do but follow their imagination or the planters. They wandered by themselves to the beach each morning. Their beach was too long a walk from the edge of the property line and too difficult to approach from the sea because of a string of rocks that paralleled as a fence twenty yards ashore—where moray eels and octopuses lived an undisturbed life—to prevent any strangers from joining them. As such, their sandy paradise remained deserted despite its natural beauty, leaving seemingly infinite space for their imaginary water adventures. The rest of the day languished when after returning for lunch to the villa up on the hill in the middle of the estate, they rested in bed during the contrura, as they were told, above the linen sheets with open windows. There they watched the exotic dance of the curtains led by the afternoon breeze and listened to the splashing sounds of the nearby sea. Occasionally, one would rise from the bed to hunt with a flyswatter a fly that had managed to breach the finely woven metallic screens while the other watched.

It was on that property that Alessandro descended towards the beach on an early August morning, following Achille 'Indian style' with the infamous cousin that has been previously discussed in the typewritten notes at the head of the line. To protect her privacy, I will refer to her as 'the Cousin' and will attempt to explain why, whether it was because of her physical appearance, her personality, or both, she held such an enchanted place in Alessandro's memory.

The Cousin was a middle-sized woman of twenty-something who had been adopted by the family as a young girl when her parents, for unclear reasons, had abandoned her. She had a small but shapely bosom that could be discerned through the light shirts that she wore, most often without a bra. She had an attractive figure: compact and gracious. She walked straight like a ballerina, turning her head without rotating her torso and moving her hands softly like water lilies floating over the surface of a pond. She had dark brown hair that was often adorned with a flower, or even a twig, that she had gathered from the ground. She had tanned skin that seemed to be made of bronze and smiling azure eyes that were somehow always surprised and mischievous at the same time. She had a gentle demeanour and cared for the poor and the sick, for the village idiot, for the plants, and for the stray animals that she called 'Orfanelli'[55]. Alessandro remembered how she had cried ten years before, when he was four and she was ten-something, because a kitten had died of food poisoning. And when Achille teased her for being soft, she threw her handkerchief at him before taking Alessandro with her to bury the poor creature in a large pot on the terrace where a lemon tree would provide asylum for its eternal rest.

The Cousin always walked in front of the line with a confident gait, as if she knew where she was going, not only at the moment but for the rest of her life as well. She would talk without turning, expecting the words to be carried by the breeze to those who followed. She was somewhat educated as she was studying history and philosophy at the university, but such learning had not tainted her spontaneity as she retained only a shallow impression of historical facts and prominent thinkers as if they had existed just to edify a colourful wallpaper around an otherwise perfectly self-fulfilling life.

Like most individuals with a creative disposition, the Cousin did not need much beyond the contentment of realising her life's passion, which in her case was the preference for the physical aspects that nurture the relationship between the two genders. Sex for her was an act of creation. Touching and caressing a man's body was an artistic pursuit as the winding stroke of a brush over a canvas is for a painter. For her, stimulating an orgasm was the ultimate experiment and producing it was the achievement of the supreme goal. It was a joyful event that invariably surprised and amazed her as a miracle of nature.

The two boys spent the summer with their mother in the villa. The Cousin, who had joined them after returning from her last exam at the University of Messina, was supposed to help care for them. So the three of them jauntily walked towards the beach, as we said, with her in front wearing a calico silk dress, Achille following with snorkelling gear, and

---

[55] Little orphans.

Alessandro trailing with an inflatable mattress, towels, sunscreen, and other paraphernalia in obsequious obedience to his elder comrades.

As it usually was in August, the water was pleasantly warm that day. Soon Alessandro dove to scavenge the rocks for little black crabs, urchins, limpets, sea cucumbers, and other creatures that lived in the tidal pools or, just as well, in the deeper sea that clear like liquid emerald covered an infinite world of mysteries. Alessandro was particularly fond of octopi that although shyly camouflaged looked suspiciously from their den with disproportionate eyes or swiftly swam when caught by surprise. Alessandro had learnt to catch them with ease simply by stretching his hand towards the little animal that could not seem to refrain from grasping him with its tentacles, thereby being removed from its den by its own prey. Placing the octopus in his bathing suit, knowing that the creature would stick to him tightly and not run away, he would swim to shore to show the prey to Achille and the Cousin. Together, they would then place the octopus in a tidal pool where it would find a safe corner from which it could reciprocate the stares of the humans with its own.

As Alessandro observed with satisfaction his temporary prey, his hands resting on his hips, salt water dripping from his curly hair, and his wet bathing suit sticking to his body, the Cousin approached him and posing her gracious body on a rock like the Little Mermaid in Copenhagen started caressing Alessandro's appendage that had made progress over the previous year from a worm-like appearance to a sausage of dignified proportion. 'I see that the banana is ripening!' she said with an encouraging smile while she continued to gently stroke the appendage that in turn, without respecting its master's will, had taken to expanding disproportionately like an inflatable lifebelt, causing embarrassment for Alessandro, who did not know how to react in front of his provoking Cousin and his laughing brother. Carried away by a burst of anger, he whacked his Cousin's hand away as if it was a fly and bent down towards the octopus that seemed silently disappointed in him for acting so awkwardly in such a natural predicament. He gently let the octopus release its grasp on the rock and attach to him, and then returning to the water, he let the animal separate slowly and run into the deep green sea while the freshness cooled his emotions and lessened the tension on the aforementioned appendage.

That evening after dinner, they sat on the terrace of the villa, overlooking the sea, with their mother. The Cousin enchantingly noticed that the moon rays drew a path on the sea that led directly to them. 'What a romantic coincidence that the moon is laying a path towards us. Isn't it a miracle?' she said with a mischievous smile as she turned towards Alessandro, who could discern her azure eyes in the darkness barely broken by the flickering light of the petrol lanterns and smell the perfume of jasmines that lay around her neck. Appreciating that she was not seeking an optics lesson, he assented to the miracle and did not add anything.

At nights, they slept in three adjacent beds facing the balcony: Achille on the left, himself in the middle, and the Cousin on the right. He could not sleep at all that night, and instead, he observed the dance of the curtains and, through them, the moon. Suddenly, he felt oppressed by the eye of an inquisitive star that without apparent reason had taken interest in him and insistently stared from the deep blue heavens through a side window.

As he lay listening to the crickets, he smelt the scent of jasmine, and in the obscurity, he sensed the Cousin lifting his linen sheets and softly reposing by his side. With her head on his chest and her hand caressing his naked torso, she slowly moved down to untie the strings of his pyjamas, once again reproducing the marvel of the morning: turning the appendage into a ripe fruit. If schizophrenia is a duplication of personality, in Alessandro's case, it occurred according to latitude, with the upper hemisphere of his body desperately trying to assert hegemony over an uncontrollable situation in the lower one. It seemed that a complete disconnect was occurring between his two souls. As the top one searched around to see whether Achille was awake, listened for evidence of his mother's movements in the other room, and wondered what a man was to do in such circumstances, the lower hemisphere was progressively accepting the provocation and simultaneously sending messages of electric pleasure to the top that further confounded his decision-making process. As Alessandro struggled with his lack of resolution that battled with his desire to run away, the Cousin began kissing his torso and slowly progressed downwards to the point of interest and with soft lips continued the job that her hand had initiated until the appendage produced an abundance of warm relief. The Cousin's head moved up again and kissed his tightly closed mouth with her moist lips. As she rested on his chest again, she moved her right hand in between her legs and celebrated the occasion with an orgasm of her own.

The next morning, Alessandro recalled the happenings of the night before as a dream. The anger, anguish, and anxiety of the night had dissipated and he looked at his pretty Cousin with a mixture of disgust and awe. In truth, it is difficult to feel sorry for the apprentice, and neither did he unduly regret it. On the surface, his life had not been irreversibly damaged by such an incident, and in truth, in the nights following it he waited for her visits that did come a few more times. For some reason, they never crossed the sanctuary of penetration that summer. While he did not know how to get there, she did not seem to care all that much, as she was using him as an appetiser.

One night, Alessandro observed the Cousin visiting Achille, and he realised that with him she was united in completed contact. He was tempted after that to swing into her bed while she lay asleep, but he never managed the courage to do it. As time passed, day by day and night by night, it was a summer that he would never forget with strange memories that were bitter and sweet, a sensation of affection and distance, of unspoken words, and of physical contact. In the end, he retained the impression that love is expressed by corporeal exchanges, fulfilled passions, and mechanical gestures without need for words, whispers, promises, or dreams.

* * *

'She was quite a type! She rarely came to confession, but when she did, she could make the Addolorata[56] cry!' said Don Pino.

'Of jealousy?' asked Mastro Antonio, to whom nobody listened at this juncture.

---

[56] A representation of the Madonna, where she was dressed in black in mourning for the death of Christ of which a statue is standing on the right side in the Cathedral of San Giorgio in Pizzo.

'I often wondered whether her stories were true or whether she made them up to test and provoke me,' continued Don Pino. 'And to tell the truth, she succeeded on a few occasions!'

'A few months later . . .' continued il Professore.

*   *   *

Alessandro was spending an afternoon at a friend's house where on the lower floor the boys had created a boxing ring. Instead of ropes, there were boundaries taped on the pavement to mark the battleground. As the host had received for Christmas boxing gear for two, the boys took turns contentedly punching each other around the flank, in the face, and the mouth: Anywhere above the belt was in limits. Alessandro was not into this type of activity, but pressured by his peers, he took his turn. After he put his helmet on and fitted the gloves, he positioned himself in front of his opponent, who was a short guy who seemed to be made of iron. When the gong rang, he received a swift blow to the middle of the face and immediately found himself on the ground, where after recovering he observed warm drops of blood dripping from his nose, spotting his trousers.

The host panicked and yelled at the short guy, who being completely unsophisticated did not know better than to punch in the face the son of . . . And then he called, 'Mariuccia . . . Mariuccia!'

The daughter of Carmelo Natti, with whom we are already acquainted, came down from the servants' quarters. When she noticed her prince on the ground in such miserable conditions, she looked at her master who had just called for her and at the short guy who had hit her prince, and as was customary for her in such circumstances, she blushed.

'Mariuccia, please take care of Alessandro. This idiot hurt him accidentally by a blow to the face. I am sorry, Alessandro. Please forgive me. He did not know who you are.'

But Alessandro could not care less. To start with, he did not care about boxing. Then he did not care about the host, as he was there solely because he did not have the assertiveness to decline the umpteenth invitation. Thus, he was happy for an excuse to be relieved of this boring company in the care of Mariuccia.

It was a cool March afternoon. The air was crisp and the windows were open. The curtains swayed according to their interminable waving dance and Mariuccia held a cold, moist cloth to his nose. She had been at the home of the host for a few months now to learn how to become a servant to a notable family in this little town close to Pizzo. Such a profession was perfect for her, as she was agreeable and happy to follow and execute orders with the nicest attitude by nature, although not necessarily with the highest ingenuity.

It was obvious to Alessandro that she remained seriously concerned for him. It appeared that she had momentarily forgotten her love for him and had turned her attention solely to his bleeding nose and his pants stained with blood. While she was busying herself with pressing his nose and wiping his pants, he could see from above her perfect bosom, fresh and genuine, firmly contained by her simple dress yet plump and budding.

He felt a sudden need to lie down on Mariuccia's bed on account of some kind of psychological dizziness that has helped many men in similar circumstances. As he lay down with Mariuccia sitting by his side and pressing his nose that was no longer bleeding, he stretched an arm towards her forearm and squeezed it gently.

'Thank you.'

Mariuccia did not reply but instead turned her eyes down towards the blanket. Encouraged by her passiveness, he adjusted the pillow against the headboard and sat, looking at her one more time as he slowly advanced his hand up her arm past her shoulder and to her neck. Then he placed his hand under her chin to straighten her head while her eyes continued to look downward. As she continued to avoid his eyes, he kissed her on the lips and kissed her again as he gently lay her at his side. He kissed her mouth, her neck, and her ears, then he opened her legs, and without removing her underwear, but instead taking it aside, he made love to her. And so it was that, together with Mariuccia, Alessandro lost his virginity in this strange circumstance where his friends were happily throwing punches at each other one floor below, while he had a swollen nose.

Mariuccia is no longer a servant. Instead, she lives in Pennsylvania where she has been a soccer mom for many years, and in fact, she is now a soccer grandma. One of her granddaughters looks very much like Alessandro and she is a legendary soccer player. The soccer star's father also looks very much like Alessandro, but Alessandro never knew this as Mariuccia was sent to America to live with her uncle's family a few weeks after the occurrence.

Many exploits of similar shrewdness followed as the kitten quickly turned into a skilful predator, but of those it is not worth reporting.

Then a girl appeared who carved an indelible mark in Alessandro's life. She was a classmate who sat a few seats behind him. She was pretty and shy and Alessandro had barely noticed her in the beginning, perhaps partially because he had already learnt that relationships were rarely casual among peers and often turned into thorny affairs while those with older women were less likely to burden him with complexities. But as time passed, he began to sense warmth behind his shoulders, and whenever he turned to examine the sensation, he would see two big brown eyes rapidly returning to the pages of an open book. He also noticed that during lunch hour, she often dwelled in close proximity, more than coincidence would have predicted, and that quite often she searched her reflection in a window to adjust an insubordinate curl of her thick black hair. One day, perhaps on impulse, Alessandro went to her, and fixing his hypnotic eyes on to hers and gently but firmly holding her right arm with his left hand, he simply asked, 'Will you come with me to the Marina this evening for a walk?'

That evening was a particularly beautiful one. There was a crescent moon discreetly peeking through silver cumulus clouds and the gale from the sea was warm and fragrant. A few bats could be seen noiselessly circling around distant lampposts while the only light discernible along the beach was the phosphorescence of the froth atop the breaking waves. There was an inoffensive mild brackish scent that completed the pulsing hum of the marine serenade and its echoing repercussion all along the shore. When he arrived at the Marina, Gianna was already waiting for him. She had run from a controlling father and a protective mother to obey Alessandro's order. She was beautiful in her simplicity and grace without the enhancements that women often use to outline their features at the expense of freshness and natural beauty.

Alessandro was preoccupied when he arrived as he found himself eager to get this affair over with. He was irritated with himself for inviting her out on an impulse and was silently regretting having done so. He sensed that she was too young and simple for him and that since she roamed in the same crowd he would have no emotional space were they to unite physically. Yet he felt stuck because he did not know how to reverse the course that he had set and how to halt the inevitable. So they left their shoes close to a boat anchored on the beach and walked barefoot along the backwash.

As they walked into the night, Gianna touched his hand and held it as they walked further into the darkness. Then she whispered, 'I love you', and clenching his right arm with both her hands she pressed her head against his chest. This cuddling reminded him of the long sleepless nights that he once had with his mother agitating at his side, and he felt sorry for the new friend as he had done for his mother back then. He circled his strong arm around her waist and gently lifted her light body towards him and kissed her. They walked further into the darkness, and when they found a spot that was silent and secluded, they made love.

When she whispered once more that she loved him, distracted by the moment of passion, Alessandro returned, 'I love you too.' They spent a few more moments together afterwards holding hands until, like Cinderella, Gianna suddenly began to run home where she knew her parents would be waiting, suspicious and cold. Her father would slap her across the face as he had done before, but this time at least, there would be a reason.

Alessandro did not love Gianna, but as he observed her graceful figure run with trepidation and disappear into the darkness, he considered that for the first time in his life he had reciprocated the confession of love, and this made him uncomfortable. 'What does love have to do with this?' he wondered, as the poor young man had never considered what might seem obvious to most human beings—that a physical and emotional relationship may, in fact, embrace each other. He questioned what had happened and what that exchange of three simple words could mean.

He returned home that evening, bearing a sensation of emptiness and dissatisfaction. He wished that he had not played this hazardous game with such a simple and trusting soul, and an ominous presentiment ascended upon him.

But it was too late. Gianna was in love with him and was determined to never leave him. She waited for him at the school entrance. If he pretended not to see her, she waved at him. If he endured in his show of absentmindedness, she would persist by calling his name and waving at the same time, building embarrassment over the annoyance. At times, she would try to carry his backpack or hold his hand or answer for him when his peers addressed him. He started to dread lunch hour and he began sinking his head into books during the free time, pretending he had to catch up. After school, regardless of what commitments he would invent to excuse himself, she would accommodate around them and he could not be left alone. Although he tried again and again to discreetly convey that he wanted his freedom back, she did not comprehend.

Left with no other choice, he began to neglect her and to act in her presence as if she was not there. He would flirt with women even if he did not care for them, make jokes and allusions of dubious taste, and not answer her questions. When he saw her sad eyes looking at him with stupor, he felt pain and guilt inside but marched ahead bravely and ruthlessly, against his own character and disposition, because he did not know any better.

One evening, a few months after the fatal walk along the beach, he sat with another pretty woman in a little veranda at the Marina. It was late spring, and the heat was starting to make him swelter. They did not see her approach when suddenly Gianna appeared in front of them. Alessandro saluted her politely and dismissively at the same time, but she did not leave and instead stood in front of them, looking at him. To put an end to the unbearable embarrassment, he excused himself from the other acquaintance and holding Gianna's arm tightly dragged her away to a private corner. Before he could speak a word, she asked, 'Why are you doing this to me?'

'Doing what?' he replied, faking ignorance.

'I mean it, Alessandro. Why are you acting like this with me? Why don't you respect me? Why do you go out with other women? Do you think I am blind? Do you think I do not hear what people say? Do you think I do not know where you were last night and the night before?' She went on and on while Alessandro, shaking his head and covering her mouth with his hand, tried to shush her.

'Gianna,' he was finally able to interject. 'I do not love you! I am sorry. It was all a mistake. I am really sorry!' he said all in one breath.

At first, she looked down at her feet and stopped talking. Then she turned towards the sea and the setting sun, and with tears in her eyes, she said, 'I love you so much. I cannot live without you. Do you understand?'

Alessandro laughed and replied, 'Yes, you can. Why would you love somebody as reckless as I am? You are better than I am and you will find a better person for yourself. Just go home and let me be. Let the scutch dwell in the spear grass and the roses bloom in the fields of heaven.'

Satisfied with his masculine conclusion, Alessandro returned to the other lass who had been waiting with crossed legs and a cigarette in her hand.

Sunday morning, the second day following the unfortunate episode, Alessandro's mother came into his room and with the transparent whisper of an angel she said, 'Sandro . . . Sandro, are you awake?' She had a newspaper in her hands, and as he turned his head, she asked, 'Isn't Gianna T . . . a friend of yours from Vibo?'[57] As he looked inquisitively at his mother with an elbow propped up on his pillow and his head turned, he thought he heard her say, 'She killed herself yesterday.'

He sprang from the bed and grasped the newspaper from his mother. He saw the picture of his pretty friend and lover, smiling with the enthusiasm of youth. Her beautiful dark hair flowed down her neck and shoulders and her face bore the simple expression of the evening when she was waiting for him at the Marina. The article stated simply that she had turned on the gas in the kitchen while her parents were out. When

---

[57]   A town close to Pizzo where the regional high school is.

a neighbour eventually smelt the odour of methane in the common stairwell of the humble building where her family lived and called the fire department, it was too late. She was found sitting with her eyes wide open, her head against the ceramic tiles, and her arms hanging on both sides of her minuscule body.

'Yes, I knew her,' said Alessandro as he covered his eyes and face with his open palms and it is possible that he cried.

Alessandro never told anybody of his relationship with her beyond what some friends might have suspected. He did not talk to anybody because he did not know what to say that could restore her life and his own. For the first time, he had experienced the irrevocable. He saw a sharp separation, an insurmountable gap between what had been until then—a carefree youth and a sudden and inevitably embittered future. He felt irreparably guilty. He recalled the last time he had seen her and reckoned how easy it would have been to hold and comfort her, to talk rather than dismiss, to play along, to do anything that could have avoided the irremediable. And he did not know that he was only partially to blame because he was too young and too inexperienced and ignorant to understand the complexities of life and anticipate this disaster. In the end, disgusted, he solemnly swore silently to himself that he would not use the word 'love' ever again.

*   *   *

'I remember that story,' said my father. 'I remember how upset all of you boys were, and I recollect that when you dressed up to go to Vibo for the funeral, you wanted to wear the black wool suit in spite of the heat.'

'Yes, I remember it too,' I said. 'But I did not know that it had anything to do with Alessandro. He never confessed anything about her to me, as he never mentioned to me any of the other stories you have been describing. Yes, there were rumours about a relationship between the two of them, but there were always groupies surrounding him, and we assumed that she was just another one of them. I don't believe we had ever seen him showing intimacy with her in public or any other girl for that matter.' As I was mixing the last third of my negroni, I pondered all the secrets that my friend had kept to himself and the pain that must have accompanied them. I wondered why he never shared any of this with me or, as it seemed likely, with anybody else till his confessions to the Professore.

'She was a nice and simple girl from a humble and religious family,' added Don Pino. 'They were upset when the Sacerdote of her dioceses said that she could not be blessed in church and should not be buried in the regular cemetery because of the nature of her death. They asked for my help, and we went to the police captain to intercede. At first, he refused to help. He was from the North and did not understand our customs. He insisted that contrary to us Terroni,[58] he was accustomed to following the rules. In the end, our persistence wore him down, and as he turned his back to us and looked out the window, he said, "I have signed it already, but if you want you can cross off 'suicide' and write 'accident'. I will not go over it again. I am done with this." 'She was so pretty in the casket in a white dress that looked almost like a wedding gown, and so many flowers that had come from known and unknown places.'

We shook hands with the old men and went home. That evening, we had dinner on the terrace overlooking the sea. It was already dark when we started our meal, so we kept the indirect lanterns in the adjacent room alight. A rectangle of light, piercing through the partially open shutter, preserved a domain of whiteness in the wall otherwise obscured by the night. There stood our friend, the gecko that like several generations of its ancestors patiently listened to our stories, old and new, narrated by voices that echoed those of decades before, spoken from these same chairs by our own ancestors, and that would remain intermingled with ours in the memory of time. Our dinner consisted of a light antipasto[59] with local delicacies, a light course of rice with seafood, fried surici,[60] and watermelon all drowned under generous bottles of ice-cold Critone, while

---

[58]   Disparaging expression that people from the North use for Southerners meaning 'those who are soiled with dirt by working in the field'.

[59]   Antipasto means appetisers.

[60]   Surici means literally 'mice', but is in fact a local name given to a flavorful fish that is caught ashore of Pizzo, characterized by protruding sharp teeth like those of a mouse.

my fish had found peaceful rest in a marinade of vinegar and lemon for the following day.

After the first bottle of wine, Alessandro's story had assumed a selfless place in the back of our minds while the conversation had taken up a much more serious topic: an in-depth discussion of my hairstyle. According to my mother, who had initiated the painful topic, my hair was not appropriate for my age, my professional status, or my overall reputation and at the same time was a desecration of the entire family's decorum. I should admit that I am not fond of going to the barber's, of awaiting one's own turn; the anxiety associated with the ranking on the waitlist which is never clearly defined, the idleness of sitting in a crowd of strangers while they pretend to read *Vogue* or other preposterous magazines, the small talk with a random grandma while her grandchild runs around and disturbs my own reading, and all of the other distractions that kindle my previously described restlessness and disrupt my preferred status of self-absorption. As such, I deal with the affairs of my hair with passive procrastination until peer pressure becomes unbearable or the hair grows to be so disorganised that I am forced to succumb to the tenets of civilisation.

With years of experience in the academic world in my favour, where patience and unresponsiveness are the most effective tools to circumvent strong opinions from powerful minds, I docilely listened to the various reiterations from my father, uncle, and other family members. I waited for them to grow tired of such a topic and move to another territory, thus postponing the fatal decision to another day. But this time, the conversation went awry. My uncle, a prominent banker, emphasised that in his world countenance in the finest detail is of the utmost value. My father noted that due to a congenital abnormality I lacked hair in a portion of my nape and that such disfiguration was highlighted by the presence of long hair around the deficiency. It was Don Pino, however, who added the final straw.

Don Pino had come for dinner at our home that evening. He wore completely civilian attire save for the white collar around his neck, which had been pre-emptively loosened. Since I was a young boy, he consistently, fiercely, and even shamelessly stood by my side. He even gave me candy during lent with the justification that—to break my hesitation—Christ had more pressing plights to worry about during that time of the year than policing a child's stomach, and in any case, He could not see because he was covered by a white sheet.[61] However, in this critical moment of my life, Don Pino said, 'Forgive me, Giuseppe.' It should be noted that he never addressed me as Signorino because he considered it to be condescending. 'I think your mom is right. This time your hair is too long and too messy. Do it for her and I am sure that Somebody up there will one day remember your sacrifice.'

Realising that I was left standing alone without allies and not even Carmelo Natti in whom I could seek refuge for a nouvelle rebellion, I reasoned that in any case I would not have patience for bingo games, and with the intention of avoiding Alessandro's conundrum, I accepted the teachings of history. I capitulated and said, 'Okay, Dad. Please tell Signor Leonardo that I will be there at eight in the morning.'

Don Pino was a man of slightly above average stature, but because of his outgoing personality, his stentorian voice, and his unravelling spirit, he soared like a giant over any conversation. After the group had established the acceptance of my fate, we turned to listen with pleasure to his stories. After a few moments of listening silently, I suddenly, following an incoercible impulse, interrupted him by asking, 'Don Pino, where do you think Alessandro is now? Do you think he is doomed to burn in hell forever?'

A silence fell upon the group while Don Pino collected his thoughts. The stillness was finally interrupted when my uncle, perhaps to buy time for his friend or maybe simply to interject his typical cynical life view, stated in a harmonious voice and a low tone that well suited the darkness of the sky, 'Maybe that would not be so bad. When I die, I would rather go to hell than paradise! That is where the interesting people dwell after all! Can you imagine how boring it would be to be with saints, monks, nuns, and preachers for eternity? With the obvious exception of Don Pino, of course, whom however, I see having a better time in hell with the rest of us!' With that, we all, except for my mother, raised another glass of ice-cold Critone and drank in approval.

---

[61] Southern Italian costume to dress the Cross with a white drape during lent.

'I do not see evil and good, paradise and hell as distinct entities,' added my father thoughtfully. 'To me, they are all facets of the same concept, different sides of the same coin. The same goes for God and the Devil. One could not exist without the other. In the end, in the heavens, things must be just the same as on Earth where there is no curtain separating good from evil or paradise from hell. Rather, these opposites intermingle into a down-to-earth purgatory.'

It may not come as a surprise that Don Pino had not chosen a life of devotion to the Church of Christ following an incoercible vocation. Rather, he embraced the Church in compliance to a commission from his parents who, belonging to the lower class of Southern Italians, felt that the only avenue for their son to escape the proletarian life in which he was raised was a commitment to the Mother of all Mothers. Don Pino was an obedient boy who recognised the value of such a strategy and submitted to their wishes accordingly. Being deeply honest on the one hand, yet completely devoted to his humble parents on the other, he accepted this responsibility in good faith. With the professionalism of a doctor who cares for the physical welfare of his patients, Don Pino perceived that his duty was to respond to the spiritual needs of his constituency by serving as an ambassador for the message of God rather than enforcing the teachings of the Bible as a zealot of His army. Thus, as a seasoned diplomat, he did not have to believe in the message to be able to transmit it effectively to his own constituency.

Don Pino also applied reciprocal logic to the biblical teaching that God created man in resemblance of His own image. He pictured God reflected in bigger magnitude in His own image and, therefore, mused that He was at least as benevolent and lenient as the priest himself. While it was easy for Don Pino to sympathise and empathise with the sinners, it was extremely difficult for him to devise penitence proportional to their sins, and in the end, a few 'Pater Noster' and 'Ave Marias' was as bad as a punishment anybody would get. These outcomes had the benefit of encouraging confession and redemption, but perhaps that came at the cost of the sincerity of remorse. This is to explain why it was not easy for Don Pino to place Alessandro in any ethereal sphere. He surely admitted that the boy, whom he remembered very well, was not exactly a St Francis. But on the other hand, he recollected Alessandro's agreeable demeanour, easy-going personality, smile, and warmth, and Don Pino could not imagine God punishing him for eternity.

'You know, before dinner I was at the bedside of a true sinner! Boy, did he do a lot of ugly things in his life! And now that he is departing, he confessed it all to me. He was remorseful and scared like a little boy. He held my hand and asked me if I could save him from hell. The man had killed on commission, had abused friends and foes, men and women just to protect an unclear value of personal interest confused with churlish honour. He had hurt others without reason, and suddenly, on the verge of death, he was afraid and regretful, perhaps even remorseful—or at least trying to be. Inside of me, I was cynical and I wondered, "Isn't it too late? Isn't it convenient to change at the last moment to bargain for salvation?" But then I asked myself, "Who am I to judge? What if he is really penitent?" And I sentenced him to say a few Pater Noster. And when I realised that he did not even remember the words, I dictated them to him until his soul was finally saved. This is why I believe that if a God really does exist, He had to create the Devil because He Himself, the infinitely Benevolent, would not have the will to punish anybody as I, His humble servant, in my more limited benevolence could not do it.'

And he concluded, 'I do not know where Alessandro could be. As for me, I hope that he is an angel in paradise. He was one of the finest boys I have ever known, and I have faith that God would feel just the same. But if he did not repent, which knowing him is a distinct possibility, and the Devil did his job, he may now be in hell, having a good time with all those fine people who could not comply with the rules of the Church, even though they never hurt anybody purposefully in their life, as Don Giusto was saying.' And raising one more glass of Critone, we washed our throats once more. This time, we drank in honour of our lost friend and all like him, whom we could not clearly place in either heaven or hell, assuming that such entities even exist.

As we toasted, I looked up at the transparent sky with all of its stars pinned in it and at the Milky Way, and I remembered my conversations with Alessandro years before. I remembered our questions, and I thought that perhaps he would now have the answer to all of them and wondered if he would ever share them with his old friend.

'Why did an elusive character like Alessandro want to leave autobiographical notes?' I asked. 'It is so discordant with his personality. He did not care about life along its complete course. He avoided closeness to women and men. He cherished seclusion. Why did he feel the need to leave a legacy? Why did he want to open up to il Professore?'

'Perhaps it was a reaction to the way he spent his life. Perhaps in his nihilism it was a regretful attempt to communicate and recollect the lost opportunities. He needed reassurance that his life was not going to be completely wasted,' said Don Pino.

'Life comes in bitter-sweet pills most of the time,' added my father. 'But if we do not feel alone, and we are able to share with others the bitterness, our suffering gains value and becomes purposeful. I think in the end, Alessandro needed some validation, as Don Pino said. He needed to leave a wake behind him that would give some purpose to what he considered to be a purposeless life. I do feel the same sometimes.'

After Don Pino departed, I left my father and uncle on the terrace where they were enjoying the breeze and an after-dinner drink and I retired to the den, waiting for the inspiration and energy to pick up the phone, either the Blackberry or the land line, and dial home to America. But the energy that I attempted to summon did not seem to transmit to my hand that sat passively on the side of the armchair.

Looking up, I saw the life-size portraits of my ancestors, who, dressed in impressive uniforms, were as usual staring at me unblinkingly with an undecipherable disposition. And I wondered who they really were in their long-gone lives. I realised that although I had grown up with those images on the wall and they felt so familiar to me, in reality I had never met a single one of them. Some had made history while others' history had been embellished for them by generations of family legends. In that moment, I could not refrain from thinking that although my genes and traits came from them, they would be hopeless strangers to me forever because not one of them had left a note or a message for the generations to come as Alessandro had. I imagined myself one day hanging on the wall with the same equivocal expression, and a distant progeny of mine in the remote future would be sitting on the same chair and asking exactly the same question, 'Who was he?'

That night, I did not call home. There was no specific reason except that my hand never mustered sufficient strength to dial the number. After being woken up from my preliminary doze in the armchair by my mother, I followed her suggestion and retired to my bedroom while the church bells reminded us, once again, of the pace of time.

V

Three Ladróns, a Knife Fight,
and a Murder

In the morning, as I had promised the night before, I dutifully dragged myself to the barber's shop that looked into the Chiazza just a two-minute walk from home. As is the case with most endeavours in Pizzo, the shop offered an experience beyond the one suggested by the white, red, and blue striped column twirling around at the front door. This was likely on account of the double life that the Napitini endured: the one adopted to cover the practical needs of existence and another the imaginary existence that stretched towards the limit of one's dreams to compensate for the bareness of the former. The barber's shop was owned and operated by two brothers who were a great deal fonder of music than they were interested in other people's manes. In particular, Leonardo was a recognised authority on classical music, a proficient organ player, and a composer of religious litanies.

Discordant with Leonardo's reputation as a musician was the opinion that Napitini reserved for him as barber. Upon stepping through the door, each costumer would become aware of the fifty-fifty chance of falling under the craftsmanship of Leonardo, who held indisputably a deterring reputation as Figaro. Awoken by this bitter reality, an intoxicating wish subsequently arose in each customer that he would be subject to the brother who was the lesser of two evils. But no matter how heavy this dilemma might weigh over each customer's mood, this downside of Napitinian life hinged upon Leonardo's shortcomings, as for many aftermaths of history, yielded the unexpected benefit of bringing out the best in the citizens of Pizzo, providing undisputable evidence that courtesy could be at least occasionally uncovered within the Napitinian genes.

In fact, when the customer's turn finally came, and if the adversity of destiny this time pointed towards Leonardo, the victim with the utmost cordiality, enthusiasm, and affability would become unusually polite and display a prolificacy of efforts to encourage the second in line to move ahead of him. The latter, of course, would vigorously offer the same option to the next, who could not refrain from turning the favours to the following one, and so on. 'Prego[62]! Prego!' they would say to the next. 'Go ahead! I am in no hurry at all! In fact, I may take the opportunity to run over to Ciccio's store to buy the newspaper so that we can all find out what is happening in the world!'

On this particular day, I was the one least equipped to resist such determined outpouring of politeness. As a result, I had the privilege of learning about Bach, Beethoven, and Handel while my greying hair lazily snowed on to the floor to the rhythm of a Strauss Waltz and my head assumed the well-renowned Easter Egg configuration *a la* Signor Leonardo.

As the masterpiece was coming together under the concerned looks of the bystanders, il Professore, who must have been informed by a man with a moustache that I had entered such premises of my own initiative, came belatedly to my rescue. Without the customary salaams and bows, he announced, 'L'Avvocato was brought to the hospital as an emergency during the night. He may be dead by now.'

Although I did not intend to belittle the dramatic impression imposed on us all by this dazzling prologue, I was influenced by my cautionary impulse that was the result of years of clinical practice. I gently advised that it might be precipitous to declare anybody dead before having a chance to check his pulse and asked, 'What happened? What was he complaining of?'

---

[62]   I beg you!

'Who knows? I learnt about this from the road sweeper this morning, who said that Donna Filomena, who lives in front of l'Avvocato's house, told him that she saw an ambulance leave his house at around two in the morning.'

'Strange', I replied. 'I did not hear any sirens last night, although we live quite close.'

'Well, there is no reason to wake up the whole town if the streets are empty and people are sleeping in the middle of the night now, is there?'

'Or maybe he was already dead,' comforted Leonardo, who by then had hurried to complete his job and with a brush was dusting away from my clothes any remembrance of my beloved curls.

I was unwilling to declare the poor Avvocato, who just a few hours before had been expectorating with Herculean strength, dead based only on second-hand impressions. I quickly donated a generous tip to Leonardo as I checked myself in the mirror to ensure that both ears were still in their proper position, and carrying my oval of a head upon my shoulders with as much dignity as possible, I left the barber's shop with the intention of gathering more intelligence from the dwellers of the Chiazza in contempt of regulations intended to protect one's privacy, which may be applied elsewhere but had never landed upon the shores of Pizzo.

Il Professore and I walked the few steps towards il Gatto, where the usual crew was already discussing the events of the night.

Sig. Belvedere took a cigarette from his mouth as soon as he saw me and said, 'Did you hear about l'Avvocato? With all of the smoking he has been doing, he must have had a stroke—like my father! I told him many times that he should smoke cigarettes with a filter!'

Ciccio Percuoco, who had been distracted by the turmoil from his own arguing with himself, came close to us and respectfully bowing in front of me added, 'Yes, he rolls his own cigarettes with the newspaper sheets, and he uses Avanti![63] That cannot be good . . . with all respect!' Ciccio

---

[63]   Italian newspaper with a rocky history.

Percuoco in spite of his humble upbringing was an avid and perspicacious newspaper reader.

Donna Rita, the pharmacist's wife who had just heard the news and had come to join the conversation at il Gatto with the same intent to gather useful information about this interesting case, thought differently. She added 'indigestion' to the differential diagnosis since l'Avvocato was known from time to time to shower after dinner without waiting the compulsory three hours that restore the body's resistance to contact with water—a phenomenon yet to be discovered by the practicing medical or scientific communities but long recognised among the *comari*[64] of the town.

Mastro Antonio added that it could have been an episode of colicky pain caused by gall bladder stones since this was a very common problem among lawyers who had their stomachs lined with hair[65] since they had to be ready to digest stones in their professional activity.

As was characteristic of his cynicism, my uncle, who was walking towards the tavolino with my father, finally suggested that the whole affair likely represented a desperate attempt by l'Avvocato to flee from town to avoid further subjection to il Professore's stories.

Il Professore, in turn, insisted that by now l'Avvocato might be solidly dead, but that in case he was not, we should hurry to do something to save his life. With this, everybody turned eagerly to me, simultaneously promoting or demoting me, depending upon the point of view, from Signorino Giuseppe to *il Dottore dall' America*.[66] It was decided by the

---

[64] Comare(i) = gossipmonger(s).

[65] Derogatory Italian expression directed towards those who like some lawyers can digest almost anything in the ethical spectrum. Although the linearity of the logic of this argument may be obscure, it closely aligns with the way some judgments are presented and accepted in such circumstances.

[66] The doctor from America.

group that I should rush to visit l'Avvocato at the hospital in Vibo[67] to save his life if it wasn't too late.

As I began protesting that American citizenship did not ascribe supernatural powers and that l'Avvocato was probably in better hands under the supervision of the hospital physicians, Dr Riga appeared and came to my rescue. He told us that it was he who had visited l'Avvocato the night before and that he had diagnosed the poor man with pneumonia. He had called the ambulance to take l'Avvocato to the hospital for a chest X-ray and antibiotics on account of his high fever and dull chest sounds.

'We should go see him together later today. I just called and they say he is doing better after taking the antibiotics. We can visit him in the early afternoon.'

Since it was still quite early in the morning and the excitement had been extinguished by Dr Riga's unembellished explanation, we all sat at the tavolino, where my father, my uncle, and il Marchese had been dwelling and watching the gathering with sceptical stares. Since it appeared that we had nothing else to do but wait for the appropriate time to visit the poor Avvocato, il Professore continued Alessandro's story . . .

*   *   *

. . . Alessandro had an uncle whose name was Don Antonio. He was a wealthy landlord in the inland. His property spanned miles of hills and valleys, peaks and troughs, green meadows and golden wheat cultivations, lush corn fields, orchards, vineyards, olive groves, and scattered centennial oak trees that covered with their shadows boundless spaces where cows grazed, cocks fought over hens, foxes appeared and disappeared, and dogs sighed as they waited for something to happen. It was here that Alessandro spent long summer days throughout his childhood and adolescence reading the classics: *War and Peace, Madame Bovary, East of Eden, The Lady with the Little Dog,* and other long interminable stories

---

[67]   The non-identical twin of Pizzo—another little town that rests on top of the hills, few kilometres away from Pizzo.

in synchrony with the way life appeared to him at those times under the shadow of the old oak trees.

Dispersed throughout the land were many farmers' settlements. There, children who had never worn a shoe climbed trees, guided sheep to pastures, milked cows, and led distracted mules. With those children, Alessandro spent timeless days searching for wild strawberries, *asparagi*,[68] or mushrooms that were compliments of springtime, summer, or fall, respectively. With them, he hunted with slingshots or helped their fathers harvest the crops and carry them to the farm on a carriage pulled by a good-natured but imperturbable donkey. The farmers looked after Alessandro with benevolence, listening reverentially to his suggestions that were born of enthusiasm and love for their land from his educated, albeit naive, soul.

In the middle of the property, at the summit of the tallest hill, stood the mansion where Don Antonio lived with his wife, Teresa. More than a palace, it was a country farmhouse. The ground floor consisted of large rooms adapted into warehouses where hay or large barrels of oil and wine emanated distinct smells into the darkness. There were animal shelters, kitchens, and shops buzzing with labourers during the day and watched over by grumpy dogs during the night. On the top floor rested the family living quarters. It was on this level that there was a large room with windows that stayed open from spring to fall, where a breeze continually flowed from the valley below. At night, the darkness was complete, save for a few migrating lights carried by peasants returning to their shelters under the brightness of the Milky Way.

There was no electricity in their home then, but the quiet darkness was broken with the flickering of gasoline lamps that attracted moths and the geckos that ate them. Occasionally, a bat paid a serendipitous visit and flew around, grazing the ceilings, until a servant could chase it out with a broom. It all happened, night after night, with the naturalness of a recurring scene that belonged to a staged performance. Each character, animal or person, was an unintentional participant, sharing with each

---

[68] Asparagus,

other an intangible fable in the immense silence and solitude of the countryside.

Tales told by the old farmers enhanced the living performance. In local mythology, the fables were embellished by stories of wolves with human hands, turkeys with red eyes who smoked cigars, ghosts that ate children and hid under their beds, foxes that could speak, and bandits who were heroes. Later on, in the depth of the night, darkness would win and only the hoot of an owl or the call of a nightingale seldom pierced the silence from a distance.

On this particular summer morning, Don Antonio sat with his wife, Donna Teresa, eating breakfast at a massive wooden table under an ancient oak tree. Mulberries surrounded them, serving as a fence to shelter them. On his left side sat the twelve-year-old Alessandro, who had just inquired about Bruno, the dog that had been following him faithfully for the last few days while he was roaming up and down the hills or resting to read under the oak trees. Alessandro had not seen Bruno at all that morning: not at the bottom of the marble stairs where the animal normally waited for him and not in the groves where the dog normally followed him to find fresh figs and grapes for breakfast.

Bruno was an unsophisticated dog who had never learnt to bark properly. Instead, he would cough up guttural sounds at times of his highest excitement, or he mostly whimpered to demand attention. He followed Alessandro around, day in and day out, being always right by his side as if he were led by a leash. Likewise, he stopped when Alessandro stopped and resumed as soon as he did. It was simple companionship without expectation—save for an occasional slurp from the canine's warm tongue, which was reciprocated by a scratch behind the ears.

'I had Guglielmo shoot him this morning. It killed a hen . . . the darn beast!' said Don Antonio.

Alessandro accepted the ruling because he knew Bruno had transgressed the law of the land, according to which he had been justly executed. But he did not feel hungry any more. Rather, he stared at the corner where Bruno used to wait for him to finish his breakfast, before joining in the activities of the day with his wagging tail and canine smile. He imagined a blackboard with an eraser sweeping Bruno away, and it appeared to him that the essence of life was only the impact of scrawls made by chalk over an indifferent slate.

The whisper of the breeze was soft and caressing on the summit of the hill on that early summer day, and no words were needed to break the peace. But soon there was the hint of the noise of an engine from far away, which gradually grew until from behind another oak tree a car appeared. The vehicle slowly continued across the courtyard and then turned around to stop in front of the table.

A man of about fifty, dressed in velvet trousers, a checkered shirt, and a wool hat, emerged from the back door while the driver continued on to park the vehicle under the shade of the same oak tree. The man was Mastro Gennaro, one of the head farmers and a person highly regarded and trusted in Don Antonio's kingdom.

'My respects, Donna Teresa,' he said, removing his hat and approaching the table. Looking at the scrutinising stare of Don Antonio, he added, 'Some scoundrel poisoned the dogs at the Granatari.'

The Granatari was a remote patch of land, a few hills apart in the inland direction of the property. There, cattle were left to graze during the day along the lush banks of a small creek that originated from a natural spring. The cows mastered the routine by stepping out of the shack where they spent the night, then slowly found their way, in a circle, up and down the gentle slopes around the creek and the little swamps until the sun moved from one side of the sky to the other and it was once again time to return to their shelter for the night. The dogs had little to do but follow the cows around with disinterest, only occasionally checking on them with the back of their eyes before being shortly distracted by a distant sound or an unusual fragrance.

'Sit down, Mastro Gennaro. Please take a bite. We have the best plums and figs today and even grapes that my nephew went to gather himself. Have some eggs or the pie that Donna Teresa made with her own hands.' Mastro Gennaro sat as he was told, although he was obviously not hungry because he must have had breakfast already. Regardless, he respectfully took a few olives and a spoonful of scrambled eggs on to his plate and slowly shoved a little piece at a time into his mouth while he waited for orders. Nobody spoke.

Donna Teresa never dared to speak. She was too stupid and ignorant to utter words to a conversation of substance, too inept and naive to contribute to a practical dialogue, and too fearful of the irritated glares of her husband to emit any unnecessary sound that might remind him of her existence. She had been overindulged throughout her youth, being raised in an all girls' boarding school away from home after Nonna sent her away during the family's troubled times. There she was taught to recite interminable chains of rosaries and to knit the rest of the time— both skills of hardly any value in the countryside.

The whisper of the breeze had regained control when Don Antonio finally stated, 'Mio caro,[69] Mastro Gennaro, I am confident you will take care of this unfortunate circumstance. You have my blessings.' Mastro Gennaro rose, gracefully bowed towards Donna Teresa, and putting his hat back on his head returned to the car.

A few days later, after breakfast, Don Antonio grabbed a cane that had been resting at the side of the table, put a straw hat on his head, and turned towards Alessandro. 'Come with me. I will show you what happens when some people do what they are not supposed to do.'

A different car waited for them under the shade of the old oak tree. The driver opened the back door for Don Antonio and Alessandro, who without questioning followed his beloved uncle. They drove a few miles up and down a dusty road, leaving a red cloud along the way. Alessandro cranked down the window and enjoyed the cool morning breeze for those few moments before they arrived at the bank of the creek of the Granatari, just a few steps from the shelter where the cows were kept.

The moos of the animals suggested that somebody had forgotten to open the gate to let them out this morning. Alessandro noticed a few people standing just a few yards away from the shelter under the olive trees. Don Antonio exited the car first, and Alessandro followed.

---

[69]   My dear.

Slowly they approached the shelter. Behind the last bush, Alessandro saw a small truck covered with dust. A dead man sat in front of it, his shoulders leaning against the hood with his head tilted up towards the sky and his empty eyes staring unaffected right into the morning sun. The windshield was shattered and another dead man leant his head against the steering wheel while a third body lay a few steps away, as if its owner had attempted to flee under the shower of bullets.

The silence was absolute as was the stillness of the scene. It seemed that the world had ceased to exist in synchrony with the life of those three men. Following the gaze of the first dead man, Alessandro lifted his eyes towards the top of the olive tree. There he noticed the gentle movement of the swaying branches as a reminder that a breath of life had been left in that forsaken corner of existence. With this thought, the young Alessandro was awakened from his surreal nightmare.

The police captain approached Don Antonio first, and scratching the nape of his neck, he explained, 'My people waited for the ladróns[70] all night. They arrived at one in the morning. From the darkness, we intimated a halt. In response, one of them fired against my man who had asked them to stop. My man turned on the lights of the police car and we responded with fire.'

Don Antonio turned back to the dead men, as if to assure himself that they were in fact lifeless, then turned back to the police captain. 'Where are they from?'

'From the mountains around Serra San Bruno. It is likely that they had stolen cattle in that area before.'

Turning to Mastro Gennaro, who stood a few steps from the captain, Don Antonio said, 'Make sure they get a decent funeral and burial. I will pay for it.' And with that, holding his cane by the shaft, he returned to the car. Alessandro, who had not whispered a word, followed closely and wondered where the lives of those three men, and that of Bruno, would be now that they had departed from their bodies.

---

70   Thieves.

*　　*　　*

Three years passed.

Alessandro had left the soccer field where he had just finished playing a very good game. His team had won the game as a result of his performance. He had taken control of the offensive strategy and as a result scored three goals. It was an away game against a team that was housed up in the mountains, where people dressed a little differently, spoke somewhat differently, but thought very much differently.

It was a shiny day and a positive one. It was the kind of day that would remain imprinted on a youngster's memory for no good reason, save for its beauty, poetry, and simplicity. And it would have been so preserved in Alessandro's memory had it not been for a strange accident that awaited him down the dusty path that led from the soccer field to the parking lot where the cars that were supposed to carry him and his friends home sat.

Two men that resembled the infamous characters in Collodi's *Pinocchio* were seemingly waiting for him. The Fox stood taller and skinnier, leaning slightly forward, as if the breeze from behind was too much to endure. The Cat, on the other hand, stood short and stout as he compensated for his companion's stance by leaning backwards with his shoulders against a post and one leg bent to rest his foot on the same post while he kept his hands in his pockets. If there had been any doubt, it became clear beyond a reasonable doubt that these characters were waiting for Alessandro when the skinny one dragged his feet towards the centre of the path and the stout one released his hold from the supporting post and followed his friend as he approached them.

Alessandro, good-natured as always, thought it best to smile at the two characters, thereby recognising them as members of the opposing team. His smile, however, froze when he saw the Fox bring forward his right hand, armed with an open pocket knife. Simultaneously, his stocky companion took his hand out of his right pocket to present a further warning: an unopened pocket knife.

Alessandro saw out of the corner of his eye that a few members of the other team had gathered around a nearby bush. They were seemingly distracted in chatter, and he could not see anyone else who could help. The Fox stepped forward with his knife exposed, aimed just below Alessandro's belt. As he continued towards Alessandro, he allowed a few words from his mouth, 'So it seems to me that you assume you can come here to the mountains and dispose at your pleasure of the peasants? Do you think we exist just to be pushed around by morons like you? Show me what you can really do, man to man. This is what I call a fair game!' Turning to the Cat, the Fox ordered, 'Give him the knife! Let's see what he can do!'

Alessandro had never been much into *machismo*,[71] nor was he particularly into fighting with strangers for any reason, especially over completely unqualified principles. But he could not think of a way out of this fight, save for declining the offer of the knife and offering instead some pretence of apology.

As he rapidly reflected on how best to handle the situation, he was suddenly pushed from the right as Peppino's voice came to his rescue, 'What is this quarrel about? Are you stupid? Don't you know who this is?' Peppino, who was Alessandro's teammate and a long-time friend, approached the Fox and whispered into his ears.

Whatever was said, it had an immediate effect. As the Fox put his weapon back into his pocket, he said with the utmost reverence, 'I am asking your forgiveness, Your Excellency. I am truly sorry. I am not sure what went through my head. Please forgive me so that I can be your servant from today forward.'

The stout feline looked with bewilderment at his friend and also returned his shut knife to his pocket. Grabbing the Fox's arm as if to guide him away from an embarrassing scene, the Cat opened his mouth in a cowardly smile and ever so subtly bent his chin forward. As he was moving away slowly, dragged by his friend, the tall menace turned back one last time towards Alessandro and begged, 'Forgive me. Please do not tell anybody about this and I will be thankful to you for the rest of my life.'

---

[71] An attitude in agreement with the traditional ideas of men behaving strong and aggressively, a common stereotype of Southern Italian men's behaviour.

The day was not totally ruined by this incident, and Alessandro was able to put the episode in the back of his mind as he resumed the path towards his car, his hometown, and his future. In fact, he did not make much of the whole incident at all, almost forgetting it had happened completely until one year later another unfortunate event forced him to recollect and appreciate what that moment meant.

*   *   *

By the age of sixteen, Alessandro had matured more than any of his peers, and as was previously mentioned, he bore a natural ease with the gentler gender, which drew them to him, like flies are attracted to sugar. On one hot summer day, he relaxed in the shade of a straw canopy which marked the entrance of a bar that faced the splashing waves and salty winds of the sea. He held a straw in his mouth, which dipped into a glass of cold soda, and he wore a pair of dark Ray Bans sunglasses that were quite in line with the fashion of the time. His skin was perfectly tanned under his light shirt that was opened just so, further contributing to his image of being a perfect playboy. As he scanned the landscape for potential prey, he waited in the comfort of the shade. The record player behind the bar blasted predictable music, as was demanded by the young generation whose taste floated adrift the romance of rehashed lyrics.

The sun was high in the sky and the shadows tightly followed their owners, including the one of a pretty girl in her teens who appeared suddenly in front of him. She had big dark eyes and red lips that sat in the middle of a dark bronze face, like a strawberry on top of caramel gelato. As she walked across the aisle, she was oblivious to everything but the path she followed to the counter where goodies were served. Yet Alessandro caught a brief, meaningful glimpse that was cast in his direction—one of those fractional movements of a woman's eye that only experienced men can recognise and interpret.

With the utmost naturalness, Alessandro asked as she was passing by, 'What's your name?'

Her name was Marilena and as it turned out after the ice was broken she very much liked to talk. And so she talked, and she explained and she elaborated everything about her family: that they lived inland and were just at the beach for the day . . . the age of her sisters and brothers . . . the gossip of her little town . . . and that they had brought the family dog with them to the beach . . . and that the dog was pregnant and would soon have puppies as she had a year before . . . and that she liked the puppies very much but last year some had died before they had had the opportunity to name them because her mother was against giving dogs Christian names and preferred the names of flowers or plants . . . and on and on she went.

Alessandro soon became weary as he wondered how this plethora of information could possibly have pertained to the original question. As he began looking for a polite way to end the conversation, a young man of about twenty came directly towards him with anger in his eyes. He took Marilena by her wrist to push her away from the tavolino, and standing in between her and Alessandro, he grimaced a warning. 'Stay away from my girlfriend or I will teach you a lesson you will never forget.'

As he had a year before, Alessandro experienced the uneasiness of dealing with strangers and his own indifference towards quarrels that originated from serendipitous encounters. Like most aristocrats, Alessandro perceived people who had not been properly introduced within his own close circle of acquaintances to be characters of a different species entirely, rather than true human beings, put on this Earth with the sole purpose of giving life to the surroundings in his world. While he earnestly respected all people in principle, he had trouble interacting—for better or worse—with these lower classes without proper introduction, save of course in the case of pretty girls when this psychological barrier often did not feel completely insurmountable.

But this time, he did not let it be. With the most agreeable voice he could manage, he said, 'I am sorry. I asked for her name and she volunteered much more. What is wrong with that?'

The visitor pulled his pants up, puffed up his chest, and turning his hand into a fist replied, 'I will show you what is wrong with that.' Right as it began to seem that the situation was progressing towards a regrettable dispute, other people in the bar gathered around, and Marilena, holding her boyfriend's right arm with both hands, dragged him away as he continued to stare at Alessandro with unforgiving eyes.

Nothing further would have been said about this unfortunate episode had it not been for a car that screeched to a stop in front of Alessandro as he was walking with two friends along the beach later that evening. From the car emerged three men who swiftly grabbed Alessandro. One held his chest while the other two, each embracing one of his legs, threw him into the car. The car skidded away as fast as it had arrived and disappeared towards an isolated stretch of beach called La Pineta.

Like Alessandro, who was too stunned to react, his friends also lacked the reflexes necessary to intervene before it was too late. As soon as the car had pulled away from their path, and they had a split second to process what they had just seen, they ran to their own car, which sat just a few hundred metres away. They jumped in and pushed the accelerator to propel themselves into the incoming darkness of the night. Peppino, one of the two friends whom we had met in the previously mentioned episode following the soccer game, had witnessed the episode in the bar that morning and recognised one of the strange men as Marilena's boyfriend.

There are not many places around Pizzo where young boys might go to solve their disputes. Several predictably go to La Pineta, in contrast to the better designed plans of professional criminals who choose instead to avoid obviousness. To Alessandro's loyal friends, it was therefore a reasonable assumption that the attackers had gone to La Pineta, where things are quiet at night and where only secretive lovers meet and other activities that hold an implicit assumption of tactfulness take place. The two boys had, of course, been in that place many times before for easily imaginable reasons.

They drove knowledgably into the familiar underbrush and scanned for their friend in the sandy and soft beach that was illuminated by their headlights. Though it all happened too quickly to consider, this was in fact quite a courageous move given that Alessandro's friends were boys of the upper middle class who were not brought up with the violence that was acceptable, and possibly encouraged, amongst the youngsters of the working class who had much to prove to themselves and to the world by crafting their own rules. They carried no arms. They had no plans. They were just following an instinct that told them to search for their friend, much to the irritation of the couples who were caught in various stages of a long established performance and looked at them with the red eye of hyenas caught in action.

Perhaps fifteen minutes had passed since they had begun searching the Savannah of Pizzo for their friend when they saw the stumbling figure of a man emerge from the darkness. He was dragging his leg and holding his right cheek with both hands. As the car's headlights fully illuminated the figure, Alessandro's slim physique became clearly visible. The site where Alessandro had been released from his premeditated punishment was a silent spot, close to the beach near where the pine trees ended.

The moon had already taken control of the dusky evening and only the murmur of the sea interrupted the silence. Alessandro's face was swollen with bruises and boasted a torn lower lip. There was blood on his shirt and hands, and there were scratches along his forehead and forearms. When they peeled back his shirt, they saw that more scratches and bruises covered his entire chest and abdomen.

Yet the three friends felt almost cheerful just like when a great fear is suddenly relieved. Even Alessandro smiled slightly at first. Pressing a handkerchief against his torn lip, he then laughed hysterically, as if the entire episode had not happened to him but instead he had heard of it as a testimony to the foolishness of youth.

Peppino joined the laugh and yelled, 'I guess you better watch those peasant women and their pimps from the mountains!'

Alessandro took a seat at the bottom of a pine tree and looked at the moonlight's path across the gulf. Placing a stick in the better preserved part of his lip, as if he was smoking a cigarette, he said, 'Do you know what will be even funnier? Donna Giovanna's face when she is presented with the current version of her grandson's adored face!'

But for some reason, that thought immediately extinguished the laughter from everybody's spirit. Instead, each of the three friends became suddenly pensive.

'There is no way we can take you home in this condition, Alex,' pronounced Peppino. 'She would have a heart attack.'

Nobody talked for a long while. Cars intermittently drove in and out of the Pineta, slowly and furtively carrying couples that had no better place to go. Alessandro thought about how busy the night was under the shelter of darkness. He had never personally been to La Pineta for the above-mentioned purposes as he had lived a privileged life where he had the luxury of experiencing the forbidden in the cosiness of comfortable homes and country villas without the need to resort to such degrading means. Yet he considered that these encounters performed in the subterfuge of the night, away from the civilised world, bore their own appeal and perhaps even a romantic flavour. He felt a sense of arousal, in spite of his condition, thinking of what took place in those busy alcoves of pleasure.

'I think we should take you to Don Antonio. You can stay there until you look a bit better,' resumed Peppino. 'We can tell Donna Giovanna that you decided to go to the villa to get some peace in the growing heat of summer. We can get your stuff. We will say that you called from the beach and that you did not want to go all the way back home because it was easier to ask one of us, who were already in Pizzo.'

Alessandro acknowledged that this was the only thing to do. Donna Giovanna would not believe such a story, of course, but she would accept it as she was becoming used to taking Alessandro's independence. She would probably suspect that he, in deference to the legacy left by his illustrious ancestors, was out on a romantic escapade, as reports of such adventures had begun to creep up the marble stairway of the mansion via reliable men with moustache.

It was nearly eleven at night when the three friends arrived at Don Antonio's house at the top of the hill. Mastro Gennaro, who had heard the rumble of their car, was waiting for them under the oak tree with a rifle in hand. He was barely dressed with his pants buttoned summarily and his dishevelled shirt half open around his hairy chest.

By the time the car finally came to a stop in the middle of the front yard, two peasants, each with a shotgun of their own, had joined Mastro Gennaro under the oak tree. Peppino, who was driving, lifted his left arm out of the car window with the open palm and turned off the headlights. Alessandro was the first to come out of the car. As he stepped out of the back seat, he cheerfully greeted, 'Good evening, Mastro Gennaro. How are things on the old farm?'

In truth, Alessandro was not doing so well. After the adrenaline rush of the evening had begun to recede, a throbbing pain had crept from his lower jaw up to his right temple and was rapidly spreading to his eye socket in one direction and his upper nape in the other. Despite the increasing pain, he knew that real men in these mountains were expected to make light of adversities. Complying with these machismo expectations, he feigned lightness while he surrendered himself to protection by the tentacles of his uncle's far-reaching power.

Mastro Gennaro and the two peasants encircled Alessandro while the two friends, who had subsequently emerged from the car themselves, watched from a respectful distance. One of the peasants lit a kerosene lamp by scratching a match against the rough palm of his left hand. Once illuminated, he lifted the lamp towards Alessandro's face, which by then was hiding the excruciating pain of its owner poorly.

'Who did this to you?' asked Mastro Gennaro.

'Somebody who did not appreciate my wit, I guess!' replied Alessandro.

Mastro Gennaro, in turn, did not appreciate Alessandro's witticism. Turning to Peppino, he repeated, 'Who did this to him?'

Peppino, who came from an upper middle class background and who had therefore lived a less sheltered life than Alessandro, precisely sensed the purpose and gravity of Mastro Gennaro's inquiry. He also knew that he had no choice but to explain exactly what had happened. As he nervously prepared himself to rehash the narrative, Alessandro began to feel dizzy and reached for one of the peasants' shoulders with his left hand. Mastro Gennaro interrupted Peppino with a wave of his hand, and offering his arm to Alessandro, he said apologetically, 'Come on, come on. Let us get you some rest first. We will figure out what is to be done later.'

They slowly walked up the stairs to the living quarters. By the time they arrived at the top floor and prepared to knock, the door swung open to reveal Don Antonio flanked by a servant, sort of a butler, holding a gas lamp.

Don Antonio looked at his beloved nephew without betraying any emotion while Alessandro tried unsuccessfully to build a smile on his sore and swollen face. Don Antonio scanned his nephew slowly. He saw that his black curls and pale forehead were soiled by sticky blood and observed that his transparent blue eyes and long eyelashes remained the only parts of his face that were not disfigured. Raising his right hand tenderly, he slowly caressed the least damaged part of Alessandro's face. When he drew his hand back, he looked at his own fingers that were now stained with his nephew's blood. He examined the scratches on Alessandro's neck, and he opened his shirt where more bruises and scratches could be seen. Without saying a word, Don Antonio turned back into the living quarters. Holding Alessandro's left arm, he led his nephew to an armchair in the parlour that was enlivened by a cool breeze let in through the open balcony.

He made Alessandro sit and said to the butler, 'Bring him some whiskey with ice.' Then turning towards Alessandro, he asked, 'What about Donna Giovanna? Does she know about this?'

By then Alessandro did not feel much like talking. Instead, with the index finger of his left hand, he pointed at Peppino and gently waved his remaining fingers, silently soliciting his help.

Peppino answered for his friend. 'No. We told Donna Giovanna that Alessandro wanted to come to stay with you in the mountains to escape the heat down by the sea. We made her believe that he wanted privacy to spend time with a respectable girl, if you understand what I mean.'

Don Antonio did not acknowledge Peppino's words. Instead, he continued to look intensely at his beloved nephew. 'Does your father know?'

'No,' Alessandro replied.

Don Antonio was a very handsome ageing man. He still had dark hair with sprinkles of grey. He had a face with gentle features, very dark skin tanned by days spent patrolling his vast dominion, and a small mouth that was flanked by dimples, which when he smiled displayed a row of perfectly white and regular teeth. His gentle face appeared to be constantly smiling, giving him the appearance of the kindest variety, save for his black eyes that seemed to project streams of fire when he stared. When he focused his attention, he had the stillness of a leopard pointing at its prey: No movement in the face or body, not even a blink, could be observed.

After spending a few interminable moments looking this way at Alessandro, Don Antonio turned to the butler, took the crystal glass of whiskey, and gently lifted it to Alessandro's lips. He forced the boy to take a few sequential sips and then said forcefully, 'I need you to tell me how this happened to you. Then you can rest. You seem like you will be fine, but we will call a doctor tomorrow morning.'

Again, Alessandro waved at his friend while imperceptibly shaking his head. He finally explained, 'I do not know who they are. Just that they were some guys from the mountains. Peppino knows who they are. There was a quarrel with one of them over a girl in the morning. He threatened me then, but I did not pay attention. But in the evening, they kidnapped me while I was walking on the beach. They took me in their car and drove to La Pineta. While two were holding me down, the girl's boyfriend punched me over and over. Then they tossed me out of the car and drove away.'

Alessandro did not realise then that this confession was a death sentence. The only missing piece was the identity of the attacker. But that would be easy enough to discover. Peppino knew the people of the region well, and he could give Don Antonio and Mastro Gennaro enough details to satisfy the question.

'You go to bed now and get some good rest, Alessandro. I will call a doctor to the house in the morning,' said Don Antonio.

As the butler walked him down the hall to his room, Alessandro heard his uncle's voice say, 'Mastro Gennaro, please make sure that such a thing never happens again. You may go with my blessings.'

The following morning, Alessandro woke up with a very swollen face. He could not open his left eye and he had pain claiming his attention, which came in turns—from his nape, chest, face, and head. Yet, overall, he felt well and relieved. He lay resting in bed for a while with his pillow raised against the headboard. He looked around with his right eye and observed discreet rays of light from a deferential sun poking through the venetian blinds, brightening the room. He thought about how strange the events of the previous day had been. He thought of Marilena and her boyfriend. He considered how strange his reaction had been.

'Did he really care that much? Did he attack me just for his pride? Or was he really concerned with protecting his girlfriend?' He asked himself whether he could or would ever do anything like this for a woman. 'Would I ever care that much? Wouldn't it be nice to care that much for someone?'

He thought of Marilena's gentle smile and warm eyes. 'Maybe she was really important to that young man,' he thought. He touched his swollen features and thought that, perhaps, there was something to be learnt from the happening. And it was a broad lesson: not just about respecting another man's girl or about abiding to similar puritan concepts. Rather, it was a revelation that it may be possible to care for another person to the point of passion and foolishness. The sweetness of that thought touched ever so briefly his insensitive heart.

The young peasants, who used to be the boys with whom Alessandro had played in his youth, came to visit and chat with him. His wounds impressed them as if he was a war hero and they were proud of him. They did not want to hear that he barely had anything to do with the fight: It was no use attempting to explain that he had passively received a beating. They imagined Alessandro fighting for the rights of manhood. They unanimously voted in their hearts for him to be their future master: the heir of Don Antonio.

Three uneventful days passed until Peppino came for a visit. He communicated that Don Antonio had paid Donna Giovanna a visit to personally comfort her and tell her that her dear Alessandro was enjoying the countryside with hikes in the mountains with the peasants to relish the coolness of the mountain air and that Donna Giovanna was happy to know that he was with his beloved uncle. Peppino reported that all was fine with their friends in Pizzo and that they all wished him well and were waiting for his return. They were arranging a sailing trip to the Eolie

Islands, Panarea, and Vulcano upon his return. They would spend a few summer days swimming in the deep blue sea and fishing, having dinners on the beach, and hiking up the mountains where goats had been grazing since the times of Odysseus. Peppino continued describing the perfect life that awaited Alessandro's recovery and subsequent return to Pizzo until Alessandro finally interrupted him, 'So, any news about that Romeo who beat me up?'

Suddenly, Peppino's expression changed. He looked inquisitively into his friend's eyes as if to ask whether he really wanted to know. He sighed deeply and turned his face downwards to stare at the floor. Quietly, he delivered the few words that changed the course of Alessandro's life.

'They found him drowned along the beach in front of the Pineta two days later. The police say that it was an accident.'

Alessandro caressed his swollen face with the palm of his left hand. He pressed on the sore spots as if to revive the pain, simultaneously reviving the actions of a dead man.

'You know very well that it was no accident.'

Peppino interrupted him immediately, 'Alessandro, look at me! It was an accident. Case closed!'

'What about his family? Did he have a family?'

'He was the only son of a widow. She knows that it was only an accident and so does his girlfriend. Believe me, nobody will ever dare to question this.'

Alessandro shook his head and sarcastically asked, 'Is my uncle going to pay for his funeral?'

Days passed, one after the other. Alessandro was recovering physically, but a new ailment that would be with him for the rest of his life had settled into his young soul.

At first, he wanted to act. He knew that he had to speak up. He knew that justice had to be served. His upbringing had instilled in him the importance of civilisation's vindication over passive acceptance of the forsaken land's brutal practices. All he had read and dreamed was of justice and fairness. He thought of confessing his crime to the authorities, which consisted of allowing such brutal events to evolve. He recognised that he had known all along who his uncle was and what he was capable of. He thought of the episode with the ladróns and the knife fights. He thought of the frightened face of the Fox when the name of a family with power was whispered into his ear. It all seemed so clear to him now.

He questioned himself for accepting being brought to Don Antonio rather than going home on the night of the kidnapping. Weren't the consequences obvious? He wondered whether he had subconsciously hoped for the unforgiving righteousness of the land for the sake of revenge. It was this power that turns against the weak, the innocent, and the defenceless when he becomes troublesome, which destroys the subordinate when he raises his head like the lion to the mouse in Aesop's fable.

He wanted to confront his uncle, but he did not have the courage. Instead, a deep apathy won over his principles. He realised that there was no justice of any kind, no matter how severe and righteous, that could bring the poor lover's life back. He realised that, like Bruno before, the poor man had succumbed not just to the harsh law of the land, but also to a deeper rule governing life itself—a rule that was even harsher with its indifference for human existence, the inexorability of its actions, the senselessness of its causality, its lack of predictability, its absolute absence of meaning and accountability to a Higher Entity. He thought himself a coward that could not bear to stand the fight of life or assert the will of humanity against the crushing silence and darkness of eternity.

. . . And he gave up.

VI

The Death of Nonna

'Don Antonio was a reasonable man and a man of principle, but he belonged to another generation,' continued il Professore. 'He was as harsh with himself as he was with others. He received the ultimate punishment for his last crime because Alessandro after recovering never went back to visit him. They never talked openly about what happened, but a few glances between them sufficed during those dreadful days. Alessandro never talked to anybody else about this incident. He maintained for the rest of his life a clandestine feeling of guilt. He was remorseful for conspiring in a crime he did not commit. He did not share his anguish even with his dad. But keeping it all to himself, he found ways to self-inflict a punishment that was crueller than the one any court of law could have enacted because it was aimed at his own self-destruction without chance for parole. A few months later, Don Antonio suffered a stroke and nobody knows what he knew and understood during the few months that followed before his death without ever seeing his beloved nephew again.'

'I do not think Alessandro was guilty of anything,' said Mastro Antonio generously, failing to understand the depth of Alessandro's anguish. 'How could he have predicted what was going to happen? Don Antonio was a country gentlemen and nobody could have expected . . .' While Mastro Antonio was filling the background, I thought of my old friend and of our relationship that had started just a few months following this incident. And I began to understand. I endeavoured to remember the cheerful aspects of his personality. And I remembered his clear blue eyes, and for the first time, I understood how much pain had been disguised by his beautiful smile. And I remembered the words he spoke when I drove him to the train station so many years ago on his way to another life: '. . . But now it is time to forget the past and move on!' I do not think he ever did and no matter how fast he ran he never succeeded in outrunning himself.

It was Dr Riga who roused me from those reflections, saying, 'Well, I think it is time to drive to Vibo and pay a visit to our good friend, il Signor Avvocato.'

*   *   *

Walking towards Dr Riga's car, I noticed a bumper sticker on it, stating in Italian: 'Non sono un comunista'.[72] Without being asked, Dr Riga felt an obligation to explain, 'Il Professore glued it in here a few years ago.' No further explanation ensued.

As soon as we entered the car, Dr Riga took a deep breath and so did his car, as it was an old Fiat with a hoarse voice and a smoky exhaust pipe in perfect harmony with its owner. It was furnished with sticky cloth seats impregnated with tobacco smoke and discoloured by the sun. There was a little statue of St Christopher hanging from the rear-view mirror as if it had been executed long time ago and forgotten there without a decent burial. The ashtray was full of stumps and there was a portable one on the floor also endowed with similar garments. On the dashboard, there was a pack of cigarettes and a lighter: 'I decided to quit smoking!' Dr Riga said. 'Of course, I made this decision several times before in my life, but this time it is for good. Please take this pack with you and hold it as a keepsake.'

Distractedly, I replied, 'Are we picking up Don Pino? He wanted to come with us.'

'Ma siamo pazzi?'[73] replied Dr Riga 'If we show up with Don Pino, l'Avvocato will have an heart attack and all the chances he has to survive

---

72 'I am not a communist!'
73 'Are we out of our minds?'

the pneumonia will vaporise.' He continued, 'Who wants to see a priest at their bedside when someone is sick? As a doctor, I never visit a patient accompanied by a gentleman dressed in black. It is bad business. Either the patient dies as soon as he sees the omen or if he survives he will hate you for the rest of his life for the stupid prank.' I agreed.

Dr Riga's thought held an impeccable logic, and I experienced embarrassment for my tactlessness. But I had no time to verbalise my regrets because Dr Riga, who was quite chatty on that beautiful September afternoon, started a new conversation.

'Do you know? I really admire you! You personify what I wished to be when I was young. You know, I had dreams as a young doctor. I really wanted to make a difference: not just being a country doctor exchanging chickens for an aspirin. But now, I am just vegetating as most of us do. I was a different person then . . . I have never been a believer in God or any of that nonsense, but I always wanted to find something a little bigger than life as it is. Once I went on pilgrimage because I was curious and hopeful. I went by foot across our Italia hoping to acquire the inspiration I did not have.

'It was a trip I took with some friends. Down the hills from Camaldoli, through gentle streams, up other hills and beyond, we reached the foot of a rock on top of which like an eagle stood the convent of La Verna.[74] We were a peculiar assembly. Tonino's life was based on dogmas. He abhorred doubt and did not wish to question the basis of anything although he loved to built arguments and discussion around it. A good foundation was of the outmost value to him whether it was right or wrong. He could have been a lawyer. He loved to argue in favour or against anything as long as he had a starting point. Turning from atheism to Christianity was just a matter of fact decision for him. He believed in God just as much as he had believed that God did not exist just a week before. When I asked why he changed his mind, he did not know. He shrugged his shoulders and told me that it did not matter. Until then he had been wrong and

---

[74] La Verna—a Franciscan monastery in Tuscany where St Francis received the stigmata in 1224.

now he had seen the light and he would stick with it till the next gale would impel him somewhere else.

'Tonino had organised this pilgrimage across Umbria and Tuscany to reaffirm his new faith—a walking tour in which we were going to visit monks, those folks who take faith seriously, those people for whom God is not a weekend distraction, but a daily occupation: the pros of Christianity. In particular in La Verna, we wanted to visit the Franciscans, up there where St Francis had spent time to be the closest to God thanks to a gift by il Conte Orlando di Chiusi.

'Behind Tonino was silently following the lanky and slim Lo Spillo.[75] Nobody knew what he thought about this extravagance or as a matter of fact about anything else. This was because he did not like to converse much. He preferably nodded. He loved all of us: each one representing an idol to him. So he never argued about anything. He was just happy to follow. If an argument lit up among us, he would straightaway try to calm the spirits by finding common grounds that did not really exist. Slightly bent forward under the weight of the backpack, there was nothing else particular about him that could improve his description. Yet we all felt there was something funny about him, which deserved a nickname. So we simply called him Lo Spillo. He ended up working in a shoe store and I heard that he became more assertive than he used to be, assertiveness that he used skilfully to argue the qualities of his shoes during sell-out days, and perhaps he is the most successful among all of us.

'After him was Angelo. Like the name suggests, he was the mystical among us. It would not be an overstatement to disclose that he truly had faith or even better that faith owned him. For him religion, prayers, meditations were only pretexts to rejoin with his inner soul which in his case was the only thing that mattered. For him, believing in God was not a choice. It was a natural phenomenon. It would have been like saying that you have to believe that the heart beats for the heart to beat. In other words, he was just the opposite of me.

---

[75] 'The pin'.

'I was closing on the small procession of pilgrims. I was appended to the group as a vestige of Tonino's previous days of atheism before his conversion. Contrary to him, I firmly believed in doubt and there were no foundations that I did not feel compelled to question. I never comprehended (and I will never know) whether God exists or not. I am an agnostic, and I will always be. It is not my choice as faith was not a choice for Angelo. Tonino had asked me to join and so I went. Agnostics do not discard experience. In fact, I always wanted to "meet God", and this sounded like the ultimate opportunity. After all, we were only seventeen.

'The sun was shining and the birds were singing. The stream whispered under the chatty trees. Yet none of that disturbed the silence of the place. Indeed, those mischievous sounds were underlining the magnitude of the silence that was growing on us and like a magnifying glass was making La Verna bigger to our eyes and our souls. Nobody talked, and then, suddenly, an hour away from sunset I felt happy in a way I had never felt before. "Perhaps," I thought, "Angelo is right. God is there looking after us, no matter whether I believe it or not."

'The monks at the monastery were cheerful and hospitable. They fed us with soup, biscuits, and wine. From the terrace in the cool breeze of the evening, dominating the valley, I was remotely listening to Tonino's words. "This is the real life. This is where we should all live—close to the creation of God without distractions. As il Conte Orlando said to San Francis, '*I own a mountain that is much remote and wild and that it is too suitable for those who want to be contrite; it is far away from people and it is good for those who want to live a solitary life. If you would like, I would happily give it to you and your brothers for the wellness of my soul.*' The brothers made the right decision. It takes strength to give up the vulgar rewards of life, to live in poverty, to wear sandals all year round in the snow and in the mud. To sleep on wooden beds without mattresses . . ."

'For some reason, the spirituality of the moment was broken by those words, by the concept of the brothers sleeping without mattresses. It seemed to me too much of an affectation. And I thought, "You can be close to God and yet sleep like a decent human being!" And suddenly, I could not appreciate what strength could be involved in living up there—away from the heat of the valley, the traffic, the careless eyes of people staring at you in the metro, the stink of crowded places. It felt more like an indulgence. Which one was the real life? Away from the daily challenges of a regular existence, which included exams, professors, and parents, or here, taking care of vegetables and praying when tired of attending the garden? Reading and dreaming in the conducive silence of La Verna? What good did all of this do and to whom? I felt that more than strength this choice was a sign of weakness.

'As the evening came, we were given the choice to sleep on regular beds or on boards. We all chose boards. Perhaps each one for a different reason: Tonino out of principle, Angelo because he could not care less about his body, Spillo out of empathy, and myself out of curiosity. But this was the farthest I reached towards a spiritual life. The following night, I made sure to have a real bed to sleep on and I never worried about those monks again.

'I became a communist because it was a more practical choice, perhaps less lofty but more likely to do any good. I continued to believe in doing the right thing, in equality, in decency but not because a transcendental force did order me to. I believed in it just because it made sense. Why do we follow the traffic rules (when we do)? It is not because of their ethical significance, but simply because they make sense and they help us coexist. Nobody claims that God invented red lights and yet we all observe them because they simply make sense,' he concluded, and this was a remarkable statement particularly when offered by an Italian!

But the story was not over: 'My parents wanted their son to be a doctor, and in the end this is why I become one. I went to the University of Rome, and after I graduated I wished to expand my knowledge to help people who needed it the most. I went far with another two young doctors. I ended up in Mongolia. It was under the Soviet Union then and they needed doctors. The communist party had organised a group of volunteers . . . It took days to get there through different countries on the old trains . . . There was still third class then. Sometimes the train would stop for a day in a remote station and I remembered Chekov's stories. But we did not have to bribe anyone to continue when the time came. It was summer and a pleasant one. We would sleep in the steppes till the train was back on track . . . so to speak.

'Finally, as we arrived to our destination, I wandered away from the base camp towards the mountains and across the highlands. I remember that soon the scenery became superb yet desolate. The silence encumbered majestically and it was overbearing. In fact, it was not even silence but emptiness. Distant sounds emerged: The yelp of an animal, the screech of a highflying bird, the mumbling of a creek, and the sneezing of the wind were the measure of such emptiness. It felt like I had reached the boundary of humanity, one step from that infinite spirit I had been longing for. And there was a sense of instability in my footsteps, indecision about whether to proceed or return, a sense of frustrated expectations towards a spirit who does not want to communicate, the bitterness about a distance that cannot be overcome across space and time, the indifference of the mountains towards a human being irrelevant to the majesty of their existence.

'That was just the beginning of a very spiritual time, though brief. The nomads had heard of the doctors and they had come from distances and set their gear around the portables where we were supposed to practice the art of medicine. They would wait for days till it was their turn to be examined. There was no hurry. It did not matter where the cattle grazed, and it was all the same to them.

'I remember the eyes of the suffering. I cannot forget the old couple that came for a visit. She was jaundiced and had advanced cancer of the liver . . . They have a lot of hepatitis there! It was obviously untreatable particularly with the resources that they had. I simply told them through the translator that there was nothing to do and she should prepare to die. They accepted the verdict in peace and dignity and they thanked me for telling them what they already knew. When I walked afterwards out of the portable, I saw both of them sitting on a massive stone. He was rubbing her back. She was looking up at her mountains. When I came back, the stone was bare. I never saw them again.

'I continued to work hard. They, those nomad people, did not seem to know about weekends in that timeless place. Distances were described by days needed to get somewhere and time by how far one could go in a given period.

'Soon it became a useless routine. I could see people even make a diagnosis but could not do anything about it because there was no money, no hospitals, no nurses, and no infrastructure. Eventually, our time was over, we went back to Ulan Bator and I never saw again that desolate place. I called it a "parenthesis" in my life and I moved on.

'Yet I still believe that one has the responsibility to use life as positively as possible. There is an old Jewish expression that says: I hope that I will leave this world a little better than the way I found it . . . I am not a Jew, but I made this motto part of my life. Even if nothing great is going to result from this stance, it will give me comfort one day to think that I did something, no matter how little, to make the world a better place. A Chinese parable talks about an old man planting trees that take decades to grow. When a young boy asked him why would he do that since he will not live long enough to enjoy their shade, he replied: "See those beautiful trees giving shade and shelter during the hot summer days? Somebody planted them for us a long time ago."'

Dr Riga continued, 'When I came back, I took over my father's practice working as a family doctor. But I did not forget all the charitable ideas. I have been trying to keep up with progress in medicine even though it is not easy here. I attended meetings to update myself and I bought books about cardiology. I like the heart problems most, and they are so common here. I tried to take care of people as well as I can even though they are not always grateful. Once a patient told me after I explained to her that she had a very bad case and there was little I could do to alleviate her symptoms (she had cancer, but we did not use that word then), she said, "You know, my dear Dottore, I was just fine till I came to see you. Are you sure that you are not making me sick?"'

And again he continued, 'You know, as you get older you become increasingly cynical. I do not even allow professional courtesy any more. I used to. But there was a family, both physicians with three small children. I did not like them because they would bring their kids to be seen only when they were extremely sick rather than earlier on. I disrespected them because I felt they were negligent. Finally, when the mother once protested the professional courtesy and insisted on paying, I charged her. In the end, if she did not care about her children, why should I care about their finances? The day after, I received a note from her husband thanking me for charging them. They had been reticent to take advantage of my services because it was free, and so they tried to postpone visits till utterly unavoidable. From that day on, their kids had the best care! So, as you can see, good intentions do not necessarily yield the expected results.'

And so on and so forth, Dr Riga continued this casual and disconnected conversation, venting upon me years of loneliness by sharing with a colleague the secrets of an isolated professional life.

As I listened while the car gasped its way up the mountain with the spectacular view of the Gulf of Santa Eufemia on my right, I concluded that Dr Riga was not a bad person after all. And looking out of the open window, with the fresh breeze entering the car, I watched the beloved Pizzo that sitting on its rock above the Tyrrhenian Sea appeared indeed smiling under the fresh September sun.

When we entered the patient's room, l'Avvocato, who was wearing a clean nightgown from under which two hairy and skinny legs connected him to a shuffling pair of slippers, pushing a pole from where the intravenous fluid was hanging, rushed towards us. 'Dottori miei! Thanks for coming! You have to do something right away. They are killing me here! You got to save me! No smoke, no alcohol, I am afraid I am going to die here if you do not help me . . . Or perhaps even worse, I am afraid that I will not die and will be stuck with this puritan nonsense!'

From his words and from the vigour with which he was wrangling for his sustenance, it was obvious that the antibiotics were already having a dramatic effect and he was doing significantly better.

Dr Riga looked at the chart hanging at the bottom of the bed with the vital signs scribbled on it and showed to me a dramatic drop of the line in the temperature chart pointing towards normality. Without looking up, he said to l'Avvocato, 'I am sorry to tell you this but you are done smoking whether you like it or not . . . unless you prefer to die. To help you out, I will quit myself. Giuseppe is holding my last pack of cigarettes as testimony! We will quit together, "mal comune mezzo gaudio"[76] as they say. But if you solemnly promise now on the grave of your ancestors that you will quit, I will take you down to the bar for a coffee and a Sambuca.'

---

[76]   Sharing a pain turns it into partial happiness.

Considering that he had no choice at least till he was in the hospital and that one of two perquisites was better than nothing, l'Avvocato mumbled, 'Andiamo.'[77]

As we were helping him put on his trousers and reclaim his shoes from under the bed, il Primario[78] entered the room, having heard from the nurses about our arrival. He was an elderly gentlemanly figure with cultivated grey hair, wearing a long white coat and an open shirt with a gold necklace shining on the tanned skin. It was of a fine texture and it held a simple cross pretty much like the ones given to children on the occasion of their first communion. Likely it had been sitting on his chest forever, since the time when his mother put it on him decades before. He showed no affectations or mannerisms but with natural warmth came towards me, smiling. Il Primario shook my hand vigorously. 'Please come to my office. I can show you the X-rays. It is a real pleasure to meet you. I heard so much about you. It is a real honour!'

Therefore, while Dr Riga who was completely uninterested in the diagnostic evidence kept fixing the appearance of his friend, I followed il Primario in his office, where he pulled a film out of a brown envelope and hung it on a viewer. It clearly showed that the diagnosis of pneumonia was correct, since it showed a fluffy infiltrate in the upper lobe of the right lung. 'This is the X-ray from this morning. It is just the same as yesterday and not worsening. Since the antibiotics were started last night, our dear patient already defervesced,' he said with pride. 'In a few days, he will be back running around like a school boy.'

Being il dottore dall'America, I felt compelled to add value with my presence, and I started a dissertation about potential differential diagnoses and how cancer must be ruled out in a smoker and how a bronchoscopy with 'lavage', a tomography, and a bunch of other technological wonders could help rule out anything that my fervid imagination could think of.

Il Primario listened with admiration to my dissertation, while Dr Riga, who had come to inform me that the patient was ready to receive the

---

[77]   Let's go.
[78]   Department chair.

promised panacea at the bar, stood close at my side, proud of being an acquaintance of mine. Finally, as I completed the presentation, il Primario with the most reverent and gentlest demeanour humbly stated, 'Yes, of course, we could do all of these tests, but to be honest, the patient has just a classic case of Klebsiella pneumonia and maybe we should just follow his course since he is doing better and wait for the additional tests unless he suddenly worsens.'

Surprised, I asked him how he knew with such certainty the cause of the pneumonia. 'Are the bacterial cultures back already?'

To which he simply replied, 'No, but I have seen enough of these cases in my years. They are not very common, but they are very typical in their presentation, with the pink sputum, the X-ray appearance. We will have the result of the cultures tomorrow.'

Sure enough, a few days later the results confirmed the diagnosis and l'Avvocato was back in the Chiazza with his friends expectorating with renewed strength after being saved from the grave by an X-ray, a few doses of antibiotics, and an experienced doctor. He even stopped smoking in front of us at the table or at least most of the times, particularly when Dr Riga was around. When I reported to the others the remarkable simplicity with which l'Avvocato had been treated, Dr Riga pointed out that the solution to the escalated spending for health care was simple: train better doctors. As I was regretfully sipping the last drop of my negroni, I wondered how come nobody had ever thought of it before. Another feather for the hats of the wise men of Pizzo!

But I am getting ahead of myself, since that same evening after returning from the hospital we were sitting at the tavolino reporting on the conditions of l'Avvocato to his friends when il Marchese politely expressed the desire to listen to the continuation of Alessandro's story. Therefore, il Professore resumed . . .

*   *   *

After leaving Pizzo to attend law school in Milan, Alessandro only rarely came back to the hometown and, when he did, it was primarily to visit with his Nonna. The truth was that he had always been Nonna's favourite and he reserved a tender feeling for the invincible lady who was feared by everybody else. So he was caught by surprise years later when his father called him, while he was partying in Milan: "My mother is dying and I am going down to Calabria to see her. Do you want to come with me?" He was used to his father's dramatic tones and accustomed to react with composure after several previous false alarms, but he knew that this time it was going to be for good. She had been sick and mostly bedridden for a while with advanced cancer, and Dr Riga had given up on treatments. In fact, he was the one who had sent the call to Milan. Yet Alessandro could not believe that Nonna was truly going to die. By then, he had just finished law school and he was not young any more. He had experienced the death of friends because of accidents, overdose, or suicide. He had lived a quite stupendous life more than most had ever had a chance of experiencing. Yet Nonna's death appeared like a milestone for which he was not prepared.

He spent a long night driving to Calabria with his father. When they arrived, his father told him that he would not enter Nonna's room. 'When you are sick and old, if everybody in the family starts coming to see you, you realise that you are dying.' Alessandro had always loved his dad, although his logic had puzzled him in several occasions. Instead, he readily went to Nonna's bedside. She looked weak, but her mind was quite sharp.

She seemed happy to see him, and although her breath was heavy, she managed to whisper a few words of admiration, 'You have always been the handsomest boy in this little town and you are getting even more so each time I see you. You are almost as handsome as your uncle who died in the war.' She maintained a grieving love for her first son.

Sara took advantage of him being there and left for a little rest while he sat at the edge of the bed close to his Nonna. At intervals, his dad put his head around the door without being seen; he had the embarrassed look of a man with tears in his eyes. When Nonna believed she was alone with her beloved grandson, she grasped his hand and said, 'Alessandro, I do not want to die!' As if she was falling off a cliff, she grabbed his arm so as to build a bridge between the days that had gone and the days to come—a bridge she knew she could not cross any more.

What an amazing sight! For the first time, he saw Nonna overwhelmed with fear! This woman that had looked down at war, tragedy, and humiliation with the dignity of a princess had now lost her composure to a most natural milestone of life. He was disturbed by her fear. He had witnessed death all around him throughout youth, but he had always managed to rationalise it—to keep it at a distance as if it was the avoidable consequence of unwise behaviour, of a preventable mistake that could be circumvented by the prepared mind, something that did not pertain to him or to anybody with a strong and thoughtful disposition. But Nonna's trepidation, who had been a fearless master of her and others' lives, was undermining now the grounds of the last of his certainties.

'So don't die! You look just fine to me!' He smiled reassuringly, and she responded with a smile. They understood each other, and there was nothing more to say.

That night, Don Pino came and sat at Nonna's bedside; his eyes were moist and his speech was interrupted. But he discussed the beauty of life and the benevolence of the Omnipotent, how death is a beginning and not an end, the joy that expects the virtuous souls of those who had done so much good on this Earth. He recounted all the great things that Donna Giovanna had done, and everybody standing around the bed had a good time remembering and contributing their own anecdotes and long forgotten stories.

There was no formal confession because there was no real need for it. Nonna did not believe she had ever done anything wrong or at least anything that she could not argue herself without unnecessary mediation with the Omnipotent when she would cross the gates of heaven. A Pater Noster was recited by all, including Nonna, who looked around with composed suspicion. Often she would turn her eyes towards Alessandro for reassurance, and he smiled at her and made a gesture to urge her to be patient as if the two of them were conspiring to mock the audience and playing out a prank to entertain them, as if all was just a farce, a jest to keep the relatives and friends amused.

Eventually, after Don Pino had finished his part by drawing a cross over her forehead with the holy oil, she cheered up, relieved from such forced austerity and composure, and turning to him, she said, 'I think now is the time to drink the famous bottle of champagne about which we talked a long time ago!' And a chilled bottle was indeed brought, and each one had a sip of the cold beverage.

That night, Alessandro lay in a small bed adjacent to Nonna's room, where he had slept since he was a child. In the night, while he was comparing the tedious silence with the voices of the past, the door opened and Nonna's head peeked into the room just as she had done every single night since he could remember. She was just checking to make sure that he was in bed safe. 'How are you?'

'Fine.'

'Bonu, bonu' were the last words Alessandro heard from her. In the morning, when he woke up Nonna had died.

They had set up a funeral parlour in the den. It looked imposing. A large shiny coffin was sitting in the middle of the great room with pictures of several ancestors guarding it competently, since they had already gone through this ultimate experience.

He was surprised by the ease with which the old heavy desk had been removed together with the rest of the furniture in the noiseless hours of the early morning. The den was twofold empty, first because of the removed furniture and second because of Nonna's departure from her lifeless body that was passively accepting a death she had not agreed to.

Nonna lay in the coffin with a sarcastic smile; in fact, it was a silent laugh that echoed in the room as a reminder of the futility of life and a memento that time was created to materialise the predictable, unalterable fate of life retreating into death. Everything was still, including Sara, who sat on a little chair at the end of the coffin as a loyal dog protecting its master. Tears silently flowed from each eye. With a handkerchief, she would occasionally wipe them off. Then when the handkerchief was soaked, she would stand, and after crossing herself in front of her master, she would wobble out of the room to return a minute later to sit on the same chair, holding a new and dry one.

Relatives, friends, acquaintances came and left. Most had something to say that was received by a complacent smile by the close family, whoever happened to be there at the moment. Alessandro spent an incalculable amount of time there; he had been searching for the most appropriate feeling to display in front of others. He could not decide; he could not sort out what he was experiencing save for an inexplicable anger that came with a sensation of impotence and an overwhelming disgust towards life and what it may or may not represent. He recollected many moments of his youth shared with Nonna, and as his eyes began to feel uncomfortably moist, he deflected his gaze across the window to grab a little of that deep blue sky that was hovering above with its indifferent clouds searching for an explanation or a simple sign, just anything from Up There.

Alessandro returned ever less frequently back to the hometown after Nonna's death, as returning was not necessarily nurturing to him. Mostly, he came back for brief summer breaks, and in those occasions, he tried to reconnect with old friends who happened to also be there, returning to their roots during the summer whenever they could. Once he rejoined Peppino and accepted to go out at sea with him and his young daughter on Peppino's small family boat.

As they were leaving the shore on a hot summer morning, the noise of the outboard engine dominated. Yet the words that Alessandro heard were well defined: Peppino was informing him about his life as he was turning the boat towards the open sea. 'Obviously, in this situation I cannot make long-term plans.'

As it had been the case years before, Alessandro had no clue either about the origin of the sentence or where it was leading. It had been a fundamental characteristic of Peppino to think aloud when he wanted to be asked. Although Alessandro did care very much about Peppino's state of affairs, at that moment his thoughts had been frozen as he was distracted by the examination of the old friend. He appreciated the persistence of Peppino's habits that had endured for a decade. Peppino had not changed a bit since he had last seen him years before. Obviously, he had changed physically; he had gained a little weight and the white had begun to settle on the side of his head. They had just passed the thirty years of age milestone. But not much else had changed—not his unfussy behaviour, his words anticipating his thoughts, his myopic gaze towards the distance when talking to someone. He talked as if he was not thinking of his own, but he was rather reporting notes from a distant world or a distant time—as the captain of a deserted ship searching the horizon for land, which he knew was never to come with the scrutiny of an expert whose skills will never become useful but nevertheless were magnificent to demonstrate.

Lost in those thoughts, Alessandro did not follow Peppino's statement and neglected to ask what he had meant. But just like years before, Peppino continued his train of thoughts, dropping the net deeper in the clear waters of the morning thoughts. 'In September, I have to decide about the separation from my wife.'

'Why are you thinking of separating?' Suddenly Alessandro emerged from his stupor, realising that this was no casual conversation and that Peppino had brought him in the middle of the Gulf of S. Eufemia that morning not to run from the heat of the smouldering beach but from a deeper fire that could only be quenched by the roaring sound of the outboard engine, driving him away from his pain.

'While I was in Rome, I worked for seven years every day, on weekends, never home. I almost never saw either her or my daughter. Because of my work I had to be available all the time . . . had to be prepared to travel all over. Yes, sir! This is the life of an officer of the Carabinieri. You go where the investigation takes you, where they send you. I was sent to America: North and South or to the Middle East, then to Tunisia, to Libya, and then Tripoli months after months, and now I have been just redirected to Messina to head the anti-Mafia taskforce. She does not want to move there and she wants to stay in Rome with Carla. She does not like little towns.'

'Could you ask to be transferred back to Rome?' There was no answer, and Alessandro knew that the conversation was over. What needed to be said had been said, and like a brief eruption of the Stromboli, the fire and the lava subsided and only a cloud of smoke was left to drift away from Alessandro's thoughts. It would have been sensible to ask about the deeper reason for the separation, but Alessandro knew that the question would have further embarrassed his old friend in front of the little Carla and that in any case that question had no answer in Peppino's mind. Ironically, this man accustomed to detective work could not and perhaps did not want to understand the intricacies of his own life. He recognised that Peppino's pain for the separation was deep because he still loved his wife and daughter. It was also bitter because it had been served to him unexpectedly, and he could not react because his own thoughts had been paralysed.

The roaring of the engine dwindled and then stopped. The boat stalled in the middle of the Gulf where the Tyrrhenian Sea is dark blue and deep. 'Here the water is clean. Let's swim.' Peppino jumped first, then went in his daughter and then Alessandro. They swam around the boat with the cold currents cooling their bodies. Carla kept close to her dad because she was afraid of the depth and of the mysterious darkness below. Peppino kept her close while the sun with a benevolent smile caressed her blonde hair floating over the dark blue of the sea. And for a moment, the horizon was forgotten and its emptiness surpassed by the crests of the waves mischievously tapping the sides of the boat. Carla was seven and full of joy as she laughed at her own fears and swam between Peppino and Alessandro in a day that she would never forget.

Alessandro never saw Peppino again; he might have gone out on the boat to scrutinise the horizons a few more times before his daughter had to go back to Rome. After that, he did not go back to Messina or to Rome or anywhere else, but he shot himself in the old family house in front of the disapproving portraits of his own relatives and a little statue of Jesus, holding his heart with his right hand. Nobody knew why he did it, and Alessandro was by then too far to participate in the grief. He just heard of it third-hand, from a friend of a friend, several months later, so distant he was from the life of the little town that was becoming ever more removed from his own soul. Meanwhile, Peppino's secret was buried with him while the people coming back from the cemetery discussed the horrors of clinical depression . . .

'Yes, things have changed. Nowadays, they bury the perpetrators of suicide in the cemetery just as any other creature of God. And I think they should,' said Mastro Antonio. 'It is not their fault if they cannot bear the pains of life.'

Don Pino said nothing, but he nodded his approval; in the end, it was one of his achievements in a life spent as a compassionate shepherd.

VII

A Trip to Monte Carlo

A narrative about Pizzo would be incomplete without mentioning Joaquin Murat and the castle named after him. Most will remember Murat as a flamboyant monument to narcissism in Tolstoy's novel *War and Peace*, as he rode his horse before the battle of Leipzig, contemplating the enemy's line ready to cross his own version of the Rubicon in support of Napoleon's dream. Unfortunately, the French Army was conclusively defeated. Thus, contrary to his more successful Roman colleague, the die that he had cast did not settle auspiciously on the gaming table of life as it had the one that brought glory to the Caesar. After a few more battles, the life of Joaquin Murat, the brother-in-law of Napoleon Bonaparte, the Marshal of France, the First Horseman of Europe, the Duke of Berg and Cleves, and the King of Naples and Sicily, would have gradually whimpered into complete oblivion if he had not decided to finish it according to his own style, which in turn resulted in preserving for Pizzo a place in history.

After being defeated in the battle of Tolentino, while attempting to protect from the Austrians his interpretation of the Kingdom of Naples and Sicily, Murat fled to Corsica where he was joined by a handful of loyalists. There, he plotted against the reinstituted previous monarchs by stirring an insurrection from the region of Calabria. Therefore, upon landing at the port of Pizzo on Sunday, 8 October 1815, Murat attempted to rally support in the town square, the same glorious Chiazza that has been the centrepiece of our story. But the crowd was indifferent at best or hostile at worse. Soon the forces from the reinstituted King of

Naples, Ferdinand IV, arrested him, and he ended up being impeached for treason and ultimately sentenced to death by a firing squad.

It is taken for granted by most of the locals that his body was buried in the Church of San Giorgio just in front of my home. Indeed, on the floor of the centre aisle, just a few steps past the entrance, one can see a tombstone with his name on it. For years, the Napitini have tried to confirm that the bones buried in the church belong to the historic figure, and they have been negotiating with authorities in Italy and in France, laic and religious, to create a monument in his honour and just as well another one to honour his beloved wife, Caroline Bonaparte, who on the other hand had nothing to do with the whole ordeal save for being his consort.

Thus, admirable efforts have been made by our beloved little town to gain the deserved role in history by being obsequious to the one whom they had earlier betrayed. But isn't it the way life goes? Think about how insignificant that whole affair would have been if Murat had passed undisturbed and unharmed through Pizzo. And whom would the castle be named after? As history cannot be constructed with 'ifs', we will put to rest this daunting question by simply maintaining our gratitude for the French hero who gave his life for the celebration of Pizzo.

It is also said that when the Napitini were offered a reward for arresting Murat, they unanimously chose Pizzo to be promoted to the rank of city. And this is why this little town is still called La Cittá di Pizzo.[79]

Il Castello[80] was paradoxically called after the name of its victim because it is the place where Joaquin Murat was jailed and eventually executed after five days of imprisonment. History tells that Murat walked with a firm step to the place of execution. With his eyes uncovered, he proclaimed, 'I have faced death one too many times to fear it.' And when all was ready, he ordered to the firing squadron, '*Soldats! Faites votre devoir! Droit au cœur mais épargnez le visage . . . Feu!*'[81]

---

[79] The city of Pizzo.

[80] The castle.

[81] 'Soldiers! Follow your duty! Aim at the heart but spare the face . . . Fire!'

The castle was erected in the fifteenth century, by the order of Ferdinand the first of Aragona, as a fort rather than a true castle on top of the rock facing the Gulf of Santa Eufemia, and it consists of two large towers linked by very thick walls built to protect the town of Pizzo from attacks coming by sea. On one side, it stands on a precipice that extends all the way to what is now called the Marina and used to be the port of Pizzo. Towards the inland, it is separated from the rest of the town by a moat, and it is connected to it by a drawbridge. Mysterious tunnels were built during the centuries to link the fort to different areas of the town or the coastline below, of which very little is currently known, rendering them even more mysterious and fabulous.

Besides various disputes of ownership among generations of feudal families, it appears that the castle was never used for the intended purpose, except for standing as a scarecrow at the top of the steep cliff to deter Saracen pirates. It can be assumed that this was done successfully since there is no account in history of any pirate attack against Pizzo. However, it failed to scare crows, robins, bats, or other flying creatures that have contentedly colonised the cracks in the walls for the last few centuries.

In 1835, Alexander Dumas visited the castle and called it, 'a Homeric station of the Napoleonic Iliad'. On 3 June 1892, the castle earned its own position in history as the Italian Government turned it into a national monument.

In modern days, il Castello Murat is a venue for intellectual activities while serving the primary purpose as a tourist attraction. The cell where Joaquin Murat was hosted and the site where he was executed are there as mementos. The guide will proudly show to the distracted tourist the holes in the wall, which are supposed to represent the first round of firing when the former king of Naples and Sicily was originally spared by the ambivalent squad. The castle is home nowadays to several cultural activities, to a museum recounting the last days of its illustrious victim, to a youth hostel in the lower floors, and to peaceful recess for bridge tournaments in the upper floors. Most importantly, it is the refuge for bats during the day and crows or robins during the night. For the locals, it is a place to observe the sunset while looking towards the sea from the terraces on top of the towers. It is also the place from where the town can be observed dispassionately as the passers-by go back and forth along the Chiazza towards lo Spuntone about which we communicated a few chapters ago.

Il Castello boasts its own bar where several specialties are prepared, which are probably more ancient than its own history, among which is the famous latte di mandorla. It was there that I met il Marchese the morning following the visit to meet poor Avvocato at the hospital of Vibo. We had tacitly adopted the habit of meeting there to enjoy a latte di mandorla and then walk together to the Chiazza to visit with the rest of the old men.

In response to my greetings, he displayed the composed and insincere smile of a person who has not experienced happiness for a long, long time. I was used to his melancholy, and customarily, I would not have paid much attention to it, but recently it appeared to me that his dejection had grown deeper and thicker as if a wall of emotions was separating him from the rest of us. Even the jaunty tapping of my shoulder with the cane was gone, while sighs and distracted looks towards the horizon had taken prominence.

We sat on a little stone bench on one of the terraces of the castle, and we sipped silently the latte di mandorla that was brought as soon as I appeared.

The previous night, I had spent sleepless hours thinking of Alessandro and wondering whether I should contribute a recollection of my own, related to his time away from Pizzo. On the one hand, I felt an urge to share the events, but on the other, I refrained from reporting because of the awkwardness of some facts that included not particularly elated aspects of my own conduct during those years.

Upon waking up, I had decided that it was not worth bringing the story up, particularly in the presence of my father. I had made peace with myself until, sitting in front of il Marchese, an impulse brought me to say, 'I did see Alessandro once, after we had both left Pizzo. It was during the summer before the last year of medical school. I was studying for an exam and I decided to go to Milano for a brief period of time to visit with some friends who were also in medical school. At that time, Alessandro had just finished law school and I heard about him from common friends although nobody knew what he was currently up to . . .'

'Wait,' interrupted il Marchese. 'I really want you to tell me all about this, but I think you should wait till we are with our friends. It would not be fair to skip this part. I think by now all of them, perhaps with the exclusion of your uncle, are engrossed by this story. Is there any reason for not sharing it?'

Lying, I replied, 'No reason at all. I will be happy to.' And one more time, walking down the ancient steps, cane in one hand, handkerchief in the other, il Marchese led the way and I followed, avoiding helping him as he very much preferred to be treated as the youthful and handsome man that he used to be.

Life was flowing as usual at the tavolino. The good old men were already basking under the sunrays that were piercing through the autumn breeze. Among them, and to my disgrace, were of course my father and my uncle who were about to hear some aspects of my youth that up to then I had kept discreetly concealed. But the keenness to share this salient element of Alessandro's story was too intense to refrain from divulging it. At the same time, I was enticed by the desire of keeping Alessandro alive a little longer in our recollections by building another chapter of his life.

It was il Marchese who upon sitting in the aluminium chair, positioned for him by Angelo's son, announced my wish to contribute. Everybody was there except l'Avvocato, who was still restlessly pacing the ward in Vibo, carrying along the pole with the intravenous remedy while complaining about the lack of the true necessities of life.

Curiously, I was not concerned at all about the presence of Don Pino, who was also going to hear about my juvenile misconduct, since as we have previously revealed, he was the least likely to be taken aback by the creativity of sinners.

Therefore, I started by saying.

*   *   *

In the summer of . . . I was in Milano visiting with friends who were also in medical school. We were studying together in preparation for the last year of medical school. I lodged at a friend's apartment, striving to quench the heat of the hot summer days of the Padana plains with cold tea, a fan, and regular trips to the washroom where I submerged my head under the running water. My routine was simple. I had no plans except for studying during the day and going out with friends at night in the downtown district which was almost completely deserted in the middle of summer, allotting a pleasant feeling of undisputed ownership of streets and venues. It was nurturing for me to spend time with old friends, and I intended to remain there for at least a fortnight before returning to my usual routine.

One Friday afternoon, my host was away for the weekend and the apartment belonged entirely to me. Lightening started to enliven the atmosphere. Thunders and a twirling wind followed, which turned the suffocating burden of summer into chirpy mountain air. I went out in the balcony to savour the first big drops of rain, the electric smell of the soaking dust, and to enjoy the spectacular fireworks, compliments of the powerful summer storm, when the phone rang. I had been instructed to answer phone calls, alerted by the possibility that my host himself may try to reach me.

In synchrony with a prolonged thunder, I heard, 'Giuseppe, is it you? It's me . . . Alessandro . . . Do you remember me? I heard you are staying there. How are you doing? It has been a long time since we heard from each other.'

It had been indeed several years. We had floated adrift from each other without good reason. We were living in different places, taking different career paths, distracted by different romantic adventures, mostly lost in the world of youth that is wasteful, disorganised, and without deadlines.

I was of course quite thrilled to hear his voice. For a while, we talked about irrelevant things from the common past. We illustrated with some affected condescendence the paths that each had taken, minimising our successes and emphasising shortcomings as good old friends do to revive the jovial cynicism of youth. Soon, however, we reached the status of current affairs, and there we paused, searching for the next topic to approach.

It was Alessandro who came up with a suggestion: 'Listen, I am spending time in Monte Carlo. It is great here, a lot of fun during the day and even better at night. You should come. I promise I will take good care of you. I swear we can have a fun week or two . . . just like the old times, and then you can go back to your studies. Come on, we live only once, don't we?'

It should be clarified that I have never been a person of strict principles, being quite open to almost anything that could stimulate my curiosity and lust for adventure. Because of that, it was suitable to firmly hold on to few principles to compensate for the lack of determination on all other matters. Therefore, my studies, my career, and my future had merged into a compensatory mechanism to justify other depravations by providing a consolidated purpose to an otherwise purposeless existence. In other words, as long as I abided to a fistful of goals dictated by conventional wisdom during the day, I felt absolved from all other sins of indolence and prodigality in which I dwelled in the afterhours.

As a consequence, I acted like Pinocchio who was incited by Lucignolo to travel to the Land of Toys, and with just the same firmness, I resisted his early insistences to yield to the subsequent ones. In earnest, it was also true that I could not decline the offer from my beloved friend, whom I had not seen for so long. And the desire to see my good old friend's smile, to share with him a few more hours of childhood thoughtlessness was too appealing. Thus, I packed a few items and went to the train station to arrive the following day at Monte Carlo.

Alessandro was waiting at the train station. He drove a flamboyant red Ferrari convertible. He was perfectly tanned and wore a white tennis shirt, and with dark Ray-Ban sunglasses, he looked just the same as he did the day I drove him to the train station in Pizzo when I had last seen him.

As soon as he saw me, he smiled and gestured for me to jump in the car while the passers-by looked on. He did not own the Ferrari, which belonged to a reach American lady with whom he had made 'friends'.

We drove along the coast. We stopped at bars and walked along the beach and we recalled the old good times. He told me that he had managed to finish law school to please his dad, but he was never going to practice law. He also said that he was not going to take the licensing exam and was instead going to spend the rest of his life as a gigolo along the Italian or French Riviera and find occasional jobs if necessary. He referred to this with the outmost naturalness, and I had no reason to believe that he was not serious. Yet I took it lightly and joked about it. I teased him for his cynical demeanour that had not changed in all those years and suggested that he just needed a little more time to mature and 'get on with the programme'. He smiled condescendingly and did not argue further. However, since evidently I was unduly prolonging my sermon, he touched my shoulder with the Ray-Bans that he was holding by one band, and pointing to two pretty women walking in our direction, he said, 'What do you say? Should we offer our company to these lost souls?'

The two pretty ladies did indeed look like neophytes of the French Riviera, looking around as if they were missing something, laughing between themselves for unclear reasons, and giving the impression that they were trying hard to find something to do. With his usual politeness, Alessandro approached them and asked them whether he could provide any assistance since they seemed lost. And because they clearly looked American, he addressed them in his grammatically proficient though heavily accented English.

It always fascinated me to observe how every woman who had the occasion to interact with Alessandro immediately related to him, whether by directly falling in love, by accepting his company, or simply by being amused. I never saw a woman walk away from him annoyed at any of his advances. It must have been a combination of naturalness, self-confidence, and of course physical appearance. With the passing of the years, Alessandro had become a master at relations with the opposite sex. Perhaps the true secret was that in reality, he truly did not mean anything beyond what he verbally offered. He really was never in desperate need for companionship or expecting anything specific from the other gender beyond what the latter had to spontaneously offer to him. He simply enjoyed and felt comfortable in such interactions. And I am sure that on this occasion he really meant to help the two pretty strangers independently of where the good deed would lead.

It turned out that the two girls had just arrived in Monte Carlo with their boyfriends and they were quite younger than they appeared to be from a distance. They were looking for a nice place to eat, which was not too expensive, or perhaps a nice nightclub to have a drink and fun according to the liberal standards of the Old Continent. So after a little chat and a walk along La Corniche, we reached their boyfriends and with them continued to a nice restaurant with tables fitted on a terrace over the sea.

Alessandro introduced the four tourists to the owner and told him to take good care of them. As we said goodbye, I could see some sadness in one of the two girls' eyes as she said to Alessandro, 'Thank you so much. I hope we will meet again!'

We continued to walk and talk, interrupted once in a while by similar non-reportable distractions, till evening descended and our stomach reminded us that it was dinnertime. At dinner, we sat at a table along the beach. The breeze from the sea was warm and pleasant, and except for the crowds that were quite different from the ones that lingered around our table in the old times in Pizzo, the atmosphere was just about as cheerful and relaxing. We had wine of course and a little food, neither of us being hungry, but we were rather interested in telling stories to each other now that the ice had been broken and detailed recollections were spontaneously being revived from all corners of our memory.

Alessandro had been living in Monte Carlo for a few months already. He lived in a small apartment near the lady friend, who was married and spent as much time in the Riviera as she could to stay away from her rich but boring husband. According to Alessandro, he was a generous man who was very keen to maintain his other half content and who only rarely visited. Nevertheless, it felt inappropriate for Alessandro to live directly with a married woman. Most importantly, this excuse was particularly convenient as Alessandro was in no disposition to limit his freedom by sharing his own life with anybody.

It appeared that the lady was also taking good financial care of Alessandro, not letting him miss anything he needed to conduct a dignified life. At the same time, she was so deeply in love with him to accept any compromise as long as she had a chance to see him once in a while and be held in his strong arms. I am not sure why I thoughtlessly asked him if he loved her or nurtured any sort of sentiment towards this lady benefactor. Alessandro simply replied, 'I do not know.'

That night after a few bottles of wine or other liquor, we ended up in a nightclub. Following few additional drinks, a drunken American, who heard us speaking in Italian, jokingly asked Alessandro, 'Do you know how you can tell that an Italian is around? . . . Because the garbage bin is empty and the bitch is pregnant.'

I had not witnessed Alessandro being confronted before in a way that would not be of the outmost deference. I was therefore nervous about the outcome of this conversation and at the same time curious to observe Alessandro's reaction. In the cloudiness of my inebriated thoughts, I tried to prepare for a fight or more preferably for a decorous flight if circumstances would allow. But then, there were girls with us and I felt compelled to avoid acting as a coward although that would have been my natural predisposition. In fact, I had no intention to confront a stranger on a topic of complete indifference to me and expose myself to the ridicule of an awkward dispute. This predicament bothered me even more than the potential bruises. But nothing of this kind was going to be necessary. Alessandro calmly stood up, looked straight in the face of the stranger with his cold blue eyes, and with an affected melange of Southern Italian and British accent asked him, 'So whatta is wronga with itt?' To which everybody laughed.

The next thing I remember, the American, who meant no offense but who was simply not exceptionally versed in the diplomacy of international exchanges, was sitting with us, chatting about something that happened in New Jersey when he was young while both of us, though coming from well-to-do families, having very little experience in scavenging for food or engaging in illegitimate relationships with females of other species, exerted the outmost imagination to teach him how to steal scrap from garbage cans and get as many bitches gravid in one night. Things of course rapidly deteriorated into other topics that would be inappropriate to relate to the younger, tasteless to the middle-aged, and trite to the mature audience, and therefore, I will spare the reader this unessential information.

We never saw the American again, but I muse, imagining him happily stealing grub from bins and procreating happily with any specimen of the opposite gender across mammalian species in disregard of any Darwinian principle but on account of his Italian friends. Above all, I trust he is not serving in an embassy or consulate not only in Italy but any other country possessing garbage cans or bitches.

That night we became so drunk that the women we were supposed to protect had the unsatisfying task of taking care of us without expectation for gratitude as neither of us remembered the later phases of that night.

Therefore, the following morning I woke up in a tidy hotel room, lit by the sunrays through the fine and transparent curtains, with the smell of pine trees and other evergreens and a pretty girl at my side of whom I had no clue who she was.

'Good morning,' she said in American accent with a big smile, 'you were very funny last night and very witty!'

I did not know how to reciprocate, and the best I could contribute was 'I have a huge headache. Do you have something for it?' And with a bigger smile, she held her left arm up, her hand gently waving towards a little table, right by the balcony, on which a few brioches and a carafe with coffee in it were waiting.

She got up, and through her transparent nightgown, I could see her beauty even better. I felt the need to perform, and I asked myself what had been done already. But I could not recollect anything. I wished to call her back in bed and initiate the process of love making, but the headache, the fact that I had no protection, and that I did not know who she was, not even her name, made me hesitate. At the back of my mind, I heard our glorious national anthem, and I saw bersaglieri[82] passing over barricades for the sake of our beloved Italy, but I just could not reproduce the level of national heroism that led to the unification of Italy during il Risorgimento.[83] Rather, slowly, scratching my hair and pulling up my boxers, I walked to the little table where she was already serving me coffee.

Trying to avoid being excessively impertinent, yet to satisfy my growing curiosity, I asked, 'What happened last night?'

---

[82]   Elite corps of the Italian Army.
[83]   Political and revolutionary movement that lead in the mid-1800s to the unification of Italy.

She giggled and replied, 'You were so drunk and tired and had no place to sleep. Ophelia, my friend whom you probably do not remember, went to sleep with Alessandro and so I took you with me and let you sleep here, and you slept like a baby but snored like a wounded lion.'

'Did we do anything else?' I said timidly and almost apologetically in either case, whether we did or did not do what I guessed would have been expected by such a predicament.

And she smiled and said, 'Why don't we just have coffee now? Do we really have to have this conversation as our way to get to know each other, my dear Jewyseppe?'

I am not sure why, but on hearing my name sweetly mispronounced according to the American perception, warmth entered my chest, and for the first time I looked at her as if she was a human being and admitted, 'You know, I do not remember your name', which was an understatement since I did not even remember meeting her.

But this sudden warmth brought also an uncomfortable feeling of cosiness and relaxation that did not align with my obsessive compulsive personality.

When she said, 'Shirley', an uncomfortable suspicion started to creep into my mind. I had never been with a prostitute, but I knew that they were masterful in making a man feel comfortable as they take care of his wallet, and as I looked at my pants by her side of the bed I noticed that the back pocket looked quite flat.

Without even thinking I yelped, 'Where is my wallet?' At that, she became startled, and looking around inquisitively, she pointed to the bedside table on my side of the bed where, in fact, the object of my anguish was peacefully resting.

'I am sorry. I thought I left it in the nightclub,' I quickly recovered with the hope that I did not offend her. But then another thought came to me. Why was the wallet out? Who took it? Did she remove it from the pocket to take my cash? As I sipped my coffee, I thought of an ingenious way to inveigle her interest in a picture of mine of 'when I was young' which

I carried in the wallet and which represented me at the age of sixteen, while I had currently reached the Mathusalem's stage of three and twenty. Courteously, she looked with interest at the picture of me and my friends at the beach holding a soccer ball, while I had the opportunity to open the wallet and find out that the money was just exactly all there.

Being relieved of this despicable suspicion, I looked at Shirley one more time with sympathy, and I wondered why this woman took me in her bed for the night. As she was looking at the picture, she said, 'You were a very cute boy and you are turning into a very handsome man!' For some reason, the word 'man' struck me. I had never thought of me as a 'man' in the sense of somebody who had closed a part of his life and had moved on to another stage.

As I took a more perceptive look at her, I started to realise that I was sitting in front of a woman who was between thirty and forty years old, beautiful under all possible aspects, but at the same time showing subtle signs of ageing depicted by a few extra wrinkles on the side of the eyes and in her forehead. The thought that I had slept, without knowing, with somebody who must have been at least ten years older intimidated me, and holding her hand, I asked, 'Shirley, what is happening next?'

'We are supposed to meet Alessandro and Ophelia at the Marina for lunch on our boat before we sail away.'

It turned out that Shirley was a married woman who was spending a vacation cruising on the private boat of her friend Ophelia, which was a hundred and twenty-foot yacht anchored ashore of Monte Carlo with a crew of three. Ophelia, her friend, was a white Anglo-Saxon princess. She was not ugly, and in fact, objectively she could have been described as beautiful except for some stiffness in her body and in her expression that made her seem more like a marionette carved in wood than a human being. Her big blue eyes were always staring, the forehead would not corrugate, and the eyebrows would not move as if they had been painted above the eyes. The mouth was tiny, and when she tried to smile, it opened symmetrically and mechanically like a curtain in front of a stage closing with the same propriety after showing two rows of white and shiny teeth. And she was a decent girl; she used proper language and never cursed. Nobody was a bad person to her, even those who in fact were; she would ask, 'Poor dear, why did he do this sort of thing?' She said that her grandmother taught her that she had to learn to be polite without lying; for instance, if a mother was showing off her ugly baby, one could say, 'Wow, that's what I call a baby!'

I did not understand at the beginning how Alessandro could endure such hypocrisy and small mindedness, but he treated her specially and kindly, more than he had ever done with any woman before. Not that Alessandro was ever rude to women, but he acted mostly detached and absent-minded, as if they were pets around him that needed some occasional attention, patiently waiting like dogs for a few scraps from the table.

With Ophelia, he was almost obsequious; he pulled out the chair to facilitate her seating, he held her jacket and helped her put it on, he would serve her food and drinks, he would turn to her to ask for her opinion about the most irrelevant things, and he smiled abundantly both when he was talking or listening to her. He even looked proud of her, and he would hold her hand when they were walking ahead of us or hold her arm to help her climb a few steps. Ophelia was his lady benefactor . . .

At lunch, the women asked how we knew each other. We did not know how to start; we looked at each other and tried to harmonise our stories, cutting most of it, not because there was anything to hide in front of these two mature women, but because it seemed boring and uninteresting for us to tell and for them to listen to the description of our past of philandering and dissipation. And it appeared to both of us that the whole content of our youth could have been wrapped in a thin envelope secured by the seal of emptiness.

After lunch, we sailed. We entertained a purposeless journey up and down the French Riviera—sailing during the day, anchoring in the late afternoon in some recessed alcove, swimming in the refreshing sea, showering, and having a few even more refreshing drinks. Although I was living and studying by then in America, I had not experienced the wealth of cocktails practiced there. This way I became acquainted with the ritual of the gin and tonic, the margarita or the mojito, or the martini or the negroni, which had been probably exported without my knowledge there from Italy a long time ago. Therefore, pre-prandial drinks became a happily anticipated moment and a wonderful cult that gave purpose to even the most boring day spent in the boat. I enjoyed the feeling that came with the sunset in anticipation of pleasure, of disengagement from anything that could be worrisome at other times, but not then when all could be forgotten just through the simple inebriation of our minds unbridled in the company of friends. And friends they were! The two women were nice as a dream and gregarious; there was no need of mine that Shirley could not anticipate without being overbearing or intrusive. There was not a flake of vulgarity in her otherwise simple personality.

Right after the first dinner on the boat, Ophelia and Alessandro retired in their cabin graciously, wishing the most pleasant of the nights to Shirley and to me. Alessandro gave me a private impertinent smile as if to admonish me not to disappoint the companion he had found for me and disgrace the reputation of our Italian ancestors.

Not knowing what to do and just left alone with the crew, Shirley suggested a dance. It was a soft night, with a northern breeze gently lulling the boat. The music had been playing throughout dinner, but I had just noticed it then. I do not remember the song, but it invited a slow dance. And I held her by her waist and she rested her head on my left shoulder.

After a few minutes, I felt that it was my duty to slowly walk my lips down her temple towards her own. My tentative and unassuming kiss was returned by a passionate and long one and by the tightest of the hugs. I concluded that I had locked on to the target or even more accurately the target had attacked me. In any case, within a few moments we were lying on a couch in a private part of the deck, where I was holding her without whispering a word. Her hugs were getting tighter and tighter, her body melting in its forms and movement into mine in such a way that this little wiggly worm and her actions sidetracked rather than aroused me.

I attempted to distract her with conversation, with the beauty of the stars, the sounds of the chopping waves against the hull, the happiness of being so far away from everything. But in the end, I succumbed to her sweetness. Her softness and her beauty conquered me, and quickly we made it to her cabin that from then on became our cabin.

In the silence of the night, with the rhythm of the pendulant boat, we gently undressed each other and we made love reciprocally and lovingly. And we did it several times that night as soon as we recovered from each refractory period like a couple on lions in honeymoon.

It appeared that she suffered from insomnia, and to entice me to share the beauty of the sleepless nights, she did her best to keep me awake or gently awaken me from what I would have considered otherwise a well-deserved sleep.

By the morning, I was way more tired than when I went to bed and I suggested spending a little longer, may be the rest of the day, in bed with what seemed to me the obvious purpose of sleeping. Shirley, who, however, had misinterpreted my intentions, warmly seized that offer, and by the end of the day, we had probably made love at least another seven times. I do not remember what happened next, but that evening, I fell asleep at the table after the second gin and tonic, and I was told that Alessandro himself with the help of a crew had to take me into our cabin where I woke up the morning after with the gentle Shirley smiling and looking at me.

This status of affairs continued for a few days, interrupted only by a few attempts to redeem the ennui by forcing upon ourselves activities packaged as touristic pursuits in the inland of unfamiliar places where we had happened to set anchor the night before. Finally, one morning I felt an irrepressible urge to jump off the boat and swim to the shore, incapable of bearing the idea that I might have another week or two to spend in that floating Alcatraz. Yet as I reflected upon the reasons compelling me to perform such risky act, I realised that it was not boredom or tiredness alone but rather unsettling warmth towards Shirley—a feeling I was not prepared to concede to. We had managed to talk in between refractory sexual moments, and by then I knew quite a good proportion of her story.

She had married a military man when she was quite young. It turned out that he was an abusive drunkard; he never made love to her but rather raped her whether she wanted or not. He would beat her up occasionally after a bad day at work. He would demand perfection in the house affairs although there was no objective metrics for it, but simply what he would find most suitable at that moment. He would wonder why the dishes were stored here rather than there, who put the garbage can on the wrong side of the road, who forgot to turn on the water heater in the guest room, and other random annoyances that could be easily addressed by relaxing the tie and the neck collar; he would drink a few cocktails and conclude the feast with a reinvigorating beating of his wife.

One day, out of desperation, she went to her cousin's place to ask for help; she was not there but her husband, who listened empathically to her, decided it was best to rape her on his own to make her forget the abuses of her husband. She never asked for any help after that from anybody, and she would still be there, in the middle of the big plains of America, if her husband had not been considerate enough to die while driving under the influence about six months before the trip to Monte Carlo. After that, she packed and moved away to the place where she had grown up and re-established contacts with old friends, and there it was that she reunited with Ophelia, an old high school friend who had made better choices by marrying a rich man and, therefore, was doing just fine financially.

Ophelia in turn had also lost interest in the romantic aspects of the marriage since her husband was a distant man too busy to give a wife more attention than his precious BMW. He was not a mean man, but he lived in his own world. Therefore, when Ophelia proposed a trip to Europe with Shirley, just as she had done several times before with other friends, the husband sighed in relief and endorsed the idea, thinking of the personal freedom that this proposition was going to bring.

A few days later, Ophelia and Shirley packed and arrived at Ophelia's villa in Monte Carlo. Shirley, therefore, had never experienced love, and the sexual element of her life had felt like a unidirectional action from the two men she had experienced, without any chances of her participation and any cognition that carnal interactions may be associated with spiritual interactions.

But she loved to love; she enjoyed most of all giving rather than receiving, and for some reason my gentle demeanour and my unassuming attempt to kiss her on the first night unleashed a passion that had been repressed for years, and within a moment she had fallen in love with me. However,

Shirley was not my type; she was an unsophisticated American woman from the Midwest. We had nothing in common, and yet I began to feel close to her. I could not resist her kindness and I wondered how a lucky man like her husband could not have learnt to appreciate such sweet gregariousness.

Time seemed to never pass on the boat. After breakfast, the two women embalmed themselves with sunscreen. Then, with thoughtful apprehension, they adjusted their bodies in the most suitable basking orientation, like compasses that sense the cardinal coordinates. The two sunflowers intuitively knew the path that the sun was about to take in the following hours with the kind of accuracy that only the most sophisticated trigonometry equation could predict. There they lay stoically like a fakir sitting on a nail bed or lying on burning coals, enduring with the utmost strength an immensurable torture for the minimal return of seeing their skin just a touch darker by the end of the day. I was left staring at the two mummies from my soft chair, sipping one lemonade at the time, till I started noticing enchanted cobras dancing around them and several pairs of arms coming out of their bodies as an indication that I was about to doze off myself. And this status of affairs reminded me of a brooding warning offered to me by an old teacher, who having ingested a few glasses of Barolo said, 'The company of women, save for sex, can be utterly boring.'

However, as time passed with the slow cadence of the rolling boat, I began to feel uneasy. What was I doing in the middle of the Mediterranean Sea, embracing an older woman, when I should have been home studying for my next exam? Besides, although by now my readers are well aware that I am not a beacon of morality in the conventional sense, after a week of that purposeless and dissipated life I felt that my time was being wasted, and like Pinocchio in the *Land of Toys* I perceived that a tail and two furry ears were growing out of my body.

I wanted to share my oppression with Alessandro and let him know that I did not want to prolong my sojourn much further. Although my efforts aimed at the noble purpose of alleviating human suffering by obtaining a medical degree could be perceived in the big scheme of things just as boring, inconsequential, and meaningless as those nights passed ashore, in the depth of my own conscience a conventional approach to life values was easier to rationalise. Thus, I wanted to return to the easy path dictated by conformity while Alessandro stubbornly continued in his self-destructing mission.

It was not easy to approach Alessandro. He, instead, seemed quite content with the monotony of the days ashore. He reclined with Ophelia faithfully by his side, watching the waves on the sides and the wake left behind peacefully by the sailing boat. Occasionally, he would get up to go find some iced tea or lemon mint for Ophelia and behaved with the same solicitude that Shirley reserved for me. Or he would stand with his arm against the mast, looking forward towards the horizon, and the same time that never passed for me seemed irrelevant to him.

Most of the day was spent sailing; only at nights we had conversations when, after setting anchor in some harbour or in a remote cove, we would rest on a stable platform and have a better chance of looking into each other's eyes. But the conversations were far from the depth of those in the old days. The presence of the women and the occasional interference of the crew constrained us, and we limited our conversations to small talk and irreverent jokes. Often I felt the urge to ask questions to him about what he remembered of our past, how he saw his future, and perhaps our future as friends. But I judged that in front of Ophelia he could not be authentic and open. It also appeared that Alessandro was becoming jealous of my devotion for Shirley. For some perverse reason, he appeared irritated when I started to give her the attention he was giving to Ophelia, as if I was attempting to take over his novel role of a devoted lover. There was even a hint of competitiveness in the way he took care of Ophelia. On my side, I grew even fonder of Shirley who was consistently warm, cheerful, and uplifting.

It was Alessandro who eventually broke the impasse after a week of stalemate. One morning, he took me by the collar of the shirt and pulling me towards himself said, 'What do you say?! Tonight let's leave the women on the boat and we go out for a drink and dinner just the two of us?'

I was happy to hear that, and to demonstrate my gratitude, I delivered a punch to his belly, which unfortunately resulted in it being harder than intended and was directed to the lower geographical region of a person's body that particularly in men is guarded with apprehension. This unfortunate accident caused Alessandro to release the grip of my collar and bend in a foetal position while holding his precious crouch. Feeling sorry, I hurried to get something to drink for him. Unfortunately, just as I was passing by, Alessandro lifted his foot to cross my path just enough to trip my movement, and I ended face down, having the previously not considered option of exploring from close distance the perfection of the teak finishing of the boat's deck.

As I was getting up to turn towards Alessandro with a reproachful stare, one of the crew pounced on me and held me from the back, not as much to save Alessandro's life as to show his muscles to the baffled women. Being unnecessarily held by this Good Samaritan, I yelled at Alessandro, 'Patto fatto.'[84]

Consequently, having set anchor in the evening in Palma de Mallorca, we happily sprang like crickets out of the boat and ran like freed gazelles into the solid grounds of the island, soon disappearing in the anonymity of the bustling crowd just as happy as children playing hooky, to find ourselves about an hour later in a nice bistro along the coast, not too far but far enough to give us the awareness of regained freedom.

We were back wondrously to the old times. With a bottle of wine smiling at us from the ice bucket and a few simple but delicious appetisers on our plates, the fatuity of the last two weeks was quickly forgotten and the old times with their conversations at the verge of existentialism were naturally resumed.

Alessandro started, 'Life is as ephemeral as the shape of clouds in a windy day. People worry about tomorrow all the time. They waste their present preparing for the future, not realising that there is no such thing as the future. It is an evolving present that we live. Every step we take turns the future into past during that fraction of a moment when the sole of our shoe touches the ground. In the end only the past accumulates with our actions irrevocably burning that potential energy that we call "future".

---

[84]   Done deal.

'. . . Terrestrial existence is a process without product except for death. When will the future finally materialise? Ten? Twenty years from now? And then what? Will the critters of hearth be happy then or will they continue to strive towards that unreachable horizon that will remain forever a step ahead of them?

'. . . The future is a distraction for those who prefer to postpone the present because they are uncomfortable with their own existence. They work hard to make themselves rich or to achieve other goals. It could be a better car, a better house, a family, a better job, or a special recognition, and this process will divert them for the time being from their internal anguish. But the truth is that they do not know how to be happy with what they have and, therefore, they postpone the confrontation with their own reality and put on hold the unhappiness by creating pseudo-goals and busying themselves to reach material milestones, fond of the illusion that their absence is the only barrier to their fulfilment. And they will continue this pursuit till only memories will be left at the table and a tiny bit of future, just enough time to regret the lost opportunities and appreciate the emptiness of what could be called a person's life.

'. . . And of course there are reverse approaches. As an opposite extreme, I will tell you about an aunt of mine. She lived in Naples. She was both a princess and an archaeologist. While she acknowledged the first, she was most comfortable with her second identity. This was because the work of an archaeologist is to revive the past and this came natural to her. In fact, for her it was not the matter of reviving but simply uncovering what was alive and well, seasoned by time like a good bottle of Barolo. The past was for her the only reality that had endured the test of time, while everything else was ephemeral and likely to vanish and be forgotten like the noise of thunders. The past also offered an additional attraction to her because it comes wrapped in history with the implicit understanding that the latter will restore justice—not the kind of justice that punishes the unjust and rewards the virtuous. Rather a justice that vindicates the truth, where for eternity the hero shall become legend and the scoundrel will sink in the hell of shame. In truth, the science that revives the life of the ancestors was a natural match for her because collimated her attitude towards her own life. She lived exclusively for the past as if the present and even more so the future did not exist. It suited her very well. Her dad had died when she was a little girl, and her betrothed also died of cancer, leaving her a virgin widow for the rest of her life. She stayed with her mother, who also lived off memories, partly of relatives and partly of the times when Italy was still a monarchy and she was a revered and envied lady. Yet in some same strange way, this aunt was one of the happiest people I have ever known since her gratification was based on perquisites that had been written in stone and that for sure would never change. Even at the moment she died, she was still telling stories about the ancient Greeks and the Romans and she was probably already dreaming that may be one day somebody would find her bones and would stick a label on them stating: *These are the bones of a princess who lived dreaming of the past till finally she became an absolute part of it.'*

Recognising my old Alessandro, I appreciated what this preface truly meant; it meant that he was in a good mood and he was inclined to chat liberally just as we did in the years of youth. Without replying directly to his foreword, I asked, 'So what is going on with Ophelia? It seems you are closer to her than to any other woman you have ever been with since I can remember.' And as an embroidered provocation, I added, 'You are solicitous with her, like a little puppy wagging his tail and peeing on the carpet when you are around her. Do you love her?'

We were sitting cosily on plastic armchairs. Alessandro extended his legs under the table, crossed the fingers of his two hands to rest his chin atop them as if into a cradle, and then he pointed his serious eyes that had turned deep blue in the dim light to look interrogatively at my face, probably wondering why would I even ask such a stupid question.

Then extending his thumbs along the jawbones as if to further support his thoughts and corrugating his forehead, he looked up towards the flickering light that was accompanying our dinner, and after giving it a little more consideration, he smiled at the tremulous bulb and said, 'Of course I don't! Have I ever been capable to love anybody? Or has anybody ever loved me? I mean truly love me, the real Alessandro G . . . ? . . . But I do feel comfortable with her. She makes me feel better. I do not know what she sees in me, but I do not think she cares too much about my looks. She treats me as if I was her teenage son. She has patience and no expectations. She likes me not for my handsomeness, but in spite of the bad personality I have. It seems likes she can see in me what I cannot decipher myself. I can tell her everything and she listens. She does not judge, but she tries to understand. I do not think she does completely of course, but it does not matter. It is only important that she tries, and deep inside, instinctually I think she does understand me better than I do.'

And after a pause, he continued, partly repeating and partly contradicting himself, '. . . She will never understand because she cannot. I did not share with her much about my past. I am really not interested in sharing old boring stories. That part of my past will be buried with me one day. Yet she senses that something is bothering me. I do not know how but she does. She knows that the handsome Alessandro is nothing more than a lost soul, a pathetically and ridiculously lonesome guy. She does not say anything. At the same time she is devoted to me. She is patient and sweet. She is there when I need her, invisible when I want to be left alone. I used to hate women like that. I was surrounded by characters like this all the time, devoted bitches who would do anything to please me, even kill themselves, . . . so to speak!' He corrected himself, 'But those women were different. In the end, they waited for me like pups at the door for nights and days till they could stare at me with their sad prurient eyes in the hope of awakening my unbending conscience. I hated that feeling of being owned. I felt like a bone that they were trying to catch and bury underground to protect it from other bitches.' He continued, 'I was selfish then as I am now, but I changed somewhat. I care less about the future. I care less about controlling what will happen, even less than before. I just want each day to pass, sooner if possible than the previous one. I do not have anywhere to go. I have no expectations save for going home and finding her, have a drink and some food, give her the only thing I ever learnt to give, which is my body, and then fall asleep till another meaningless day opens my eyes.'

'Do you think that she loves you in a special way compared to others before?' But there was no answer to this question. Perhaps he thought that he had already answered that question.

Instead, Alessandro returned to its original train of thought and looking towards me gave his beautiful smile. 'You are lucky. You possess a belief. You work hard to achieve a goal. You are going to be a great doctor, a professor one day! Like for everybody else, it is just a distraction, something to keep you hanging to the tight rope of life, but it will work for you. You will have a smoother ride than the one I am going to take. You will be at peace with yourself because you will comply with what others are expecting of you. You will be a team player in the game of life, no fears of displeasing parents, friends, relatives, a future wife, a concubine when you will have one, your kids. You will just be their puppet, and this will keep you comfortable. I know this, because I know you and I know myself. Sometimes I am tempted to take the same easy path—take the licensing exam, practice law, find a wife, make my father happy since my mother died last year, have children, grandchildren, be the patriarch and reproduce over and over the purposeless cycle of life. But I cannot do it. I cannot see myself that way. I would look at myself in the mirror one day and see a ridiculous man—a middle-aged bold and overweight clown. I cannot do that. A nurse working in a retirement home once recorded the top regrets of the dying. Most lamented not having lived a life true to themselves rather than the life others expected of them.

'"Muor giovane chi agli dei e' caro,"[85] used to say Meander. Yes, I wish I could die young and uncontaminated by life before it will be too late. I would have killed myself already if I would have had the courage. But I do not! Suicide is an unnatural thing. Vegetating, as I do, is a realistic form of self-destruction that I can handle. So I settle on the boat, looking at the time passing in the form of waves under its hull or clouds in the sky, and I peacefully wait for the end and try to kill myself slowly and peacefully like Gogol who starved himself to death.'

'Sorry to hear about your mother. What happened to her?' I interrupted.

'She died of cancer a year ago . . . ovarian cancer . . . I went for the funeral. She was still the pretty little woman she used to be. The evening, just before she died she held me close like a little child holding a doll. She whispered that she loved me and she would miss me:—*You are such a handsome young man! You always were special, so strong and smart! Promise me that you will make your father proud. Do it for me. Do not disappoint him. He has been a good and loving father to you better than I was as a mother and as a wife.* I am not sure what she meant by that, but I held her

---

[85] Dies young who is loved by the gods.

in my arms till she fell into her typical restless sleep. I caressed her hair and kissed her head. I loved her of course but not as a mother, rather as if she was a daughter. I thought that I would miss her of course, but I was not scared of being left alone. I realised how irrelevant she had been to me as a developing man, and I felt sorry for myself for never truly having had a mother but rather a childish sister. And even then, I could not relate to her except for petting her like a sick puppy and trying to relieve her from her nightmares as I did when I was a child. After the funeral, my dad spent a few days in his den going from the armchair to the window and back. I never saw him cry, but he sat resigned and apathetic. When I went to say goodbye, he hugged me, stroked my hair, held me around my neck, and kissed my head. "Good luck to you, Alex," he said. That was the last time I saw my father.'

'I developed what they like to call in modern terms clinical depression, and some friends convinced me that I needed medical help. In the end, I did go to a shrink. He told me that I have a borderline personality disorder that goes beyond depression and that I carried along throughout my life as a parasitic infection. In many ways, the shrink described pretty accurately what has been bothering me since I could remember, which is a disconnection between the reality and my inner self. I had traits of paranoia he said that made me believe that people around me do not really exist but are just images surrounding me to play games. You understand that I am perfectly aware that this is not true, but at the same time I have to remind myself of this continuously. Things seem to get worse when I receive emotional hits. Of course, he recommended medications as if pills could solve problems! The day they will find a treatment that can solve the Israel/Palestine problem or revive extinct species I will take that pill! But it is amusing how shrinks try to make one believe that by playing a little with the intensity of one's emotions they could solve lifelong problems rooted in the deepest of our soul.

'. . . A person is the result of a long chain of events that shape his moral view. In my case, brutality and tragedy were very much the daily routine. Although I have never been a bad person, I have witnessed a lot of bad occurrences. I have seen things being destroyed out of nothing. I have seen selfishness at the basis of tragedy. I have seen mocking birds being killed just for pleasure. These days I think a lot about what life really has to offer and how to find out what is optimal. I agree that one has a responsibility to use one's life as constructively as possible. It is not a religious thought, but it is a basic rule, formed out of respect for life and sort of gratitude that we are actually here and for a while able to do something in the world. But it is a demanding task too. It is easier to just decide that things are okay and go on living along the same path. Default I believe is the word. So little and yet so much time has passed from our youth in the old Pizzo. I remember the ambitions. I remember that when people did not believe in me I wanted to show them wrong, and when they finally did, I did not want to prove myself wrong. What happened to that ambitious Alessandro? How can this one make his father proud?

'. . . Sometimes I feel that I am so focused on surviving day to day that I cannot pay attention to anything else. It is like walking on a rope, where you cannot allow for any distraction to affect your steps that are protecting you from falling into the depth of an unending soul . . . and this occupation keeps you so self-absorbed that you forget to look at life as a whole.

'. . . This is why I am so happy you came. Recently, I had another of those moments when I wished I did not exist, and I felt I needed you. It was sort of a miracle to find out that you were around. I felt that I have been holding on you all this time because you were one of the few people who made me comfortable with my surrounding world and who was able to empathise with me without becoming a burden. We were so similar! Those were great times! Remember the day you sprained your ankle but you could not care less because we had won the championship? I wonder what happened to those medals. But they left a sweet memory!'

I suddenly felt an urge to interrupt his soliloquist exercise. 'You have to reckon that by addressing your pains and their causes you will not fall from the rope and you may even find a remedy. There is something inside you that is wounded, and one day or another you have to take the initiative to fix it. You just have to accept to take care of yourself, and I am confident that you will not "fall in depth of an unending soul".

And I continued, 'Do you keep a diary of your life? Maybe by writing all of these emotions that are suffocating your mind and trying to put some order into them, you may find your way to salvation.'

'I do not have a true story of my life,' he replied. 'All went inconsequentially from one step to the other, from a day to the other without questioning and without wilful decisions. It was a downstream flow of shapeless events, fluidity made of apathy. Yet you are right. I feel a need to leave a record of it, maybe to warn others to do not as I did. I cannot even imagine who would even read it, but it feels good to believe that some records of my person, besides a few photographic images, may survive me.'

I wish I had been smarter and more sensitive than I was then listening to those precious disclosures, and I wish I had listened more empathetically to Alessandro. Instead, as it has happened so many times in my life, I lost that opportunity and instead I tried to lighten his spirit and dismiss his anguish:

'I am sorry about your mom. She was such a sweet and elegant lady. Maybe Ophelia is taking her role! Does she hug you at night and make you feel safe?'

I realised as it came out from my mouth how insensitive and condescending my comment was, but Alessandro smiled patiently, and getting the point that it was time to play happiness, he turned to the chilled bottle, poured more wine into my glass, and raising his glass over my head, he said jokingly these prophetic words, 'Let's drink! This wine is my blood.' Then taking a piece of baguette, he said, 'And eat this. This bread is my body, Amen! Let's enjoy our last supper together!'

And following this profane ending, we both laughed, and after a generous pouring of another glass we focused on our dinner and on lighter topics till we were interrupted by an English-speaking woman who had come to our table from the bar stand from where she had been staring at Alessandro for quite a while.

With an almost full bottle of champagne in her hands, she politely asked, 'May I join you gentlemen?'

Without waiting for an answer, she made herself comfortable on a chair at our table, pouring the champagne in her glass and checking whether our glasses where empty to do the same. She was half drunk, with the other half not any soberer. She was good looking but of the aggressive and confident type that is generally less attractive to men and that does not do anything for me. But Alessandro patiently accepted her presence at the table and smiling encouragingly asked the generic questions commonly exchanged between strangers. Encouraged by this start, she turned around to another pretty woman in her early twenties, inviting her to join the table to pair the numbers. So suddenly, I had a date in front of me—young, joyful, and smiling, which quickly distracted me from the dismay that my special dinner with Alessandro had vaporised to be replaced by a call for duty—the course of the Latin lover!

Alessandro surprised me by introducing me as 'his lover' to the two ladies, perhaps in an attempt to politely get rid of them or may be just to see what effect such a statement had on them. But the new alpha woman did not fall for it, and finding it an amusing joke, she reacted by stating that all the same the woman sitting at my side was her partner but tonight they were taking a break from exclusive homosexuality. I am not sure whether, if we would have been sober, we would have found a way to politely get rid of the two ladies. It was not because they were unattractive, to the contrary. But we simply had planned an escapade from another pair of nurturing but invasive souls for just one night, likely the last night together before my departure.

But by then we were already on our second bottle of wine, and with additional champagne being poured into our minds through our insatiable mouths, the barricade against the opposite gender was rapidly crumbling.

It has been clearly shown that intoxication by alcohol limits the one-person resolve, particularly when such determination is shaky to begin with. Therefore, by the end of dinner we had been fully acquainted with the two beauties from South Africa and made unequivocally aware of their appetite for romance.

To the relief of the restaurant owner, we walked out, holding the two drunk ladies, and went for a walk along the beach according to a long-established protocol that one would expect to work in Mallorca just as well as it did in the distant shores of Pizzo during our youth and perhaps in any distant or near shore along this planet or for that matter any planet in the universe where sexual reproduction serves as a tool to propagate species.

After a few steps, I found myself alone with the young woman while Alessandro had disappeared behind a boat with his alpha female. In spite of my tipsiness, I approached the situation methodically, following procedure. I started with a romantic and genuine kiss, followed by a stroking of my hand along her flanks, up to the open shirt, and a crawl of the fingers between the breasts under her elegant bra. Proceedings continued undisturbed with encouraging moaning from my counterpart till the technical question rose in my young medical mind of how to complete the process with a perfect stranger without any protection. Therefore, with the outmost deference I asked whether she happened to carry a condom in her purse. Learning with a mixture of disappointment and relief that she did not, I felt emancipated from the need to complete the action, and therefore, we continued fondling each other till satisfaction could otherwise be accomplished, which in her case consisted of a bewildering number of orgasms.

When Alessandro finally appeared holding his woman by the hand, she looked much happier than the one who had been handed by fate to me. Later on, as we were walking back to the yacht I most casually asked Alessandro whether he had made love to her, and he just as casually replied, 'Yes.'

When I just as casually asked, 'Did you use a condom?' in an irritated tone he simply replied, 'No.'

When we returned in the middle of the night, our two women were on the deck waiting. There was a bottle of wine in the ice bucket and two empty glasses. They were jovial and treated us like mothers scolding their schoolboys coming from an adventure. They asked whether we had enjoyed our freedom and whether we were happy to be back. We both managed to mumble something and Alessandro went to Ophelia, who was reclining on a sofa, and kissed her lips; then he lay by her side, opening his right arm to let her settle in this natural cove. They relaxed peacefully for a few minutes, and then Alessandro apologised for both of them, stating that he was tired and that they were going to retire.

Left alone on the deck, I turned to Shirley, and not sure about what to say, I gave a meaningless smile. Gently she accosted me and touched my hand; then she asked: 'I know that I have no right to ask you this, but I need to know for my own protection. Did you make love to somebody tonight?'

I am not sure what happened, but this surprising question gave rise to a rebellious sense in me, an incoercible impulse to be somewhere else where there was no need to be accountable to anybody. Without attempting to control myself, I looked straight in her eyes and . . . I lied, 'Yes, I did.'

While I was curiously waiting for her reaction, she serenely told me, 'I understand. Thanks for telling me the truth, but now I cannot make love to you any more.' And kissing me on the forehead, she rose and went to her cabin.

It was the perfect night, just the kind of night that I love, with just enough of a zephyr to alleviate the heat and enlighten the spirit, with a half moon occasionally peeking through creative clouds and bright stars scattered across the rest of the free sky. And I sensed the freedom of the wind and of the moving clouds entering into my soul, lifting me away from the jail where I had been imprisoned for the last fortnight. I felt the joy of the man without responsibility, without accountability, the man I enjoyed to be. I imagined that sweet Shirley would soon be just a nice remembrance to be tenderly stored in a corner of memory. Of course, I would respect Shirley's request to leave her alone and I would act as a gentleman. I would be kind and still close to her. I would even be grateful in the future for all the good moments spent together, for her willingness to listen to my insipid stories during the tedious hours of sailing. I could be of course her magnanimous friend while I could spend the next few days on the way back to Monte Carlo, resting on the deck, reading and studying and enjoying my own company in peace.

But as I was savouring the pleasantness of the regained freedom, I felt a hand on my right shoulder and another one stroking my hair. Then I perceived the softness of a woman's bosom against my nape and the familiar perfume of Shirley.

'Just because I cannot make love to you any more, it does not mean we cannot still sleep together.'

In a few minutes, we were in our cabin and in another few we were making love like rabbits. Most aggravatingly, in a moment of passion, I confessed that I had lied and that in fact I had not made love to anybody, therefore extinguishing with an infantile impulse the passage to freedom so magisterially orchestrated just a few moments before.

The following day, the sky was limpid, the air was still, and consequently the sea was completely flat. Only a periodic chopping noise under the boat reminded us that we were still ashore. The stillness had taken ownership of everything including our minds, and we were resting, each one absorbed in the one's thoughts without saying a word. A pigeon blighted from nowhere and carefully picked at croissant crumbles sitting on the breakfast table, periodically looking around proudly with an inflated chest. Nobody bothered to chase it away; rather we were all looking at it with interest as if it was offering us an opportunity for distraction. Then, suddenly, the bird flew away, towards the pier close by, and I wished that I had wings too that could take me to the loneliness where I belonged and where I felt most comfortable.

In the following days, we made it back to Monte Carlo without further reportable events; we had a final early dinner on the boat. We had one more bottle of wine and a few more cheers and promises to see each other again. As I was about to leave the boat, Shirley started to hold me tighter and tighter. She caressed my hair, she looked at me and sighed, she touched my legs and chest, she bent her head on it, and then she said, 'I love you. I will miss you.' And I felt sorry, not as much for her as for myself, because I had lost the ability to love and I had metamorphosed into another Alessandro. I felt the need to explain to her that we were experiencing our loneliness differently; she was looking for somebody to share it with while for me it was an unbreakable sanctuary, a shelter of self-absorption, a deserted island where the silence could only be broken by familiar sounds like the whispers of the winds and the mumbling of the waves with their discreet messages and unobtrusive implications— most importantly where words did not exist.

Instead, I said, 'I would love you too if I could love at all.'

She followed by asking what I meant, and I replied with other senseless streams of words that flowed smoothly, but neither of us could understand their meaning and that I barely remember, while I remember her silent eyes looking into mine, the sorrowful smile, and her last hug. Some may wonder what happened to Shirley and me. It would be inaccurate to say that we never saw each other again and such beautiful moments passed together were never reproduced elsewhere on other occasions, but this is beyond the point of the story and we, therefore, will let Shirley's character rest in Monte Carlo where it belongs safe and sound.

Alessandro took me to the train station on the red Ferrari, and both tanned and wearing Ray-Ban sunglasses received curious and envious looks from many who saw in us the ultimate gratification. We joked a little and laughed a little; we mostly remained silent. When the train was leaving, I said goodbye from the window, and this time I won the duel and shot him with my index finger before he could raise his. And he crossed his hands on his chest and he bent his neck as if he was going to die one last time, giving to me his beautiful smile. That was indeed the last time I saw Alessandro.

Looking at the French and then the Italian Riviera from the train, I wondered about my future. I wondered about how much I was turning into another Alessandro. Yet there was a big difference; as he had said, at least I had a life to go back to, books and expectations, aspirations and the comforting feeling that if I would work hard enough something good and unexpected would materialise in the future that I could not imagine in the present. And then I compared my life with Alessandro's and how his self-destructive existence was aligned with his beliefs much more than the constructive default I was following, which did not match at all my nihilistic views. And I reckoned that, in the end, he was the one between the two of us who stood taller, who was consistent with its own philosophy while I was just deceiving myself to comply with conventionality. And I also knew that I would never have the courage to veer from my own conformist choice. But then I was still young, and if things did not make sense, it did not matter that much because there was the future ahead and I was subconsciously still under the illusion that something miraculous would serendipitously happen somewhere, someday, which would explain it all.

VIII

A Love Story

On the following day, my uncle was recounting a well-known episode about the renovation of Pizzo's old train station, when il Marchese and I joined.

*   *   *

'I remember that glorious station of when we were young. We would go there to wait for the soldiers coming from the war or our relatives coming back from wherever they had immigrated. We would go to pick them up with horse-drawn carriages. And we waited for hours and hours because the trains were never on time. But it was a beautiful station, with a bocce ball court in front under the eucalyptus trees. So we played or watched people play till the train arrived, and we were disappointed if the train arrived in the middle of a game. And there was a great bar, with granite[86] and lemonades, great panini with salami. It was a real feast.

'But like many things, the good times at the station vanished. Most young people left for the North and became immigrants themselves. Only the old men remained there to play bocce ball. With time, the poor old station withstood a few earthquakes. In spite of its resilience, after the last one, it was condemned and the trains were suspended from stopping there.

---

[86] Flavoured water ice beverage.

'A decade later, a new mayor, who remembered the glory of the little station from his own youth, stirred a great effort to raise the money to restore it to the celebrated times. Finally, when everything was ready for the inauguration, the Napitini thought it sensible to coincide the event with the return of the first train to Pizzo. Therefore, the municipality of Pizzo prepared a courteous letter to the Ferrovie dello Stato[87] to inform them of the completed restoration, offering the services of the reborn station. Unfortunately, the reply was that although the Ferrovie dello Stato were very impressed with the quality of the described renovation, since a new railway had successfully replaced the old one with direct lines all the way to the main cities, for the time being no trains were likely to transit and even less likely to stop in such an obsolete corner of the world. Therefore, the inauguration was held without trains of any sort, and the old bocce ball field is still hosting unending games without concerns about a train ever disrupting the participants' engagement.'

*   *   *

'This is what I call strategic planning!' concluded my uncle. 'It may seem a strange story, but you have no idea how many stories like this I witnessed in my years as a banker. You have no idea what people bet on without bothering to ask the simplest questions first!'

With unclear logic of association, il Dottore Riga, recounting his Chinese zodiac allegory about which he held a special infatuation, proclaimed, 'It is true that we carry so many lives in one, often unaware of what we or others will be or will want the following day. It is truly like the Chinese say, except we breathe those lives contemporarily rather than sequentially as l'Avvocato stated a few days ago. You can say the same for things around us. People live parallel lives and do not bother looking one inch past their nose till the need comes.'

As I was trying to dissect the logic within the aforementioned statement, il Professore added, 'I agree with you, and although you are speaking figuratively, there may be some truth in reality. I was thinking about what Pinuzzo, the son of the pharmacist, who is studying at La Scuola

---

[87] Italian railway system.

Normale of Pisa,[88] told me recently. We do not experience it, but in fact there is not only one universe but also several intertwined. According to the string theory, there is a multiverse where many things happen at one time, but because the different entities do not interact with one another we are not aware of it. Maybe, we ourselves have different lives, but we are aware of only one at the time. Maybe trains are stopping at the little station in another universe that coexists with ours but we cannot experience.'

Mastro Antonio, corrugating his forehead and raising his right eyebrow, interjected against this theory, 'I beg your pardon, signori miei.[89] What stringa[90] theory here and stringa theory there? That Pinuzzo is so spacey that he could not even use a stringa to tie his shoes!' Thereby settling with such eloquent, persuasive, and conclusive logic a salient and controversial topic of contemporary physics. It was later disclosed, in Mastro Antonio's absence, that his antipathy for the string theory and scepticism towards the multiverse could be at least partly explained by the fact that the pharmacist had not as yet paid him for some services he provided in relation to a country house. But we will leave this metaphysical discussion for another occasion.

While we were all absorbing in silence Mastro Antonio's wisdom in an attempt to extract some redeeming sense from the aforementioned conclusions, il Marchese who had inadvertently checked his shoelaces with composure, after scratching his sideburn with the right index finger and then moving his cane from the right to his left hand, interrupted the silence, saying, 'I also have a story related to Alessandro that I could share with you in confidence, my dear friends.'

*　　*　　*

Several years ago, I roamed the streets of life, as sometimes I still do, cognisant of the most unusual circumstance. I realised that I had died

---

[88]   Well-known physics university in Pisa.

[89]   My sirs.

[90]   String in English sounds like stringa in Italian, which means 'shoelace', hence the confusion of poor Mastro Antonio.

during that complicated moment of life corresponding to the watershed that separates youth from adulthood. I could not even recollect how and why, and meanwhile my body continued to wander around as if it was still alive.

At the beginning, I felt its stench because of the decomposition, but eventually I got used to it. Funny thing is that nobody ever noticed. Once a guy was upset with me because inadvertently I cut the line, and he grew even angrier because I did not bother apologising. How would he know that for dead people these are frivolous niggles? As I was trying to get into the conversation, he got close to me as to punch me, but when I looked at him with my empty eyes, he stopped, and when we stared at each other and he met beyond my pupils the abyss of bleakness, his anger turned into fear, and he backed up and disappeared in the crowd. Funny thing how the living fears us, the dead!

Of course, I still had a wife then, who tormented me with intrusive sweetness and care, who told me that I should take more regularly my stimulants to improve my mood as if you could temperate the atmosphere of the dry desert by painting it green. And when she looked at me, she still could see in me the man who had long gone. Sometimes her care made me wonder whether I was still alive, but then a quick look into the mirror to see my own corpse and my silent eyes clarified things, and I did not feel sorry or sad. I just did not feel anything because I was dead.

And of course, I had a lover . . . actually more than one. Nice women, all telling wonderful things to me about me. All convinced that they understood me more than anybody else, as if there was anything to understand, but missing the fact that I was not there because I was dead. And this partly was my fault. I misled each one of them by pretending I cared, and I misled my wife also, pretending I cared. Why did I lie? It bequeathed a recollection of what life used to be. It reminded me of my youth games, of the excitement I felt for the scent of a woman. It is not that I missed those things, but the contrast interested me. It was odd to see how little I cared about those same things that drove my earlier life. And yet I was still quite young compared with what I am now. I was in my late thirties.

But then, listen to what happened to me! I met a woman while spending a vacation at the bath of Catulle in Sirmione. She was quite young, in her early thirties and pretty. She wore a kind and simple conduct, natural in expression, fair in judgment, confident in the tone of the voice, as it is unusual for a young lady. She had a charming smile and she looked to me as alive and as enthusiastic as a Bambi. No surprise, I was attracted to her, and for a moment I forgot that I was dead.

We were talking while we sat upon velvet chairs in a hotel lobby. And we had a drink. I had a glass of wine and she had tea. We were having a pleasant conversation that I could not repeat in detail, but it was something at the same time frivolous and thoughtful when suddenly, out of the blue, she asked me, 'Do you ever experience days when you do not feel like doing anything?'

I said, 'Yes, of course, all the time. But why did you ask me?'

'Don't know . . . I often want to ask this question, but I do not know to whom. You made me feel comfortable. I thought you would understand.'

It was then that I realised that she was just as dead as I was. This is also how we became lovers. But this time it was a different kind of affair.

It was a complicated affair; first, because she was married and she had a young son. She had left her husband and child at home, encouraged by her doctor to take a break to recover her nerves since she had been quite spent during the last few months. Baths were thought to offer astonishing solutions for health problems, and such solutions were more likely to succeed the more impalpable the essence of the problem; therefore, bad humours following a pregnancy, which in later times would have been called post-partum depression, were among the ailments most likely to be addressed by the salty and warm waters.

As a second complication, she was from Pizzo and from a visible family. She had come there because it was a place popular among the upper class from our parts and close to Milan, where she frequently spent time to be close to her husband and son. It was a place far from the eyes of our peers, except of course for those who happened to be there coincidentally. She had no specific expectations by coming to the baths since she had simply succumbed to the habits of the society to which she belonged, to the enthusiastic recommendations of the family doctor and the tender encouragement of her husband.

Third and most important, she was not there looking for romance. Rather, the innocent soul fell into the trap of love as candidly as a starving mouse in the presence of cheese. But as you very well know, these meek and naive women, when they fall in love unarmed, cause the most problems for the seasoned predators, for those hunters who can cruelly kill powerful lions but cannot execute their cubs. You just do not know how to get rid of these meek women; you feel sorry and protective, and you postpone the dismissal till it is too late, and before you know, you are just as in love and trapped.

After the drinks, I asked her to come for a walk along the lake and she agreed with a smile, but she wanted to change into more comfortable attire. We walked to her hotel while the sun was about to set over Gardone. A thin and cool breeze softly refreshed the air. Nobody seemed to be around, spare for a few dogs sniffing around or cats furtively crossing the road to hide under a bench or behind a tree. A few couples were walking at a distance, and the gravel under our steps with its crushing sound caused the only disturbance.

When we reached the hotel, I offered to go up to her suite to wait while she changed. She did not refute, and furtively, we walked across the lobby. We went up two flights of stairs and entered the place. It was by then dusk, and I walked towards the balcony in the drawing room to open the window. I stepped out to admire the evening and the view of the lake with the newborn lights from the distant towns along the lakeshore and from ferryboats crossing the lake. The breeze had turned into a sustained yet gentle wind that was muddling my hair and provocatively rearranging hers when she joined me to oversee the scenery.

She had not even started to change. She looked around as if she was surprised to be there. The beautiful creature then rested her hands on the rail while the stretched arms held the rest of her tiny body straight. Her neck was slightly bent forward and the head was leaning down. Her stillness and silence and the appearance of meditation aroused tenderness in me. I had no bad intentions when I had come up to the suite except for the simple desire to be with her all along, not to miss any moment with this beautiful and unassuming woman. But her naked neck, the fluttering dark hair over it, the meditative look induced me to touch her shoulder. She shivered at that touch although it was not cold, and this shiver induced me to hug her gently first and tightly after. She did not resist and the hug continued for an undetermined time. She kept looking down while I touched her skin with my lips and kissed her neck, and unhurriedly my lips moved along her cheeks till they met hers and we kissed. It was a gentle and not passionate kiss, the kiss that a girl would give a baby doll that she holds in her arms. But after that kiss, another followed and another with increasing passion. Her body yielded to my stronger one; she let herself be held against me tighter and tighter. She leant her head against my shoulder, her arms around my neck, and she kissed me of her own initiative. Then she looked straight into my eyes with a corrugated expression and asked, 'Can I trust you?'

Just as two negatives make a positive, two dead people can make a living soul. Suddenly, I did not feel alone any more; by holding this meek and defenceless woman in my arms, I gained a strength that I had not experienced for a long time. We did not go for any walk that evening, but we spent the night in her suite and for several nights afterwards. During the day, we took long walks along the lakeshore or we took a ferryboat to the other side of the Lake of Garda, to the hills above Gardone; we visited Il Vittoriale,[91] and we visited orchards to the east of the lake or hiked the mountains to find wild mushrooms. Throughout those activities, we talked and talked. It was a natural exchange, spontaneous and honest such as I had never experienced with my wife or other women before, and I do not know why she could extract the best out of me.

'Do you know I think I am starting to love you?' she suddenly said.

I did not know what to reply, and without saying anything, I held her with my arm around her waist and we continued to walk in silence. It was only after about a quarter of an hour when we sat on a bench

---

[91]   The Vittoriale degli italiani (The shrine of Italian victories) is an estate in the town of Gardone overlooking the lake of Garda where the Italian writer Gabriele d'Annunzio lived from 1922 until his death in 1938.

overlooking a small pier devoid of boats, washed by gentle waves that had been stirred by the evening breeze, that I whispered, 'I love you too.'

She told me her story—that she had been married through an arranged marriage at a very young age to a man she barely knew. Her husband was a good person who treated her with devotion, but he had entered her life through the wrong door. He was quite older than she was, and she felt he had bought her with his money through her parents rather than conquering her heart with the flowers of romance. He also was a practical and honourable family man, a successful businessman. He had rebuilt from the ruins of war the family business. He had lived to restore the respect and honour that the family deserved. But he was shy in personal matters and uncommunicative.

The honeymoon was spent in Milan where his business was. They went to La Scala a few times, but he was distracted and eager to leave before the end of the opera to avoid the rush at the end of the performance. He would take her for short walks at the Giardini Pubblici.[92] But they had nothing to say to each other. He was absorbed in his own worries, and even if she asked about them, he would simply reply, 'Nothing important. Nothing you would care about.' And he would add some non-sequitur such as 'It is so strange how people expect things that they do not deserve . . .' or 'I believe I have always tried to do my best. Hopefully, some day we will see the results.'

It was soon apparent that there was no reason for those walks; there was no joy in being alone together with his wife but rather an imposition on his time and on his emotions, and he found shelter completely in his business.

Time passed and a baby boy came; it took years for this to happen. But when the miracle occurred; she realised that the excitement experienced during the gestation had rapidly been tainted by conflicting emotions. Why bring to life another miser? Would the life of the poor boy be just as insignificant as her own was? After the boy was born, she carried him around with a love tainted by sadness, as if the boy had an incurable

---

[92] Public gardens.

ailment, a meagre future ahead of him, a disease called life. And she could not understand the excitement around her, the congratulation for the masculine creation, the vague promises of unending happiness, of future fulfilment of indeterminate expectations. She was soon diagnosed with post-partum depression or whatever might have been called at those times and she was sent a few months later, just after her son had turn one year old, to the Baths.

I held her in my arms and felt sorry for her. I heedlessly made promises I had never made before, confident that they would be forgotten as soon as their sound had dissipated in the crisp mountain air. Yet, deep inside, I realised that I meant every word I said and that I loved this innocent soul.

She was worried about her baby boy, whom she had left at home; she was worried even about her husband, whom she was betraying for a little corner of happiness, and she was worried about me and worried about what would happen after those few days of fulfilment. The only person she was not interested in was herself. Each night, she held me tight, and she snuggled around the curves of my body not falling asleep till late. And when she did, she would have agitated dreams. She would produce gentle squeals; she would say words that made no sense. And I would touch her breasts gently to make her relax. She would draw a deep sigh and would go back at least momentarily into a peaceful sleep.

One time, she asked me in a whisper, 'Am I just one of your many women?' And since I did not reply, pretending I was asleep, she continued, 'I do not care. I am grateful for the happiness you give me.'

When the time came for her to go home, we spent the last day walking along the lakeshore, silently holding hands. In the previous days, we had been worried that somebody from our place could see us and we avoided any public show of intimacy. But that morning, we forgot about any precautions. I held her tight close to me while I rested my back against the railing of a pier, and I told her that I loved her and that I would for the rest of my life.

'I know!' she said. 'But after today, you will forget about me. I want you to. I cannot hurt my husband and I have a little boy waiting for me. It has been a beautiful dream, and I want to keep it in my heart just as that . . . forever a beautiful dream.'

I accompanied her to the station, and after the train disappeared in the distance, I felt a sense of relief. Perhaps she had been right; the path we were going to embark would have been impossible and painful for us and for others. I recognised that she was right and I was just as happy to return to my previous Pygmalion's free style.

But such relief did not last long. Walking back to my hotel, I retraced our steps. I went by her hotel where I had spent the last fortnight and looked up at the window where we had been so happy for a few days of eternity. I looked at the little tables outside where we had coffee in the morning, at the gardens where we walked side by side and where I felt a profound desire to touch her and hold her. I recollected how simple was my happiness just when her eyes turned towards me, when I could touch her arm furtively, and how powerful was the effect of such simple contact. By night-time, I had realised that there would not be an end.

There was no solution to loneliness except for the acceptance of staying alone. Since she had left, I had been lost in a whirlpool of emotions. I spent long nights staying awake, thinking that any moment could be the one when she would go back to her husband. I tried not to feel anger but happiness for her, for him and for her life returning to normality. And I recalled all the lost opportunities when I could have told her one more time that I loved her or I could have shown her one more time how much I loved her.

I questioned my resolve. Could I go back to Pizzo and rescue her from her miserable life? Would she want for me to do that? Would I have the courage to first settle my lifelong problems with my own life? I tried to argue with myself that it was just a silly infatuation; she was just another beautiful woman and I was lucky to have had her graces for a little while and now be free without any accountability. Isn't it what the love game is all about? I wondered who would be next, and I tried to anticipate the flavour of the new conquest. But nobody could take her place even in my imagination, and after so many days of glacial solitude, by the time I had to go back to Pizzo I had made up my mind in opposite directions about 1,000 times. Finally, sitting on the train and seeing Italy pass before my eyes, I reached the only realistic compromise: 'Let's see what happens when I get there!'

As soon as I returned, I started to plot ways to see her. It was difficult to be discreet since she belonged to an eminent family, but most importantly it was impossible because she had made herself completely unavailable to strangers. One day, I received a letter from her:

My dear,

> Please forgive me from breaking my resolution to totally sever our communication in matters of love, but I need to reach out to you because I thought you had to know. My period has been delayed and I am sure I am pregnant. If this is the case, I want you to know that I want to carry your baby and I will hold him dear for the rest of my life as if it was you in my arms when I will carry him or her around. I know that you would want to care for the baby as well, but please, for his or her happiness, do not. Let the innocent soul live a regular life with a regular family. The innocent will be well cared by me and by my husband since he is a good and caring person. He or she will miss nothing. I believe that this is a gift of God to us and we should cherish and at the same time sacrifice our own gratification for his or her chances of happiness.

With eternal love,
Yours forever
Anita

. . . And this is how Alessandro was born.

. . . Love is a bumpy road, with twists and turns and a lot of loneliness. It is a force that bursts out of our ego at first, but feeds only on our selflessness. Years passed and things remained as they were supposed to. Alessandro grew up and I barely saw him on occasions. He was a handsome boy, full of spirit and confidence. He lived in prosperity surrounded by a protective family. Besides the mother, he had a wonderful grandmother and a caring father who took care of him lovingly. He had no needs and I could not even imagine what I could offer in excess of what he already had. Meanwhile, I had no children of my own and I knew I would never have. I would not even want any because I loved Alessandro and his mother and I was just as happy to know that they were doing well in the comfort of a nurturing family.

More years passed, and Alessandro left to study in Milano. Then his mother died of cancer and a little later his father did. It was then that the craving to connect with him besieged me. I frantically wanted to know where he was and how he was carrying on now that he had been left alone to master his life. Of course, I would not disclose our relationship although I had often wondered how it could have been possible for nobody to notice our resemblance: the blue eyes, the slender body, and the dimples in our smiles. I just wanted to have a chance to be close to him and offer some friendship if that could ever be possible without being too intrusive.

Since he never came back to Pizzo after his father's death, I contacted his brother Achille, who was a successful banker in Rome, with the most reasonable excuse that I was going to be in town for a personal affair and I would enjoy reconnecting with the progeny of family friends. Achille was most cordial and happy to host a pleasurable dinner at the Parioli,[93] where he lived, and I went there with trepidation.

The dinner was elegant because Achille and his wife were trying to be graceful to an old family friend and at the same time they were genuinely touched that I remembered them. Two beautiful children were running around, busy in their own world of fantasy and totally independent from the adults. There was also an aged and thoughtful aristocat that came to sniff my attire to test my rank in society and the propriety of my presence. Satisfied with the results, he lay by my side, stretching and closing its paws against my leg as if it was knitting dough. I was reassured that its claws were regularly clipped and in fact the massage was pleasant and not painful. Many other irrelevant things happened or were discussed, including the conversion from the Lira to the Euro and how there was no point in resisting this transition but rather figuring out from a financial point of view how to take advantage of it. And while Achille

---

[93] Upscale district of Rome.

kept discussing worldly matters, the wife contributed at times anecdotes about the children who coincidentally happened to be the best creatures in the world. After the appetisers and cocktails, supper was served with the usual unpretentious elegance of Roman dinners—special cold cuts from Northern and Southern Italy, seafood salad, a simple pasta cacio pepe[94] but sprinkled with grated black truffles, veal with Marsala and a touch of exotic cumin and so many other amenities that contributed to a seemingly endless dinner.

It was only at the time dedicated to the ritualistic after-dinner drink consisting of Venetian Grappa that I managed the courage to bring Alessandro into the conversation by casually asking, 'How is your brother doing?'

From the reaction, it was immediately clear that I was not about to hear good news.

Achille became suddenly thoughtful and looked around to see if the children were listening, and after looking at his wife, he turned to me and said, 'Alessandro has Aids and he is in the hospital in Milano.' Not being familiar about what Aids was at that time (it was the middle 1990s), I modestly asked what it was.

Achille stood up. 'It is a new disease. They say it comes from a virus called acca vu.[95] It affects the blood cells and when you are affected you cannot fight infections.'

When I asked where he got it, he seemed embarrassed. 'I do not know. They say that homosexuals acquire the disease through their practices, but Alessandro is not homosexual. He had a troubled life after he finished the university. I have not had much contact with him. It is not because of me. I love my brother, but he has been evasive. He visited only when each child was born but never after. It was difficult to follow his whereabouts and I learnt of the hospitalisation only through friends

---

[94] Pasta with cheese (pecorino cheese) and pepper, the true version of Fettuccine Alfredo.

[95] Italian way to pronounce HV for HIV.

of friends. I did not even know whether he wanted for me to visit him or whether he would be ashamed of receiving me. In the end I went. I found him in a good mood, almost as if he had been relieved by the burdening expectations of life. He cheered me up and we chatted about the old times, about our arguments around the old children table, our silly cousins. He even talked about an old cousin of ours, a woman we were very fond of during our youth! He asked if I knew what happened to her. Ironically I had never seen him as happy and relaxed in spite of the terminal disease. I asked whether he needed money or any other help, but he seemed in great shape, taken care of by good friends who had grown to be doctors and with plenty of reserves from the inheritance. He has been in and out of the hospital with different infections. The doctors told me that his case was progressing much faster than others and that his lymphocytes were very low. In other words, it looked like he will die soon.

'. . . A movie just came out entitled *Philadelphia* with Tom Hanks in it. It is about a man who acquired Aids. When I heard about it, I went to see it to understand my brother's situation. It is a touching story. Although Alessandro has lived a promiscuous life, he told me he never had homosexual relationships or practiced drugs. He was exposed through unprotected sex and he even knows the woman who gave it to him. She did not know about having acquired the disease. She learnt later on that she contracted the infection from a casual encounter with a guy who had been taking intravenous drugs.

'. . . It is amazing to me that I am talking like this about Alex! But this is his story. I hope you will understand and forgive him. He was always a good person. He did not hurt anybody, and although we were not that close, we sensed each other's presence and felt comfort in knowing that either was there for the other. When he dies, I will be the only one left among all the family.'

Achille suddenly ended the emotional and disconnected narrative and stared at me, scrutinising my reaction. It is impossible to explain the way I felt. You see, we make mistakes when we are young and pay for them as we grow older and older. I agonised throughout life because of the forced separation from my son. And now that I might have had a chance to be of use to him and an opportunity to develop some sort of relationship,

I was hearing that he was about to die. I could not say anything, and consequently, Achille assumed that I was reserving my judgment while I was looking for words to gracefully disguise my contempt by offering superficial soupçons of empathy. Finally, as I recovered from my reflections, I said, 'I am so sorry to hear about this! You are right. He is such a kind and generous soul. I did not have a chance to be close to him, but I did observe him grow. I would love to visit him if you think it would be acceptable to him. I will have to be in Milano in the near future anyways for business and I could drop by.'

'I am sure he would appreciate that,' replied Achille.

Alessandro had been in a private hospital room for the last two weeks. It seemed that each time he recovered from one infection another supervened. When I entered the room, my heart was thumping. A woman was sitting close to his bed reading a book while Alessandro was dozing. She had the face of an angel, and for a second, I wondered whether she was made of flesh or truly was Alessandro's guardian angel.

Whispering, I introduced myself as an old family friend who happened to be in Milano. She smiled at me and said in broken Italian, 'Io sono Ophelia, amica di Alessandro. Alessandro dormire adesso . . . Stato sveglio tutta notte.'[96]

The sunrays peeking through the curtains landed gently upon her thin lips and made her hesitant smile more radiant. There was some softness and comfort in the silence that ensued, as if we were in a sacred place. I looked at Alessandro sleeping peacefully; he had not changed much since I last saw him except for a few violaceous plaques—one on his right left cheek partially hidden by the sideburn, one in his left forearm, and another one on his chest. His handsome curly hair had been recently trimmed and he had been keeping up with shaving. I felt like touching his hand and caressing him, but I refrained, reminding myself that I was only an old family friend. I smiled at her and told her in my own broken English, 'You can take a break if you would like. I can stay here for a

---

[96]   I am Ophelia, friend of Alessandro. Alessandro sleeping now. He was awake all night.

while. I have nothing to do all day.' She seemed to understand, and with the same gentle smile impressed upon her face, she gathered a few things, placed them in a tiny purse, and left without looking back.

I sat where she had been sitting. The chair was still warm and the silence grew heavier in the room. I looked around, and the bareness of the chamber with no flowers, photos, or other comforting objects impressed me. It was just a tidy room furnished with a bed and a sofa that stood close to the window, which in turn looked out towards the crowded street with its distant noises produced by people and cars just to enhance the depth of the inner silence.

Time passed. I moved the chair that had been placed parallel to Alessandro, looking away from him in the opposite direction to allow myself to observe for the first time my son from a close distance. And I recalled . . . I recalled his mother, that gentle Anita. I admired how strong she had been in keeping me away from her and from her son to give him peace and a family for all these years, and I wondered whether it had been the right thing to do. In our time, in our place, there was no question that it had been not only the right but also the only option.

And I recalled my anguish . . . I remembered how I thought how inconsistent that little woman had been; I knew that she nurtured her love for me throughout her life, and yet she shun away from me—like a moth that craves the light but dwells in nocturnal existence, avoiding the sun. I recalled my solitude, the long walks along the shore, wondering how she was doing and how my son was doing. I recalled my jealousies and apathies, my regrets, my . . . and all those emotions that gurgled out of the Pandora's box of my cursed life.

And I felt guilty, I could not say why. Was it the abandonment? God knows how much I would have loved to take care of him. I had just been prevented from doing it. Was it remorse for creating him in the wrong circumstances? But were they really such bad circumstances? In the end, he never knew anything about it and lived the most privileged life in one of the most prominent families. Or maybe Alessandro had unconsciously sensed that he never had his true father close to him? Was I guilty for not reaching out to him earlier after his parents died and before this catastrophe occurred? But how . . . ? How could I have justified my intervention? Was my guilt due to the unsettling notion that I had given to him my revolting genes of depravation? Had I created a monster in my own image?

Then I imagined that his mother was there looking at us, for the first time seeing from the sky the two of us together and blessing us with whatever power she might have had.

These and similar thoughts busied my mind while I sat and guarded Alessandro's repose.

This meditation could have lasted for an eternity if Alessandro hadn't suddenly opened his eyes and looked at the side where Ophelia was supposed to be, and in her absence, he stared at me.

Recovering after a few seconds of hesitation, he smiled and cordially pronounced in a low but jovial tone, 'What a surprise, Your Excellency! What brought you here?'

'I heard from your brother that you were sick and I wanted to pay a visit since I was in Milano for personal business. I was a good friend of your parents, and I thought they would want from up there for me to check on you and see if you are going to behave! Now tell me, is there anything I could do for you?'

Warming up to me, Alessandro went straight to the substance.

'Dear Marchese, I am going to die. It looks like I caught a very bad cold! And a cold that comes with a stigma . . . A friend's sister has entered hospice care for advanced cancer, which has spread to her lungs. I haven't seen her in years, so I sent her a note telling that I knew it is not easy. I was told that she was offended about the fact that I tried to contact her and compare her cancer to my filthy ailment. In reality, I had just been thinking of my mother and how she had suffered from the same disease. She did not write back.

'The discrimination really hits home. People see me differently now with the exception of a few loyal friends and sweet Ophelia, who came to live with me from America since she learnt about my condition, and she has not left me since then. And thus, I am happy to lie here like a doomed bug in a Kafkaesque position, like those cicadas that come out of their hibernation every so often, in the span of decades, and cover the ground, having sex all over the place till they die right after crawling for a few yards before turning upside down. Maybe this is the deserved punishment for a depraved and meaningless existence.

'You know . . . I spent my life riding on the back of the horizon astride the twilight in between the daylight and the darkness. The present has never represented for me more than the moment when the future turns into the past—when dreams, hopes, and fears turn into memories, nostalgia, and anguish. It is as if I have never lived my own life, but rather I posed as a bystander at the side of its turbulent flow. And now that I am approaching the end, I realise that there is no logical conclusion. I realise that life can unfold passively without following a rational progression—just a series of disconnected events that fill the time till the show is over. The quest for a meaning is a pointless exercise as there was no purpose to all from the inception.'

After a pause, he continued, 'Sometimes I experience the impulse to write the story of my life, just because it did not make any sense, just to share with people its absolute emptiness—letting them know that there is no need to dwell alone in despair, to recognise that nothingness is a companion to many more souls than we may appreciate, that there is no shame in roaming in the dark labyrinth of existence, that we cannot be blamed for our prodigal and wasteful existence since we did not have any choice but life was dealt to us without any chance to chose. The Bible is like a mountain that cannot be washed to the sea. It will stand for a long time, well beyond our lives. Sometimes harsh, sometimes difficult to understand, sometimes unfriendly, but it gathers the thoughts and the heritage from so many wise men. My tale will be a small part of the legacy of humanity, but if I leave it for others, maybe they will be touched by knowing that they are not alone.'

'I wish I could entice you to write a novel, a book filled with your reflections and memories,' I said to support his train of unbridled thoughts. 'You know, il Professore is retired now, and he is *a la reserche du temps perdue*,[97] particularly of his preferred students, and you were one

---

[97]   *Remembrance of Things Past*, novel by Marcel Proust.

of them. I am sure he can visit with you sometimes and he can help you write your memories.'

That was all the time we had. Ophelia had returned and was standing at the door; it was awkward for me to stay longer. I held his hand before leaving, and it was obvious to him that I was hesitant to release the grasp.

As I was leaving, Alessandro whispered, 'Do not be upset for me! I am just fine. I am attaining what I looked for all my life which is to disappear in oblivion. I would have never had the courage to kill myself, but now that death is approaching gently and softly, I am happy to accept it and return to the emptiness where I came from and where I always belonged.'

I promised to come back, and indeed, I did a few more times since business took me to Milan more often than one would have ever expected for a retired gentlemen. But the awkwardness of such behaviour never alerted Alessandro. Instead, he made all efforts to thank me repeatedly for staying close to him and ignoring the stigma of what he called '*his shameful finale*'.

The last time I saw him, Alessandro was in pain. Yet he received me with his cordial smile crowned by the familiar dimples. Before I left, I held his hand tightly as if to keep him from falling into the eternal darkness. He smiled again, and once again he reassured me, 'Do not worry about me. I am content.' Then in between spasms of abdominal pain, he looked over my shoulders, through the window, at the silent blue sky and at its indifferent clouds, searching not for an answer any more but just a sign or just anything from Up There.

*   *   *

That evening on arriving home, Signorino Giuseppe was delivered the message that his wife, who had not heard from him for days, had called several times, insisting that he should return her calls. He reluctantly walked to the den, searching for a peaceful corner to consummate the dreaded conversation. He had been too captivated by the languid life of Pizzo to be thrown into the old reality and to confront the unambiguous conversations that his wife was about to impose on him. It appeared to him that of late he had been surfing over an immense ocean, driven by currents as if he was a bottle adrift sent by a lonesome survivor to deliver a message that nobody would care to read. The life of Pizzo that he had carried in the third person during the last fortnight had suited him, with its tolerant demeanour, the lack of expectations for decisiveness, its apathetic pace bordering into stillness and a timelessness that would have been absolute if the church bells had not taken upon themselves to carry forward the process of time.

The conversation started on the wrong foot and quickly went awry because his wife pre-empting any apologies asked unwaveringly why he had not bothered calling for the last few days and did not even bother to return her calls. Why did he only reply to her emails with succinct and trivial statements? What message was he trying to convey to her with his dismissive behaviour? And there were other questions along the same line that, although understandable from her point of view, made increasingly uncomfortable the already confused mind of poor Giuseppe.

He would have liked to explain about dogs roaming the streets searching for ghosts from the past, about flapping fish in the bag, about old friends, about ladróns and murderers, about suicides and ancestors' portraits. But he knew that sharing his confusion from past to present and then to future and offering other indeterminate arguments would not satisfy the decisive and stringent logic of his wife; her conviction was that actions are prompted by resolve, that effects are the linear result of a discernible cause.

He also wanted to explain about Don Pino and il Marchese and of noble mistakes and lost opportunities, about l'Avvocato and his habit to fold his handkerchief elegantly after expectorating half cup of a yellow greenish phlegm into it with the nonchalance of a seasoned diplomat, about the infinite plains of Mongolia, and how the village idiot and other craved people had an obscure yet legitimate reason to exist . . . And he also wanted to share how all those images congregated into the abstract canopy of his mind, how they persisted in his memory, becoming a predominant portion of his own thoughts and distracting him within the seclusion of Pizzo from his other realities anxiously waiting on the other side of the Atlantic.

But he could not even initiate this conversation. His mind seemed frozen, and it could not articulate a compelling sentence; everything seemed too abstract and impalpable and could not be packaged into a logical argument.

Therefore, after she asked him once more, 'Why didn't you call me?' he simply whispered, 'I do not know!'

The phone was hung on the other side, and the subsequent silence came as a relief for Giuseppe, who hated confrontation at the point of accepting any loss as the result of inaction. He also felt satisfaction in the reaffirmation that he could not be understood, that life is better lived alone, that he should jealously preserve the one relationship that counted—the one with one's own self, with the only entity who could understand. And with this narcissistic reaffirmation, Signorino Giuseppe left the den and went to the kitchen to open the refrigerator and pour for himself a full glass of Critone.

When his mother asked him how things were going on in America, he coldly replied, 'Tutto bene . . . ottimamente bene.'[98]

Following dinner, after the stentorian voice of Don Pino and his affable personality had vanished from the table and the night had regained its meditative mood, Signorino Giuseppe walked to the den, away from his relatives, searching for the silent company of his ancestors. He carried in his right hand a crystal cup with a few drops of grappa. He carefully set the cup on top of the desk and subsequently rested the same hand over the landline phone. He meant to call his wife to apologise. But he hesitated while he tried to compose a compelling justification for his behaviour. Suddenly, his hand released the phone, and he regained hold of the cup. He gulped down the grappa as he stood up to leave the room. It had occurred to him that his failure to articulate a reasonable explanation had nothing to do with the momentary panic and the psychological block of a confrontation with his wife. It was rather due to the fact that there was no explanation at all, that there were no gripping circumstances to redeem his conduct since his life had no logic progression at all and his behaviour was simply reflecting such reality. He recognised that there was no compelling excuse to offer to

---

[98] Everything is fine . . . perfectly fine.

his wife because his whole existence was the result of an entanglement of uncontrollable events, of passive acceptances, of actions that were rather reactions to occasional situations rather than the result of wilful decisions. Most importantly, he had accepted that there was no foreseeable solution because he would never manage to find the determination required to shift the course of his own life.

IX

Epilogue

I probably could have done a better job in reporting the events, and it occurs to me that, due to my inexperience in writing novels, this story was written upside down, from the end to the beginning. I have used this strategy previously when preparing scientific commentaries. I like to present the conclusion first and then dissect the steps leading to it. But then, isn't it the way life is? In many ways, true life starts at its crepuscule while all that precedes it is just in preparation. The revelation of its essence comes, if ever, at the end when most has passed. Only then we wish to revisit the sequence of those seemingly fortuitous events to which we barely paid any attention in our youth and yet led to its conclusion. Only then we appreciate the continuum and we wish to reconcile the causes with their effect while we attempt to weigh the significance of our existence.

In reality, someone's life is of consequence or trivial according to the scale by which it is measured. Measured in units of eternity, even Genghis Khan's existence would seem inconsequential. A few years from now, Alessandro's story, like that of all of us, will cease to exist. But while sitting at the tavolino in the little town of Pizzo, Alessandro's odyssey appeared to us just as palpable as fresh water from a mountain spring appears to the bare hands.

Alessandro's chronicle is composite and was only known by him. It would have gone lost and his memory would have gradually faded within pity and contempt for a wasted life if, by a twist of fate, il Marchese had not been encouraged to confess to il Professore. Certainly, these notes do not redeem him totally for his prodigality, but at least they offer deeper roots to the existence of 'a plant that that bore beautiful flowers but never yielded fruits' as Alessandro's dad had prophesied many years before. I believe that while we all reckoned how much of his cryptic life had passed undetected under our own eyes, we wondered how much had gone through each other's life that would stay buried under the sheets of eternity.

But let's go to the conclusion of our story.

On the last day of the fortnight in Pizzo, I met il Marchese al Castello Murat. After drinking the customary latte di mandorla and a cappuccino, instead of walking to the tavolino, we took a steep incline originating from the seaward side of the Chiazza called la salita dei morti.[99] It is probably so named because it is the path that takes to the cemetery, which resides on top of the hill and like a cougar inspecting its kingdom from the crest of a boulder patiently waits for its game. With slow steps, we climbed to the highest point, and then we took the flat road that completes the distance to the place of eternal rest.

Entering the cemetery, the visitor is affected immediately by the silence and peace surrounding the marble monuments that have been lying unchanged for decades under the shade. The pine and the cypress trees offer a fragrance of conifer as they are gently shaken by a constant breeze, possibly commanded by the Omnipotent to relieve with a wisp of gaiety the austerity and sorrow of the place.

A few steps to the right of the main entrance, a chapel stands without names at the door. There Alessandro is resting together with his ancestors.

Il Marchese gently pushed the gate built of solid iron, creating a passage for our entry and for a glimmer of light that revived the memory of the dead. In oblong compartments coated in marble, the names of Nonna, of Alessandro's father and of his mother, and Alessandro's name could be read, slowly . . . one at a time, as if they were credits cast at the end of a movie.

---

[99]   The climb of the dead.

As I was holding il Marchese by the arm, I wondered in which direction were their bodies lying. Where was the head? That lack of information bothered me as if that detail was the only impediment to my reconnection with the old friend.

As the eye adjusted to the darkness, I noticed fresh flowers at the base of Alessandro's tombstone, some fresh gladioli and in a corner a bouquet of gardenias. I also noted at the end of his mother's plate a white rose. It was a sad and lonely flower, not as fresh as the other ones. I asked il Marchese where the flowers came from.

'I come to the cemetery as often as I can. It is the only distraction I have. Sometimes I come in the morning, sometimes in the afternoon. When I have the energy, I walk an extra kilometre to the nursery to buy flowers— colourful ones for Alessandro and a white rose for Anita. Of course, I feel that I should buy flowers also for the other tenants, but then I figure that they would not be welcome. But these fresh flowers did not come from me. I am not the only one who visits the place . . .'

In fact, a few minutes later, as we were absorbed in our own thoughts, the gate squeaked and opened a little further. More light penetrated into the chapel, and with it a woman of around sixty appeared, still quite beautiful in her elegant stiffness. As I was attempting to recall the familiar look, she said, 'How nice to see you again, Jewyseppe. It has been such a long time!'

It was Ophelia, holding red carnations in the right hand and extending the other arm to give me a hug. 'Il Marchese has been kind enough to let me stay at his villa in the country when I visit Pizzo, and I have been taking advantage of the offer since I have nowhere else to go. Pizzo is a beautiful place, just as beautiful as Alessandro described it.'

The three of us sat at the entrance of the chapel. After a while, she rose and taking a broom from a corner she swept the floor inside first and then outside while il Marchese and I watched. Then she returned to sit close to us. She stared at me and said, 'You are still the same impertinent-looking young boy I remember from Monte Carlo. Shirley eventually remarried, do you know? . . . And she has two children now. She is happy back in America, but she often talks about you. You should write to her sometimes.'

I smiled and replied, 'I will someday.'

Later on, I spoke, 'I admire Alessandro above all of us. He is the only one who carried a life consistent with his beliefs. We compromise day after day. We believe that we are doing the right thing, sacrificing ourselves to follow the path pre-determined by societal wisdom. We live like puppets held by the invisible strings of conventionality, which we are afraid to break. Alessandro had everything that anybody could want, but for him, all of it was just a distraction. He understood that life has no beginning or end, has no cause or effect. It has no meaning beyond its passive flow along a river that we call time. Contrary to us, he did not lie to himself. He did what we do not have the courage to do. He looked straight in the eyes of emptiness and defied it but building an even bigger one. I am proud of my friend.'

Following my words, il Marchese smirked and said, 'Yup! He may be happy now, certainly happier than when he was alive.'

Then il Marchese seized his cane resting by the side of the marble bench. He stood up and pronounced, 'It is time to go.' Ophelia on one side and I on the other took the respective arm of il Marchese, who still distracted by his own thoughts allowed us to guide him without reticence against the obsequious act. As we exited the cemetery, he escaped our grasp, and resuming the function of the cane, he walked in front of us towards the town of the living, towards the old Chiazza where his surviving friends were waiting for him.

*   *   *

Later that morning, in an impulse to confess to my sins, I met Don Pino at the Spuntone and we sat together on a bench facing the sea. I did not even try to enumerate all the sins collected from the last confession from half a century before. They were too many and too boring to mention. Thus, I focused on the biggest of all, the wickedness that sculpted my existence: lack of faith.

I said, 'It is not just lack of faith in God, but it is a greater scourge. I do not believe in my marriage, my profession, my relationships, the bustling of people, the sunrise and the sunset, the stars and the galaxies. It seems

to me that everything is just an illusion. I cannot empathise with any
of the things that are commonly experienced by most people as reality.
The doctor calls it organic depression and he gives me pills that make me
sleep better. But at best, such medicaments are just as good as your Pater
Nosters and Ave Marias. The truth is that cynicism is not a disease but
an actuality that sits on the driver's seat, a wickedness against not only
God but against life itself . . . And there is no solution that I know of . . .
Neither I believe that there is penitence and forgiveness because I know
that I will never change . . . not because I do not want to but because I
cannot.'

Don Pino took a deep sigh, and crossing his hands over his chest, he said,
'Ego te absolvo a peccatis tuis in nomine Patris et Fili and Spiritus Sancti,
Amen.[100] . . . Caro Giuseppe, you are right. Your problem may not be
solvable and your sin has neither penitence nor redemption. Like Christ,
you will carry your cross until the end. But I know that the Omnipotent,
the Benevolent, will see your struggle and will understand your good
intentions. I am sure that He will come to you at the right time if you
could not reach Him before. He will open His arms and welcome you at
the gates of heaven. You do not have to worry about it now, but just do
your best. Your sin is a disease that cannot be cured by any practical or
spiritual remedy, but you should cope with it as we all do with our own
cross.' He continued, 'But if I can advise you on more practical matters
as an old friend who has seen you grow since you were a little boy, let
me tell you that your agnosticism in spiritual matters is justified and
acceptable because it does not affect anybody but you. However, this does
not apply to practical matters: On this Earth, you cannot assume that by
not making decisions you are not to be blamed. I see that your indolence
is self-centred. It may even be an excuse to protect yourself from engaging
with the challenges of life. You make your problems bigger because you
are afraid of confronting the little ones. Many will languish and suffer
because of your chronic procrastination, particularly those who truly care
about you and do not abandon you. Fabius Maximus[101] succeeded against

---

[100] I absolve you from your sins in the name of the Father, the Son, and the
       Holy Ghost, Amen.
[101] Roman politician and general called the Contactor that signifies delayer
       due to his tactics of deploying troops during the second Punic war against

Hannibal because he had a plan and a goal, but what is your goal? If it is to be happy, you have to go for your own gratification and relieve others from their sword of Damocles.[102] It takes courage to be selfish, but in the end it will be best for all whose happiness depends on you. If you are unhappy about things that are under your control, exert your power and make yourself content. Do it not only for your own sake rather for the relief of others' misery . . . but if you decide not to do it and to sacrifice yourself for the happiness of others, then all the same do it with all your heart and be consistent with this choice . . . You may wonder how I know what really is in your mind. All I can tell you is that a good shepherd comprehends his flock.'

*   *   *

Unfortunately, I did not value Don Pino's admonishment as much as I should have done. I rather heard the pardon of my sins and I saw the gates of heaven opening in front of me while I continued as a wanker to carry an onanistic existence of self-absorption, postponement, and hope for serendipitous solutions.

Yet I remember with fondness those days in Pizzo and those wise old men.

Nowadays, Italy is Italy as usual. The Coliseum and San Marco's square are where they are supposed to be and the Tower of Pisa is consistently leaning. So is the Chiazza with il Gatto's ice creams. So is the castle with its crows and bats and so is the Statue of Re Umberto I with its big moustache. So is the Chiazzetta with the cats and the dogs and their monotonous life. But the wise men are being decimated by the passing of time spelt out by the inexorable sound of the church bells. Their species is in its way to extinction. Year after year, several quit coming to the Gatto. Most desist for justifiable causes such as a heart attack, a stroke,

---

Hannibal targeting the supply lines and postponing direct confrontation till the enemy was deprived of strength. He is considered the father of the guerrilla warfare.

[102]   Anecdotal figure of a man named Damocles sitting on a throne with a sword hanging over it held by a horse hair to signify that power comes with anxieties and risks,

or an incurable cancer. Others disappear with less legitimate and obscure pretexts, such as a broken hip requiring bed rest and inactivity, which in turn stirs a clot that eventually stops the heart. And the lamest excuses have also been evoked: failure to thrive, a slow decay, forgetfulness of the Chiazza and of their friends.

When a few dances are left at the end of a party, as we treasure the residual pleasure, we intuit the imminent ending as we observe from the corner of our eyes the departure of acquaintances that gradually became rare. Likewise, one at a time the wise men vanish, and the fewer that remain to convene at the tavolino savour the last drops of life in the form of a Sambuca, lemonade, or a cappuccino. One does not dare to ask what happened to il Marchese, il Professore, Mastro Antonio, and all the other old wise men because the answer, no matter how obvious, would be painfully conclusive. One prefers to leave such inquiries unexplored as if the transition from the past to present, from the antique to the contemporary could be perpetually postponed.

But now it is time for me to go back to America and to say 'arrivederci' to the wise old men. It is time to return them to the past where they belong, to imagine them alive in their minuscule universe where they did and perhaps still thrive. And so it goes that, as long as a quorum of them will still be there, most ailments of life and their intricacies will continue to be discussed and comprehensively solved by these wise old men in the little town along the sea. Unfortunately, these perspicacious solutions will remain buried under the ignorance of the world that, unaware of such wealth, unrolls so much anguish and suffering upon all of us. And I am afraid that in the future those who by serendipity might get hold of these pages and might want to experience in person such nuggets of wisdom by visiting the wise men of Pizzo will be disappointed since many of them will have departed towards better pastures where, their wisdom not being required any more, they could finally rest in the deserved peace.

*   *   *

. . . As the plane climbed the sky against the sun, ashore from the coast of Calabria over the Gulf of Santa Eufemia, our visitor looked at Pizzo through the window. The little town did not seem ridente but rather self-absorbed in its own life that was gradually reverting, in the distance, to its Lilliputian proportions.

As he metamorphosed from Signorino Giuseppe to the respected American scientist, our visitor realised that he had solved none of the problems he had intended to tackle. Contrary to the original intent, he had confronted none of them but had rather put them in the back of his mind being distracted by the life of the little town. But the idea of returning to the old troubles did not falter him, because that fortnight had left him with the impression that time will solve all problems, no matter how daunting, by making all of them irrelevant in the end.

The End